BLACK ARTS, WHITE CRAFT

HAILEY EDWARDS

This is a work of fiction. Names, characters, businesses, places, events and incidents are either the products of the author's imagination or used in a fictitious manner. Any resemblance to actual persons, living or dead, or actual events is purely coincidental.

Edited by Sasha Knight
Copy Edited by Kimberly Cannon
Proofread by Lillie's Literary Services
Cover by Damonza
Illustration by NextJenCo

BLACK ARTS, WHITE CRAFT

Black Hat Bureau, Book 2

After a black witch pitched a hissy fit in Hollis Apothecary, Rue got stuck cleaning up his mess. That was the easy part. Repairing the damage he inflicted on Camber and Arden? That makes Rue wish she could bring him back to life just to kill him again. Slower this time.

While Rue is setting her new life back to rights, Clay and Asa are off working a case, but it soon becomes clear that they'll need her help to catch the vicious creature preying on locals in a small Tennessee town. She's got her hands full at home, but Rue has no choice. She must report for duty to honor her agreement with the director. Or else.

What she discovers leads her deeper down the rabbit hole of Black Hat Bureau corruption and promises that, no matter how grim the past few weeks have been, the worst is yet to come.

1

The first cupcake arrived the day after Asa left. It was delivered in pristine condition in a clear plastic box designed to resemble a diamond. I wholeheartedly ignored any symbolism associated with its packaging and devoured the double dark chocolate treat, savoring its rich cherry cordial center and candied cherry frosting.

Two cupcakes arrived the next day, both s'mores, with an incredible charred marshmallow fluff topping.

Three came the day after that, all silky lemon chiffon with tart icing and candied lemon peel curls.

Then came four.

Five.

Six.

Seven.

Eight.

Nine...

Once I accepted, deep in my black heart, that I couldn't eat that many cupcakes alone, I thrifted a plastic stool, taped a sign that read "free cupcakes" to its front, and set it on the sidewalk in front of my shop. As a thank you for the town's continued support, I began leaving the extra treats out for everyone to enjoy.

After I sampled the day's flavor. I mean, they were gifts. It would be rude of me not to eat one.

And just like that, I was back to thinking about Asa when I had a billion other things to do.

Credit where credit was due. His daily deliveries ensured I couldn't forget about him while he was gone.

Not like I had a hope of that with the bracelet he'd made for me snugging my wrist.

"Horsefly."

Jerked from my sugary thoughts, I located Arden waving her arms over her head like spaghetti noodles.

"I got it." Camber palmed the flyswatter, stalked her prey with measured steps, then swung. "Splat."

"You saved me." Arden picked the bug up with a fistful of paper towels between it and her fingers. "How can I ever repay you?" Her voice carried as she went to flush it down the staff toilet. "Name your price."

"You're broke." Camber tossed her the sample bottle of our hand sanitizing gel, made from an aloe vera base with peppermint, witch hazel, manuka honey, onion and garlic extracts, rosemary and tea tree oils. "How about you do my laundry for a month? Or wash the dishes for a week? Or just stop being a baby?"

"I'll take option two." Arden slathered her hands. "Option three ain't happening."

The horsefly infestation was more symbolism I was ignoring. Their appearance was a wake-up call that an unpleasant task was dive-bombing into my life, and it was time to stop running and face up to it. Except I had stopped running, and I had faced up to it. I had a home here in Samford, and I was Black Hat again.

What more did the persistent pests want from me? The spaghetti noodle dance?

Sweat dripped into my eyes as I finished painting the trim on the shelves that held our tinctures and teas selection. November in Alabama was warm. November in Alabama in a shop with an AC unit on the fritz, well, I had sat in cooler saunas.

That was before you factored in the manual labor of sanding the wood trim, priming it, then painting it to restore the shop to its minimalist aesthetic prior to David Taylor's efforts to redesign the space using black magic to demo everything the girls and I had labored so hard to achieve with Hollis Apothecary.

Stepping back from the wall to admire our handiwork, I scratched under my parting gift from Asa for the umpteenth time. The persistent tickle was as constant a reminder of his absence as the cupcakes.

"Stop picking at it." Camber swatted my hand. "Your *boyfriend* worked hard on that."

Never in a million years should I have told them the truth when they asked where I got my jewelry.

"He might have asked for a list of her allergies first," Arden countered. "Look how irritated her skin is."

From a box in the office, she retrieved a small tube of our popular itch relief cream. Most folks used it on mosquito bites or chigger bites in summer, but it also soothed poison oak, poison ivy, and poison sumac.

Made with chamomile, shea butter, colloidal oatmeal, calendula, hemp seed oil, vegan emulsifying wax, olive oil, rosehip seed oil, neem oil, and a little extra that didn't make it onto the label, it was good stuff.

After nudging the bracelet up my arm, she rubbed the lukewarm cream over the pink spots.

"Thanks." I studied her face, the new shadows in her eyes she worked hard to hide. "Are you still drinking your tea?"

"Yes." She withdrew. "A cup before bed, as prescribed, which makes me have to pee ten minutes later."

Firmly in mother hen mode, I might as well pester Camber while I was at it. "You too?"

"Yeah, yeah." She wrinkled her nose. "How long until we're cured?"

Never was too harsh an answer, but it was the honest one. Good thing I was used to filtering my truths.

As far as they knew, the blend of California poppy, lemon balm, ashwagandha root, lavender, linden flower, passionflower aerial parts, and red rooibos tea was to help them sleep and banish night terrors.

"One more week." I crossed my heart. "Then I'll let it go."

The girls would remember what David Taylor had done to them for the rest of their lives, but the tea the girls had been drinking since they were released from the hospital blurred the edges of their recollection of the more peculiar aspects of their abduction until their brains filled in mundane excuses for the worst of their trauma. The fact they were best friends, and shared the burden between them, meant the more they talked about what happened, the more their experience blended into a cohesive, believable whole.

Between that, and the potion Asa dosed them with prior to the paramedics arriving at Tadpole Swim, we had done all we could to help them cope with the muddled aftermath of their ordeal. Or so Clay and Asa had assured me.

The person I was becoming marveled the girls held nothing against me. But I was quick to remind myself the fine details eluded them. They would feel differently if they knew the truth. About David Taylor...and me.

Still, life in a small town meant it was common knowledge that my fake ex-boyfriend was to blame. I wouldn't have been shocked if that link to me was enough to get me written off by everyone, but I had done my job well. I had instilled in the population of Samford a wide protective streak that kept me safe.

The person I had been, the dark and power-hungry void in my gut, wasn't surprised that I had purchased the girls' forgiveness with lies and half-truths, given all the groundwork I had laid to this point.

That cruel remnant was downright proud of how I manipulated a whole town into protecting what they ought to fear.

Me.

Accused witches had been burned at the stake while townsfolk toasted marshmallows in the flames, and that inbred fear never left us. White witches blended better, with their herb gardens and medicinal gifts, but black witches didn't have a hope to hang their pointy hat on when a pitchfork-carrying mob marched to their cursed doors. They were *always* guilty of something. Usually of worse than their accused crimes.

"Your wrist looks better already." Arden capped the lotion with satisfaction. "How does it feel?"

"Yes." Camber sat on the floor to finish painting the baseboards. "How *does* it feel to be in lurve?"

"I'm not in lurve."

"Aww." She paused with her brush in the can. "Your *boyfriend* will be heartbroken to hear that."

Yup.

Never should have owned up to Asa giving me jewelry as a parting gift.

Chalk it up to a hard lesson learned, never to be repeated.

"You do mean love, right?" I measured her expression. "Or do I have to consult the Urban Dictionary?"

"She means love," Arden clarified. "Plain old vanilla romance."

"Asa is not plain or vanilla." Camber wet her lips. "He's like that streusel-topped French toast with maple buttercream sprinkled with candied bacon cupcake from day four? Day five?"

That was a mouthful. Both the description and the cupcake itself. I remembered it well. It was delicious.

"Can you confirm or deny?" Arden arched her brows. "Have you taste tested your boyfriend yet?"

"He's not my *boyfriend*." I resisted the urge to scratch my wrist. "This is a friendship bracelet."

Made from his hair. By him. Designed to ward off other men. Without any discernable way to remove it.

"Mmm-hmm." Camber clucked her tongue. "A *boyfriend*ship bracelet."

"Can you please stop saying *boyfriend* like that?" I started to twitch. "How about stop saying it period?"

For a full minute, she squinted at me, pretending to ponder her answer. "Nope."

The bell over the front door tinkled a greeting to a potential customer.

Except the shop wasn't open, and I could have sworn I locked up to prevent this exact scenario.

"We're closed for renovations." I pasted on a customer service smile. "I'm sorry for any inconvenience."

A man ambled into the shop despite the warning and perused the empty shelves.

His brown hair was clipped short on the sides but left long in a strip down his scalp to create a fauxhawk.

The rips in his jeans appeared earned rather than bought. His tee was tight over his frame but faded the way a well-loved shirt got after too many washings. His dark boots were dinged and scuffed and lived in.

Between the outfit and the thick beard, he could have been a lumberjack, if I put an ax in his hand.

Must be a tourist on his way someplace else. Whoever he was, he wasn't a local, and he wasn't listening.

"I apologize for barging in." He slid his gaze past me to Arden. "I came to visit, not to shop."

The mellow resonance of his voice caused Arden to drop the lotion with a high-pitched squeal of delight.

"Uncle Nolan?" She tackled the stranger in an oxygen-depriving hug. "How are you here?"

"Well, you see—" he grunted from the impact, "—they have these things called airplanes..."

"You know what I mean." She let go then punched him. "I thought you were in Spain."

"Surprise." He rubbed the spot as if mortally wounded. "I thought you'd be happy to see me, Ardy."

The nickname caused her to wrinkle her nose, and I couldn't blame her.

"I am." She drew back to soak him in, head to toe, as if she couldn't believe it. "I'm just surprised."

"And violent."

Done waiting, Camber rose—brush in hand—and flicked paint onto his grinning face.

"You've grown ten feet since I last saw you." He lifted a hand over his head. "You're a giant."

"I'm only five-five, Uncle Nolan." She scuffed her sneakers on the tile. "I'm perfectly average."

The girls were as close as sisters, so I wasn't thrown when Camber called Nolan her uncle too.

You didn't have to share blood to be family.

"There's nothing average about you." He planted a smacking kiss to each of her cheeks. "I missed you two troublemakers. You'll have to come out to dinner with me tonight and fill me in on the hot gossip."

Clearly used to his teasing them about living in a pinprick on the state map, they rolled their eyes.

"Are you going to introduce me—" I shoved a damp curl out of my eye, "—or should I go on break?"

Hmm.

The prospect of a break made me wonder if there were any cupcakes left on the stool out front.

"This is my uncle." Arden kept her eyes on him, as if worried he might vanish. "Nolan Laurens."

"He's a wildlife photographer." Camber jittered with excitement. "He travels all over the world."

The longing in her voice made me wonder if she wouldn't spread her wings after graduation.

The choice was hers, and I would support her dreams in whatever form they took, wherever they carried her, but my selfish heart shriveled when I dwelled on a future without the girls. And Arden would follow. Their bond ran deeper than friendship. Their witch blood, as thin as it might be, compelled them to stick together, whispered in the form of instinct that they were stronger that way.

And I couldn't deny, given recent events, they would both be safer far away from me.

"His pictures win fancy awards," Arden bragged while he groaned. "They're in magazines and galleries."

"Girls." He rubbed his nape with a tattooed hand. "You're embarrassing me in front of the pretty lady."

Pretty lady served as a reminder that handsome out-of-towners didn't know my sordid dating history.

Had I chosen a different cover story, I might have had more luck in the dating department.

Not that I wanted or needed a complication, um, a man.

Or a dae with silky midnight hair and fathomless eyes that tracked me like prey.

"Uncle Nolan." Arden detached from him and scooted to my side. "This is Rue Hollis."

A shadow passed behind his eyes, gone too fast for me to be certain, but his smile didn't waver.

Maybe I spoke too soon. Thought too soon? He must know my history, as it pertained to Arden's ordeal.

Now it was his turn to give me a once-over, and I could tell he liked what he saw, but he gave away nothing else.

Rue Hollis was fast becoming every bit as infamous as my other aliases had been.

I had kept the round cheeks of my childhood, and their always flushed appearance made me look as if I had sprinted across town to be here. Pair that with wide blue eyes and wheat-colored waves that hit me mid-spine, and I could pass for a kid fresh out of high school, though I was three times that age.

The camouflage had served me well, and make no mistake, it was camouflage. Nothing about me had been left to nature or to chance. I was the culmination of generations of selective breeding that resulted in power, beauty, and intelligence wrapped up in one girl-next-door package.

"Nice to finally meet you." He stuck out his arm. "The girls talk about you all the time."

"Nice to meet you too." I shook his hand. "I didn't know Arden had an Uncle Nolan."

The touch of his skin swept tingles down my arm that raised the fine hairs on the back of my neck.

Asa warned me the bracelet would act as a citronella candle to any men buzzing around me, but zapping *me*? How was it my fault I had to shake hands to observe social norms? I was being polite, dang it. There weren't enough cupcakes in the world to excuse an attempt at shock training me to shy away from men.

"Most of the time, she calls me Uncle MIA, or just MIA when I go too long between calls."

"MIA?" I laughed when it hit me. "I thought you were an aunt, named Mia."

"And it was hilarious." Camber high-fived Arden. "I can't believe we kept the joke running for so long."

"Thaaanks." Nolan dipped his chin. "I can only imagine what your boss must think of me."

I thought he was exactly the diversion the girls needed to get out of their heads for a while.

Given the timing, I didn't have to wonder why a long-lost uncle had chosen to resurface in Samford.

"The giggle-snorting every time they mentioned you should have tipped me off sooner."

"They giggle-snorted so much when they were little, I called them the two little piggies." He smoothed a hand down one side of his shorn scalp. "Are you busy tonight?" He flashed a lopsided smile. "Want to join us for dinner?"

"Are you..." Arden clamped a hand over her mouth, "...asking my *boss* out? On a *date*?"

"*No.*" His arm wilted to his side. "Not a date-date." He rocked back on his heels. "Just dinner. With us."

"Did you see?" Camber burst into laughter. "Just the word *date* almost made him bolt for the airport."

"I love you, Uncle Nolan, I do," Arden said, "but your commitment issues aren't only geographical."

Yowch.

"Do you smell something burning?" He sniffed the air. "Oh. Never mind. It's just me. Being roasted."

"We should have used more garlic." Camber inhaled then wrinkled her nose. "Maybe some onions."

"I have an idea." Call it guilt or call it inspiration. "Why don't you two take the rest of the day off?"

The girls exchanged a glance, their conversation wordless but their eyes bright, and I knew I had them.

"Go spend time with Nolan." I smiled at them. "You guys have lots of catching up to do."

"Are you sure?" Arden linked her fingers at her navel. "We don't mind staying."

"We made a lot of progress today." I scanned the shop. "There's not much to do until the paint dries."

"Promise you'll go home?" Arden wrapped her slender arm around me. "You deserve a break too."

"You've been living here since..." Camber's gaze slid away. "You should take an afternoon off to rest."

With Christmas around the corner, I had a prime opportunity for a grand reopening *if* I hit the deadline. I couldn't afford to miss it if I wanted to hang on to our current downtown location. Renovation costs plus payroll minus the lack of income while the shop was closed added up to a huge drain on my savings.

Never thought I would say it, but I was grateful for the Black Hat consultant check sitting in my bank account. It would tide me over until the insurance company got off its butt and reimbursed me.

"Fine." I kissed each of their cheeks. "I'll put away the paint, and we'll do touch-ups tomorrow."

"Promise?" Arden narrowed her eyes on me. "You say *just one last thing*, then it's four hours later."

"I promise." I crossed my heart. "I'll lock up after you guys leave."

Right after I sweep the floor, wash out the storage bins, and mop for the hundredth time.

"You better." Camber backed out the door, eyes on me. "I expect you to be gone in twenty."

"Yes, boss." I scrunched up my face. "Oh, wait. That's right. I'm *your* boss."

"Semantics." She flipped an imperious hand. "Are you coming tonight? Dinner is on Uncle Nolan."

"Hey," he protested without heat. "Ask a guy first."

"You owe us five years' worth of holidays and birthday dinners," Arden pointed out. "Time to pay up."

"I would love to go out with you guys." I mopped sweat off my forehead. "I'll pay my own way, though."

"Great." His grin spread from ear to ear. "Arden can text you with the time and place."

I appreciated that he didn't ask for my number, and I blamed that on the bracelet too. Anyone could call me directly if they plucked a business card out of the display. It wasn't like I kept my digits super-secret.

"Later girls, and guy."

After walking them to the door, I leaned against it, shoving it into the slightly bent frame on schedule for repairs next week. This time I made certain to jiggle the lock into place and tested it against walk-ins.

A notification from a spam-blocking app I used to track all calls to my private line lit up my phone screen. A now-familiar blocked number flashed, and I checked the time against his previous attempts at contact.

The director was a smart man. He would get the message I had nothing to say to him soon enough.

Alone in the quiet, weighted down by exhaustion, I allowed the resilient mask I wore for the girls' sakes to drop, and granted myself permission to wear my true emotions on my face where no one could see.

Guilt over what was done to them.

Fear—no, scratch that—absolute terror the director knew about Colby.

Shame over how the town treated me so well.

Anger directed at myself for thinking I could have this life.

The rest spiraled out from there, an endless loop of regret, until I couldn't hold still another second.

Proving Arden right, that I was a *just one last thing*-er, I found myself stocking the shelves that had finished curing from the night before to make the shop less naked. The gleaming nooks with uneven numbers of bottles left me twitchy, but I would get in enough trouble with the girls without caving to the urge to mix lotions to fill in the gaps. Already I would be joining them for dinner sweaty and dressed in the same dirty outfit.

A light tapping noise on the door at the back of the shop drew me out of my head.

No one else used that entrance. The girls exited out the front and crossed the street to the parking lot at the diner. All thanks to Mayor Tate issuing me one spot instead of the two covered in my lease. For the same reason, lack of available parking spots, repairmen and deliveries tended to enter via the front too.

The knock came again, louder this time, and I dried my hands before seeing who wanted what now.

Night had fallen while I puttered around in the shop, and a nearby streetlamp illuminated my doorstep.

A familiar daemon towered over me, his large hands clasped behind his back, his regal head bowed.

His dark red skin was sheened with sweat that made his onyx rosettes glitter. Thick ebony horns curled from his temples back over his head, and his hair hung loose, a curtain of black silk.

A breath punched out of my lungs when his burnt crimson eyes rose to mine, and I breathed, "Asa."

2

The reality of a hulking daemon standing on my doorstep, dressed in nothing more than a pair of yellow skintight boxer briefs that might as well have been reflective, muted my shock and kick-started my brain.

"Have you lost your mind?" I tugged on his fever-hot elbow. "Get in here before someone sees you."

"Rue." The daemon prowled inside then presented me with...a cupcake. "Brought gift."

This wasn't a cupcake from today. Wrong flavor. The delivery had been apple cider cake filled with apple chutney and topped with caramel icing. This hit me as more death by chocolate meets molten lava cake. It could give an ice cream cone a run for its money with the amount of decadent frosting twirled on top.

It was also missing a bite.

Which would explain the frosting smear on the daemon's upper lip.

"Thank you." I checked the street then shut the door behind him. "What are you doing here?"

"Clay busy." He held the cupcake closer to me. "I come alone."

Any closer, and he would smash frosting up my nose. "So, you're blaming this on Clay."

"Yes."

"Hmm." I accepted the treat. "That's convenient."

The daemon did his best to appear angelic, which worked about as well as you would expect.

According to Asa, the daemon was and wasn't him, which made addressing them problematic.

Half daemon, half fae, he considered himself dae. Too bad my options weren't as catchy. Using his logic, I qualified as either a blite witch or a whack witch, given my parents practiced both branches of magic.

"Can I talk to Asa, please?" I turned the cupcake this way and that. "I'll take a bite if you do."

The daemon raked a fang over his bottom lip, clearly tempted, but he shook his head. "Asleep."

"Asa is asleep?" I wasn't sure how I felt about the daemon seeking me out solo. "Okay, where is Clay?"

"Hotel," he grumbled. "Said we come tomorrow."

The big galoot had to be kidding me. "He didn't notice you leaving?"

"He petting his hairs." The daemon curled his lip. "He bathe them too."

Clay was created bald, as all golems were, but he did love his wigs as if they were his children.

A spark of inspiration burned in the daemon's eyes as he shoved a hank of his hair at me. "Rue pet."

Goddess bless.

In lusting after Asa's hair, I had created a monster, and I had only myself to blame.

Cupcake in one hand, hair in the other, I had a choice to make. I set down the cupcake and fished out my phone. Clay hadn't changed his number since he and I were partners, a fact that gave me warm fuzzies.

Dialing from memory, I waited for him to answer, then drawled, "Missing something?"

"I'm already in the SUV," he grumbled, "on my way to you."

At seven feet tall and four hundred pounds, he had a knack for busting captain's chairs if he breathed too hard while sitting in them. I hoped he made it to the shop without incident. Usually, he rode in the back for the extra support of a bench seat.

"Don't get huffy with me," I said as I got huffy with him. "It's not my fault your partner wandered off."

"I warned you." He blared the horn and cursed the traffic. "I told you not to mess around with Ace."

"I didn't mess around with him." I flushed under the daemon's stare. "There was no messing around."

"Ace is complicated, Rue." Clay's breath filled my ear. "So are you."

"Huh." I pretended to ponder that. "I would never have put that together if you hadn't told me."

A low growl pumped through the eavesdropping daemon's chest. "Rue mine."

On that note, this bracelet was gone the instant I got a free hand and a pair of scissors.

"This right here," Clay informed me, "is what comes from swapping spit muffins with Ace."

Spit muffins.

"That was wrong on so many levels." I cringed from the accurate descriptor. "Like, all of them."

"Dammit, Rue, this is serious."

"What do you want me to say? I didn't invite him over. I wasn't expecting him. I didn't know you were in town. No one told me." I noticed the daemon wince and eased my grip on his hair. "Why didn't he call?"

"If I had to guess," Clay said with a long-suffering sigh, "I would say he wanted to surprise you."

Aww.

That was sweet.

Crazy inconvenient, given his daemon side had jumped the gun, but I didn't hate Asa's thoughtfulness.

Voices drew my attention toward the front of the shop, and the bottom dropped out of my stomach.

"Oh crap." I passed the daemon back his hair to free up my other hand. "Hold on, Clay."

Quickly, I checked my messages, and sure enough, I'd missed a text from Arden naming a time and place for dinner with her, Camber, and Nolan. This must be them come to fetch me. From the shop. Which I had promised to leave twenty minutes after they ended their shifts. Hours ago.

"I have to get that." I turned on the daemon. "Stay put." I tapped his nose. "Don't let anyone see you."

With one final warning glare at the daemon, I loped to the front of the shop, cracked open the door, and wedged my foot behind it to prevent the girls from pushing inside to fuss at me.

Nolan, his strip of hair twisted into a messy man bun, stood with his hands in his pockets. "Hey."

The girls, their arms linked, stared me down over his shoulder, clearly unimpressed with my appearance.

"I lost track of the time." I shoved damp hair off my forehead. "I'm sorry, but I can't go out like this."

Their twin glares made it plain I had disappointed them, but I couldn't leave the daemon unsupervised.

"You're grounded." Camber thinned her lips. "No breakfast smoothies for a week."

"Two weeks," Arden countered. "She must be held accountable, or she won't learn from her mistakes."

The number of people bold enough to threaten me could be counted on the fingers of one hand. But the girls had no fear of me. They trusted me, loved me, and times like this, I felt humbled to be seen. Not as a black witch or a white witch, but as the person I wanted to be when all was said and done.

I wasn't her, not yet, but I was working toward it with every practiced smile, scripted kind word, and planned show of kindness that one day I hoped would come naturally to me rather than require so much effort and study to make it appear as effortless as the people I had chosen to emulate.

"Maybe some other time?" Nolan scuffed his boot. "When you're not grounded?"

"Sure." I hurried to agree to win the girls' forgiveness. "We can all do lunch one day."

"I'll hold you to that." He backed up, bumped into the girls, then blushed. "See you later, Rue."

"See you." I slammed the door in his face then felt warm breath on my nape. "What in the...?"

The daemon stood on my heels, the forgotten cupcake on his palm. "Eat."

Not this again. "I'm not hungry."

The spit-muffin thing had ruined my appetite.

"*Eat.*"

The daemon thrust the cupcake under my nose, leaving a daub of icing on the tip, which made him grin.

Smiling right back at him, I gripped his wrist, brought the treat closer to my mouth, then pushed out with all my might, smashing the treat between his burnt-crimson eyes.

Crumbs sprinkled onto my clean floor, and icing slid off his nose in thick plops, but it was worth the mess to see him blink out at me from behind a thick layer of chocolate.

A snort of laughter shot out my nose as the daemon wiped a hand down his face, which only made it worse.

But I shut up real quick when he smeared that chocolate-coated palm across my cheek.

"That's how you want to play this?" I sucked on my teeth. "Okay, then." I curled a finger. "Bring it."

Scooping more frosting off his face, he grabbed for me, but I ducked his arm, palming fallen cake off the floor. I threw a glob at him, nailing his shoulder, and he broke into a smile that showcased thick fangs.

We flung crumbs until they were too small to pick up and hurled icing until there was none left.

The daemon balled up the pleated wrapper and chucked it at my head, which devolved into a dodgeball-style battle. I slid in a smear of frosting and spun into a skid across the floor...right into Clay's open arms.

Dressed in his usual black suit, he looked good. The wig du jour, a neon-blue quiff, brought out his eyes.

"Um." I clutched his broad shoulders to regain my balance. "This isn't what it looks like."

The daemon, wrapper in hand, walked up to us and bounced the paper off my forehead. "I win."

"That's cheating," I protested, then bit my lip when Clay rolled his eyes heavenward in a plea for help.

"I hope you know what you're doing," he muttered. "Food fights are daemon foreplay."

Of course, they were.

What else would they be?

3

Dignity was in short supply as I drew myself taller, without first wiping off the frosting, and attempted to wield the awe my presence used to command. Sadly, I knew I had failed even before raising my eyebrow resulted in crumbs raining into my eyes, which forced me to blink rapidly and stagger, blinded by its grit.

"Go wash up." Clay angled me toward the bathroom. "Both of you."

Dragging my heels, I did as I was told, with help from my seeing-eye daemon.

"So—" I squirted one of our minty hand soaps into my palm, "—you're in my neck of the woods."

Once I worked up a good lather, I started scrubbing my face. Buttercream was a bear to break down, but the combo of lemon grass, tea tree, peppermint, and rosemary essential oils were up to the task. Even if that combination made for a very tingly washing experience, it worked wonders for opening my sinuses.

Rinsing was easy, but I had nothing clean to pat my face with. Guess I was air-drying.

"Your turn." I left the warm water on for the daemon. "Help yourself."

"We are in your neck of the woods," Clay agreed once he set eyes on me. "For two reasons."

"You need my help," I realized, ignoring the hollow ache that rang through my chest. "On a case."

Reading me with ease, Clay hooked me into a bear hug that lifted me off my feet. "That's one reason."

Face buried in his shirt, which solved the towel problem, I let the wall of his (literally) sculpted muscle comfort me. "And the other?"

"I missed you, Dollface." He kissed the top of my head with brotherly affection. "That dumbass did too."

The hollowness filled in as he held me. "Do you mean Asa or the daemon?"

"They're the same person."

Rather than contradict him, I hummed a nonanswer and soaked up his warmth. "I'm glad you're here."

"When you left, it felt like some jackass cut off my favorite arm." He released me. "This time it was more like an asshole stole my prosthetic." He stared down at me. "Ace and I are a good team, but you and me. We've seen some shit. We've been through some shit." He worked his jaw. "We've done some shit."

Each swear hit my ears like a hammer on a tiny anvil. "You really have to work on your potty mouth."

I did *not* want Colby hearing him swear as easy as breathing and pick up sentence enhancers of her own.

"Yeah." He rubbed his jaw. "There must be better words out there as yet undiscovered."

"Uh, no." I punched his shoulder and immediately regretted my life choices. "That's not what I meant."

A *plink, plink, plink* sound drew my head around to the bathroom, and a dripping wet daemon.

"Wash hair for Rue." He indicated the mass of bubbles fizzing on his head. "Hair sticky."

"He's all yours." Clay swept out his arm. "Enjoy."

The declaration brightened the daemon's eyes, and he puffed out his chest. "Rue mine."

"Rue belongs to no one," I corrected him. Again. "The bracelet Asa gave me isn't a dog collar."

There was no *if found, please return to owner* information embedded in it. Or was there?

The only thing sneakier than a daemon was a fae, and just my luck, Asa was both.

"Tell me more about the case." I led the daemon back to the sink. "What's on the docket?"

The daemon folded almost in half for me to flip his hair over his head into the shallow sink basin, where I began to pay for each and every thought I'd ever had about playing with Asa's hair as I rinsed out the suds.

"Remember when I said our case involved a wendigo in the Appalachians?"

During one of my required weekly check-ins with my team, Clay had filled me in on the details of their case. I was their sounding board, though it didn't involve black magic. Therefore, it shouldn't have involved me.

That assignment had called them away on Halloween night, hours after we closed the copycat case.

Poor Colby had been heartbroken. She still pouted because they left before taking her trick-or-treating.

"I remember being grateful I didn't have to fool with it, yes."

Wendigos resembled emaciated corpses more than anything else, with tufts of wiry fur on their ears and down their spines. Their jaws were alligator-strong, and their rows of serrated teeth belonged on sharks. Their fingers were triple jointed, and their nails cut open their prey with scalpel-like precision.

And they stank. Phew, boy, did they stink. Like durian fruit but meatier.

After I wrung out the daemon's hair as best I could, I helped him straighten to avoid an epic hair flip that would have splattered water all over creation.

"Yes, well." Clay mashed his index finger to his thumb. "We have a *tiny* problem."

"Obviously." I edged past the daemon, who admired himself in the mirror. "What kind of problem?"

"The wendigo is back."

"Are you sure it's the same one?" They tended to travel in packs. "It could be a clanmate or its mate."

"Ace tore off its head." Clay let me digest that. "This is the wendigo, spotted in town two days later."

Removing his phone from his pocket, he showed me the screen. The wendigo's neck was a mass of black sutures. I enlarged the photo to be sure I wasn't imagining things, but sure enough, a row of tall stitches appeared to be anchoring its head onto its body.

"Who would offer a wendigo medical care?" I chewed my bottom lip. "That's downright bizarre."

They were humanoid in shape, with limited speech capabilities, but they were animalistic in thought and behavior. You couldn't communicate with them. Their language wasn't replicable with our vocal cords.

It was a whole thing, decades ago, to teach them basic signs, but they were too food motivated and often ate their instructors the second the treats ran out. Needless to say, that experiment didn't last long.

"See, that's the problem." He pocketed his phone. "This was done postmortem."

While most supernatural races would be dead as a doornail after decapitation, there were a few able to regenerate *if* they got their head back on their shoulders fast enough. Wendigos were one of them. They were so close to dead, forced to feast on organ meat to survive, they were nearly impossible to kill.

But what he claimed surpassed even a wendigo's healing abilities. "Are you thinking necromancy or...?"

"The Society for Post-Life Management only involves itself in necromancer and vampire affairs."

Seeing as how the race of undead humans was their creation, really, they only cared about themselves. I didn't mind that. It took two factions off the board, for the most part. Black Hat only stepped in when an issue arose that the Society failed to handle to the director's satisfaction.

Bonus for us, the Society didn't know about Black Hat, or at least not the scope of our operation.

A necessary evil when tasked with policing the agencies responsible for punishing their own.

"That leaves black witches." I should have led with that. "I assume the director signed off on this?"

"You are our black magic consultant." A twinkle brightened his eyes. "He couldn't very well say no."

He could, but he wouldn't. He wanted me invested, wanted me active. Simply put, he wanted me back.

"What, exactly, is this zombigo doing in Appalachia?"

"Eating people." He rolled a hand. "Rewind." He tilted his head. "Did you say *zombigo*?"

"Um, yes?" I didn't see the problem. "What would you call a resurrected wendigo?"

"Nasty."

A hefty thud interrupted our bickering, and I pivoted to find Asa sprawled across the tile, unconscious. Boxer briefs stretched to their limits, the fabric puddled around his lean waist, dipping low on his hips.

And *no*, I was not ogling him. I was assessing him. Visually. For medical purposes.

"Ace?" Clay brushed past me to crouch over his partner. "You okay, buddy?"

Peridot-green eyes blinked open on the ceiling, and a line appeared between his brows. "Where...?"

BLACK ARTS, WHITE CRAFT

"You're in my shop." I shifted my weight, awkward in his presence. "Have been, for an hour or so."

For all that the daemon claimed me as his, he didn't give me the tingles.

Asa, on the other hand, blasted shivers over my skin in a prickling wave that stole my breath.

"The last thing I remember was filing our expense report." He touched his scalp. "Why is my hair wet?"

"You and Rue got into a food fight," Clay explained while examining him, "with that twenty-dollar cupcake you insisted we pick up on our way in."

"Twenty dollars?" I did the math in my head and swooned at the figure. "Per cupcake?"

"Who buys cupcakes?" Clay made a disgusted noise. "Homemade or bust."

"I can't bake." Asa let his eyes close. "I should have chosen another gift."

"Your gift was fine." I bit my bottom lip. "Better than fine. Amazing. The whole town appreciates them."

"The whole..." his alert gaze pierced me, "...town?"

"You sent one cupcake on the first day, two on the second, three on the third..." I soaked up his dawning comprehension. "There were dozens of them. I had to share, or they would have spoiled."

A laugh burst out of Clay, and he slapped his thigh, thoroughly enjoying himself at his partner's expense.

"I told you that shopgirl wasn't listening." He snorted. "She was too busy licking her lips over you."

A flash of jealousy startled me, but that wasn't my style, and I tamped it down as far as it would go.

The woman whose employee ID number might be printed on the last gift receipt I had yet to throw away had done nothing to deserve shoving designer cupcakes down her throat until icing shot out her nostrils.

Wrist itching like crazy, I tucked my hands behind my back and scratched under the bracelet.

"That would explain the bill." Asa peeled damp hair off his defined chest. "Why did you say I'm wet?"

"The daemon decided to wash the frosting out of his hair. Your hair? I helped rinse when he couldn't get out all the bubbles." I knelt beside him, unable to keep my distance any longer. "I hope that's okay."

"You washed my hair," he said softly, and he threaded his fingers through mine. "Thank you."

There was a weight to the words I didn't understand that curled heat in my belly. "You're welcome."

To cover how long our hands were clasped, I used that same grip to raise him into a seated position.

"Let's skip the mushy stuff," Clay cut in, "and focus on the important parts."

"You have no memory of leaving the hotel," I clarified, "or coming to my shop?"

"No." Asa folded his legs under him in lotus position. "As I said, I emailed accounting and then..."

"Nothing," I finished for him. "If it helps, the daemon—to simplify things, let's call him that—told me you were asleep. He said Clay didn't plan to visit until tomorrow, which, I think, is what set him off."

The barest curve of Asa's lips made an appearance. "He brought you the cupcake?"

Asa didn't hesitate over the distinction between himself and the daemon, and it made me curious.

Everything about him sparked my interest. That was how I ended up wearing a freaking hair bracelet.

"It was missing a bite."

His expression turned pensive as he gripped his ankles.

"He tried to make me eat it," I rambled. "That's when the food fight broke out."

Amused despite himself, Clay asked, "Who fired the first shot?"

"He started it." I dropped my gaze to Asa. "He kept shoving it in my face."

"And naturally," Clay continued, the natural arbitrator, "the mature response was to smash it in his."

"Yes." I tucked a stubborn curl behind my ear. "Not that I admit any fault in the incident, but yes."

"I won't file a grievance," Asa assured me. "I wouldn't want you dragged to the director's office."

"That makes two of us," I muttered, then raised my voice. "How long do we have before we leave?"

There was no question I would go. I had signed a contract to consult. I had to honor my end if I expected the Bureau to uphold theirs. The only question was what to do with Colby. As much as I wanted to order her to stay home, safe behind wards, I got the mother of all wake-up calls the last time I left her behind.

I was a white witch now. Not a black one. My power was finite, not infinite.

The things I once did without blinking required all my focus and hours of preparation to achieve.

As much as it dinged my pride in my spellwork, I had to admit she was safer with me than without me.

Given how she had saved me from David Taylor, the reverse was also true.

But the more we worked together on cases, the more exposure she would get, and the more attention it would draw to me. Just as Asa had flipped out when he understood what I had done to save Colby, there would be others just as horrified and equally unwilling to forgive me for binding her soul to mine.

She was a kid, mostly, and she didn't understand the scope of what she was asking of me.

She was also a survivor, and I didn't get to tell her how to live the rest of her very long life.

Assuming Black Hat and its zombigo case didn't get us killed first.

"We need to be gone by breakfast at the latest."

"Okay." I rubbed my forehead. "Let me see what I can do."

Depending on how long the case required, I was in danger of missing my appointment with the AC repair guy. And the electrician. The door guy too. Probably I was forgetting others after being put on the spot.

Usually, I would just call Miss Dotha, but after David Taylor cornered her in the shop and kidnapped the girls in front of her, I didn't feel comfortable asking her for the favor. And I didn't want to be told no.

Camber, Arden, and Miss Dotha were linchpins in the coven of strong, if unmagical, women I had chosen to surround myself with. They had witch blood way back in their lineage, enough to add their touches to our products, but nothing that required formal training or awareness of their latent talents to use them.

As much as I hated to interrupt the girls' dinner, I didn't see a way to avoid it in my current time crunch.

Hating to be a bother, I dialed Camber over Arden as a compromise. "Hello."

"Why does that sound like a goodbye?"

"You're an astute young woman with a good ear?"

"Quit buttering me up." Her snort blasted across the line. "What's going on?"

Here comes the hard part.

"The police have asked me to consult on another case." I let her absorb that. "I said yes."

The uptick in her breath left me imagining her panicked heart, which made me...hungry.

Gritting my teeth, I focused on Camber and pushed down that dark yearning. "Are you okay?"

"Yeah. Good. Fine." She gulped a few more quick breaths. "I just... lost it...for a second...there."

Panic attacks were new, or else she hadn't told me she was having them, and it twisted my gut.

"Breathe," I soothed her. "In and out." I listened until her inhales and exhales eased off. "Good girl."

"Can you give the details to Arden?" Her breath hitched. "I'm not..." She hesitated. "I'm not ready yet."

If the mention of the police or casework hit her this hard, her condition was worse than she had let on.

As underhanded as it felt, I made the choice to up her tea dosage to calm her mind and help her cope.

"I understand." And I hated myself for scarring the girls and then asking them to bear more.

"Know I support you." Her voice went raspy. "I would do the same in your shoes."

I was handed off to Arden before I could say another word.

"Rue?" Worry spiked her tone. "What's wrong?"

"The police have asked me to help them with another case."

"Oh," she replied softly. "You said yes."

"I did."

"Good." Conviction rang through her. "No one should have to go through what we did. What *you* did. If I could help the police like you do, I would volunteer, but since I can't, I'll do whatever it takes to free you up to consult on cases." A trembling breath left her. "You should be proud of how far you've come, Rue, that you've healed enough to want to help others. Maybe one day Cam and I can pay it forward too."

Tears pricked the backs of my eyes as she praised me for lying to her.

I wasn't some champion for her to admire. I didn't deserve her thanks. I was serving time. That was it.

Clay rested a hand on my shoulder, loaning me his strength to finish the conversation.

Superhuman hearing was truly a blessing and a curse, but I was grateful for the support.

"I expect to be gone at least a week," I began. "Can you meet the repairmen on the schedule?"

A few might allow me some wiggle room, but it would be better for my bottom line to stay on track.

"No problem." The responsibility settled on her thin shoulders without a hitch. "Anything else?"

"Stock the shelves between appointments, but otherwise, use your time wisely."

"Done and...I make no promises."

Had she ever been this eager to take on extra tasks? No. Camber had always been the ambitious one of the two. Arden worked hard and dreamed big, but she was content to support Camber and me rather than step out with her own projects or ideas.

Maybe this was what she needed right now, to take control, to have a say in what happened and when.

After David Taylor stole her choices from her, I supported her need for power over her environment.

"That's the best deal I'm likely to get." I laughed under my breath. "I'll take it."

"Oh, hey, Uncle Nolan wants to talk to you."

"Um, okay?"

The phone got passed, and Nolan came on the line. "Do you think it's wise to leave the girls alone?"

"They're both managers. They have keys. They know how to open and close."

And they both needed to reclaim the shop as a safe space rather than let one night ruin their hard work.

"That's not what I'm asking." An edge was hidden in the polite tone. "Will they be safe?"

The urge to snap at him had me clenching my jaw, and I couldn't figure out why when he wasn't saying a single thing I hadn't thought myself. I understood his concerns. I sympathized with them. I shared them.

Maybe the bracelet was working its magic on me and men in general annoyed me. Or maybe I hated for my worst fears to be voiced when I was working so hard to keep them to myself and not coddle the girls.

"They'll work half days until I get home," I decided, to ease them back into their usual solo routine. "The contractors are locals, all people the girls know and are comfortable with. They won't be isolated. It will be daylight, and the shops down the street will be open. They have their cells and a landline phone in the shop. They can call for help if they need it."

"Look, I'm sorry." He gusted out a breath. "I didn't mean to snap at you. What happened to them..."

A lengthy pause clued me in to how hard he was struggling to phrase what he wanted to say. "Yes?"

"It wasn't your fault." He didn't sound like he meant it, not that I held it against him. "I worry for Arden." He backtracked. "For both the girls." He sipped his drink. "I don't want them alone in a place where they might feel vulnerable, and I'm concerned they feel obligated to show up when they might not be ready."

Put that way, I had trouble taking offense. "I won't force the girls into work. It's their choice."

Shuffling noises broke out, and Arden reclaimed the phone. "We're in."

Pressure swelled in my chest, but I had to be certain. "Are you sure Camber wants—?"

"She wants," Camber yelled from the background, then added, "a raise."

"You drive a hard bargain." I wiped my fingers under my damp eyes. "How much?"

"A dozen cookies per week," she decided. "Our pick of recipes."

"Done." I smiled at that spark of her coming back to herself. "Anything else?"

"I demand homemade ice cream once a week," Arden announced. "The flavors TBD."

"Okay, now, let's not go overboard." I chuckled. "We have that Dickens Christmas thing next month."

"Just be thankful we got out of the Gobble 'Til You Wobble Marathon." Arden made gagging noises. "No sane person would agree to walk/run five miles, stopping every mile to eat a plate of Thanksgiving food. And forget water. Did you see they made the participants drink cranberry juice last year?"

"Last year," I recalled, "three people were hospitalized with food poisoning from the potato salad."

"I forgot about that." She grew distracted. "Dessert is here, so I need to go. Email the to-do list, please."

"I'll type it up tonight and send it over in the morning." Throat tight, I hesitated. "Thank you."

"We'll get through this," she assured me, which ought to have been my job. "All of us."

"Enjoy your dessert."

"It won't be as good as what you bake, but I'm sure I can find room in my stomach for it."

The call ended, and I dropped my head back on my neck. "I don't deserve those girls."

"You're right." Clay slung an arm around my shoulders. "I'm sure kids their age could find management positions in any shop in town. I bet the owners would listen to their suggestions and implement their ideas. I'm sure they would get paid the same and benefits would be included in the package too."

"Okay." I huffed and leaned into him. "You made your point."

Just not the one he meant to, since it got me thinking I had subconsciously been giving the girls hazard pay for years.

"You're a nurturer, Rue." He rubbed my back. "Through and through."

Goodness wasn't innate to me. I started out mimicking people who behaved in the way I wanted to act. I embraced *fake it 'til you make it* as a template for the person I wanted to become. I still had days when I felt plain fake, but moments like this gave me hope it was more than pretend change, that I was doing it.

The mantle of black witch felt most comfortable on my shoulders, but white magic sat easier on my soul.

With my peculiar lineage, I could have gone either way. Light, dark. Good, evil. Kind, cruel.

Until the director was awarded custody after my parents' deaths. Until he brought me to his mansion on the cliffs where the Black Hat Bureau hid its compound under the waves. Until he decided a path for me.

To be fair, he only knew one road, the blackest of the black, but he forced me to walk alongside him.

Yes, I could have gone either way.

And now, in embracing white magic, I had come full circle.

4

The drive home from the shop gave me time alone to stew over the biggest surprise of my night.

Namely, a certain daemon body-jacking Asa to spend quality time swapping spit muffins with me.

I wasn't sure how to feel about that, the case, or leaving the girls alone to deal with a tsunami of repairs.

As I stepped out, the wards surrounding my property hummed a steady drone that told me all was well. I was at the front gate, about to push through, when a black SUV pulled in behind me, Asa at the wheel.

Our gazes collided, leaving my skin flushed and tight all over, and I gripped the gate to steady my pulse.

He had changed in my office before we left, and that meant he was dressed to the nines.

Lean muscle covered his frame. Hard to forget that after watching him model his underwear. No amount of tailoring could conceal his strength, but he managed to hide his powerful body better than most. Four hammered silver hoops fixed into a single earring hung from each of his ears, and a ring pierced his septum of the same material. His hair had lost its sheen thanks to the oil blend in the hand soap and the daemon's vigorous scrubbing. It was clumped down his back, mostly dry, but tangled from its ordeal.

His poor hair. His poor, beautiful hair. His poor, beautiful hair that was long enough to wrap around my fist...

No.

Bad Rue.

This was how I kept getting myself in trouble.

A faint smile played around his full lips as he watched my gaze rove over him, and he returned the favor.

Muffled squealing drew my attention back to the house, where a pale face smooshed against a window.

Faster than a bolt of white lightning, Colby shot into the yard to zoom around me.

Seriously.

Who knew moths got zoomies?

With white fuzz covering her abdomen and a wispy off-white mane, she was a showstopper. Pearlescent wings blurred when she got excited, like now, and her velvety black legs kicked with excitement. Though we had agreed the uppermost set, tipped in cream, would be deemed *hands* despite the lack of fingers.

"Clay." Her antennae fluttered with delight. "You're back."

"Hey, Shorty." He grinned from ear to ear. "You miss me?"

The ward dipped in warning, popping my ears, as Clay and Asa entered my yard.

"Duh." She lit on him as soon as he crossed the barrier. "All the cool stuff happens when you're here."

Heart pinching at her enthusiastic greeting, I told him, "That's a nice way of saying trouble follows you."

Just like a certain dae had followed me, silent and stealthy, as if he were stalking prey.

"Hello, Colby." Asa stood close enough for our elbows to brush. "It's nice to see you again."

"Hi," Colby said shyly, waving at him. "Rue made detangler for you."

If there was any justice in this world, I would incinerate on the spot and be pardoned from facing Asa.

When I failed to self-immolate, despite trying my best, it proved what I already knew. There was none.

My only saving grace was she didn't out me for testing what I had mixed up so far on my bracelet.

And *no*, it wasn't just so I could catch a whiff of juicy green apple while he was gone. That would be sentimental and ridiculous.

With a smile in his eyes, Asa excused himself to the bathroom. Probably to perform damage control.

Chin held high, I launched into my totally valid excuse. "I'm starting a haircare line for the shop."

"That's interesting." Clay rubbed his jaw. "Very interesting."

"Don't make me hit you." I narrowed my eyes on him. "I don't want to break my hand."

"Seriously." He held his palms out, toward me. "I'm interested."

"You're serious?" Shocked to my toes, I forgot to be embarrassed. "You would entrust your hair to me?"

"The shampoo I use now is nothing special. I bet you could make a better version."

"You want me to magic extra shine into every bottle, don't you?"

"A spelled preservative would be nice too. Do you know how much a good wig costs these days?"

"Actually, no." I flashed a sugary smile at him. "I haven't bought a wig in a few decades."

"Not this again." He groaned with sincere regret. "I apologized then, and I'll apologize now."

Antennae twitching, Colby asked, "What happened?"

"I bought Clay a wig for his birthday. We had been working together for six months, and I had no idea he was such a huge snob. I picked a style I thought he would like, but it turned out to be synthetic, not real, and he looked at it like it was a giant rat I fished out of the NY sewers and suggested he wear like a hat."

"I wore it every day for a month," he reminded me. "I wore it until the hair fell out of the cap."

That was one of the moments when I realized Clay wasn't acting, or not *just* acting, when it came to me. He was more than the spy the director paired me up with to keep an eye on me. He truly was my friend.

"Not true." I snickered at the memory. "I rescued you when you started to resemble Friar Tuck."

"I still have nightmares," he said in a haunted voice. "Life's too short for a bad wig."

Legs tapping on Clay's shoulder, Colby tilted her head. "Who's Friar Tuck?"

"Whippersnappers these days." I flipped a hand at her. "They don't know nothing about nothing."

"We'll rent *Robin Hood* for you." Clay patted her head. "The 1973 cartoon edition."

Antennae drooping at the ends, Colby scrunched up her face. "Are bad wigs less traumatic in cartoons?"

"Much," Clay reassured her. "Plus, as much as you enjoy raiding, I think you'll like Robin."

"He goes on raids?" That got her antennae quivering. "Really?"

"Yep."

Heavily editing the tale, he skipped over the part where Robin stole from the rich to give to the poor. Far as I knew, Colby never gifted her spoils of war. She would trade, but charity? She was more of a hoarder.

To spare him from losing his audience, I shifted gears.

"Shine, I can do." I thought about the required materials. "Preservative might be cost prohibitive."

"You're thinking too small. Forget selling to the locals. You'll make a killing online."

"You sold me on the idea." I raised my hands in surrender. "I'll start researching it after this case."

"Case?" Colby zipped back to land on my shoulder. "We have a new case?"

"There is definitely a new case." I scratched her head. "I haven't decided if—"

"I'm in." She pumped her tiny fists. "This is going to be awesome."

"Ahem." Clay tipped his chin toward me. "You need to take that up with Rue."

"We're a team," Colby assured him. "She wouldn't leave me behind." She slid her gaze to me. *"Again."*

"How am I always the bad guy?" I left Benedict Arnold and entered the house. "Seriously, how?"

"Remember when you were a kid," Clay began, "and your parents told you no, and that made them the bad guy?"

"Now that you mention it—" I angled toward Clay, "—no."

The few memories I had of my parents had been weathered by time...and magic. Unlike the tea I brewed for the girls to help them cope, the director slipped bitter potions in mine when I was a child. He wanted to erase anything that came before, anything that might hold me back from reaching my full potential.

Years of my life were a blank slate he had written his own message on.

The awkward lull that followed prompted Colby to make a confession.

"I don't remember much about my parents." She hunkered down on Clay's head. "Is that weird?"

"Neither do I," I confessed, so she wouldn't feel as exposed in her vulnerability. Colby never talked about her family. Ever. A fact that worried me. But I didn't share my childhood either. "I don't trust what little I think I do." I had too much magically induced brain trauma to be certain of its authenticity. "Pretty sure I invented my loving version of Mom and Dad based on the stories I've heard from others over the years."

"I hate that." Sympathy etched Clay's face. "For both of you."

As a golem, he had no parents. He had a creator. A long-dead one. Any bond they shared had been buried with him.

"After I turned thirteen, I got recruited for Black Hat, and my..." I bit my cheek until a copper tang spilled into my mouth to avoid calling the director *Grandfather*, "...guardian wasn't able to screw with my head anymore."

And...I hadn't meant to overshare like that.

"Thirteen?" Clay boomed with ear-ringing volume. "He turned you over at thir-fucking-teen years old?"

Colby stared at him in awe then whipped her head toward me to see if he got in trouble.

"No cursing," I told them, then escaped down the hall to avoid more questions. "I need to pack."

Bile crept up my throat as I entered my bedroom and shut the door behind me.

The faint knock that hit seconds after the latch clicked made me regret ever opening my big mouth. Now that I had unstoppered that bottle, I had done worse than release a genie. I had freed a wisp of my past I didn't want to pollute my present. I had no use for pity. For better or worse, what was done was done.

Expecting Colby, I lost my train of thought when I opened the door on Asa. "Look, if you're here to—"

"—borrow a comb and detangler?" His lips twitched. "I could use your help too, if you don't mind."

A giddy thrill shot through me, and I had no idea why, but this olive branch was exactly what I needed to seal the past back into the airtight box, where it could suffocate for all I cared. I hated that I recalled with such perfect clarity how the director trained me, how I lived for years under his roof, but Mom and Dad, their faces, were remembered from the photos I had collected of them.

"It's in the workroom." I waved him back to the third bedroom.

"This is where we test new recipes for the shop." I indicated one of the stools. "You can sit there, and I can hose you down. Unless you'd rather shower? The soap your daemon used wasn't meant for hair, but I keep the good stuff in the bathroom."

"I'll give it a day or two before I wash it," he decided, "let my scalp replenish some of its natural oils."

"You're big on haircare, huh?" I caught myself before I brushed aside a few twisted strands caught on his collar. "Do you keep yours long for any particular reason? Other than exploding ovaries, obviously."

"It's tradition." Asa sat and folded his hands in his lap. "I'm forbidden to cut it except for split ends."

"Wow." I grabbed the detangler and moved behind him. "That's strict."

"Traditions often are." He glanced over his shoulder. "Does this make you uncomfortable?"

"No." I bit the inside of my cheek to keep from sounding too eager, and I instantly regretted aggravating the sore. A good reminder it was a habit in need of breaking. "I can't turn down a chance to test a new product. Your hair is gorgeous, and there's so much of it. You're the perfect guinea pig."

There. Totally valid excuses. Professional even. I was proud of me.

"Ah," he said simply and relaxed as I began spritzing the long strands.

"So..." I fumbled for conversation. "Fae or daemon tradition?"

"Daemon."

One of the first things Asa told me about himself was that his daemon father had raped his fae mother. I hadn't dug any further into his personal history after that explosive revelation. I had tiptoed around him, too afraid I might step on another landmine. But it puzzled me to learn he honored his daemon heritage.

As was often the case with Asa, I couldn't help myself. "You have a relationship with your father?"

"Not as such." He tilted his head back and closed his eyes when I began to comb. "I'm his heir."

"What does that mean?" I ran my hands through his hair to my heart's content. "Or is it rude to ask?"

"It means my father is Orion Pollux Stavros, High King of Hael, Master of Agonae."

The casual namedrop left me choking on my own spit. *"What?"*

A subtle tension entered his shoulders. "Does that matter to you?"

"Um, yes?" I fumbled my comb. "I have enough problems without adding that to them."

"The title makes me less desirable to you?"

"Much." I was, sadly, almost done with his hair. The detangler worked too well. Dang it. "Sorry."

The tension in his shoulders eased once more, and a faint vibration moved through his chest.

"Are you...purring?" I froze on the spot. "Daemons purr?"

"Only when they're happy." I heard the smile in his voice. "And you make me happy, Rue."

"We're a terrible idea." I kept my tone light. "You know that, right?"

"I'm aware." He chuckled. "Clay reminds me at least once a day."

"He's like a big brother." An urge to defend him rose in me. "No brother wants his little sister to date."

"He loves you very much." Asa twisted to see me better. "Do you know how rare that is for him?"

"Clay is a social butterfly. He likes everyone. He was my partner for a long time. That builds bonds."

"Clay is a very old thing who has become exceptional at acting any role assigned to him by his master."

A cold spot opened in my chest that hadn't chilled me in far too long. "What are you saying?"

"That you're a singularity. That's why he worries about you." He glanced away. "And your heart."

For as long as I had known Clay, he had been the hand I gripped to hold my head above the waterline.

We were friends, I knew that, trusted it, but I had never stopped to wonder if I was his only true friend.

"He cares about you too." I toyed with his hair. "He doesn't give nicknames to just anyone."

"He likes me well enough, or he did." He laughed softly. "Until I showed an interest in you."

"We're both adults, and we're entitled to make our own mistakes. Clay can bide his time and rub in the *I told you so* after we crash and burn. That ought to make him happy. Being proven right usually does."

"You're sure we'll crash and burn?"

"Oh yeah." I laughed at how fast the certainty hit me. "I can smell the smoke from here."

A thoughtful quiet settled between us as I passed him the comb.

Ignoring it altogether, he asked instead, "Would you mind?"

"I get to braid your hair too?" I bit my first knuckle. "I feel so special."

"Only three people are allowed to touch my hair. My mother, myself, and...you."

"Oh." My hand fell to my side. "Um." I tapped the comb against my thigh. "That sounds serious."

"I am fascinated with you." He softened his tone. "You have been granted permissions others have not."

We were in a long-distance cupcake exchange. I wasn't convinced that qualified as dating or much else. But I was glad to hear Asa's permission kept me from being targeted by his father.

A bitterness flavored his voice that worried me. "Others have tried?"

"They have, and Father punished them." He ground his molars. "He's always aware of infractions."

"Probably spying on you." The way the director, apparently, had been spying on me. "That sucks."

"It does."

"Dare I ask what's the cost?"

"The hand that touched my hair."

"As in how they used to punish thieves by chopping their hand off at the wrist?"

"Yes."

"That seems...extreme."

"Father is an extremist."

"Other parts of you are okay, though?"

A smile in his voice, he slanted his gaze toward me. "Define *other parts*."

"I walked right into that one." I snorted. "Let me find you some hairbands."

"I have some." He shifted his weight and dug them out of his pocket. "It pays to carry extras."

"Do you mind if I ask how Black Hat recruited a daemon prince? Lord? Duke?"

"I attempted to murder my father. He didn't take it well and reported me. He hoped a few centuries as a Bureau lapdog might teach me what it means to serve without choice, without hope, without freedom."

The fact he didn't answer my question about his title didn't slip my notice, but I didn't press.

And I didn't explain my scowl when my spam app alerted me to another intentionally missed call.

"Sorry the murder thing didn't work out for you." I cut a razor-sharp part. "It sounds like he needs it."

"I was young and impulsive, eager to avenge my mother's honor. I'll be prepared for him next time."

Next time meant he was actively plotting patricide, which would make him king. Had he done the math? Or was he so blinded by hatred for his father that he couldn't see allowing his father to live was the only hope Asa had for a normal-ish life? Murder was satisfying, but the price of instant gratification was high.

"Of that, I have no doubt." I started plaiting, careful to keep his braids tidy. "Done."

"About time."

I swallowed a yelp as I spun to find Clay standing in the doorway with Colby on his shoulder.

"I thought you were packing." Colby twitched her wings. "This isn't packing."

"We couldn't find you in your room," Clay explained, "so we followed the smell of *feelings* in here."

Heat climbed up my nape to tingle in my ears. Black witches —*former* black witches—didn't blush.

"You mean the scent of green apple essential oil."

That I hadn't bought because it reminded me of Asa. It was popular, okay? Check any haircare aisle.

"Mmm-hmm." Clay rolled his eyes in tandem with Colby. "Sure."

Letting them team up, I was starting to see, was a very bad idea. For me.

"We're done in here." I backed away from Asa. "I'll go get packing."

Colby flitted from Clay's shoulder to mine as I passed him, wings jittering. "Where are we going?"

"Tennessee, to the mountains."

Interest fluttered along her spine. "What's the case?"

"A black witch raised a wendigo zombie."

"A real zombie?" Her macabre delight bothered me. "Does it eat people?"

"Yes," I admitted after accepting she would find out soon enough, "but wendigo do that anyway."

"Why does everything eat people?" A shudder rippled through her. "They can't taste that good."

"You would be surprised," Asa murmured, "what can be accomplished with the right spices."

The urge to glance back at him after that comment twitched in my neck. "That was a joke, right?"

"He was kidding." Clay tugged a lock of my hair. "Mostly."

Eyes wide, Colby studied Asa with new interest that worried me more than the spice comment.

"Our mission—" I jostled my shoulder, "—is to hunt down the black witch and their pet zombigo before they hurt more people."

"Zombigo." Her wings tickled my ear. "You're so lame."

"Most people don't sass me and live to tell about it."

"That's a lie." She scoffed as we entered my room. "Camber and Arden do it all the time. So does Clay."

"I used to be fearsome." I set her on the bed then started packing. "I don't know where I went wrong."

"You gave up the wicked witch life," she teased. "That means no more hexing people who annoy you."

"Ugh." I *almost* missed the days when I could wreak havoc without conscience. "Don't remind me."

"I've never been to the mountains." She walked a circle then settled in the center of my bed. "Will there be snow? Ice? Sleet? Hail? *Oh.* A blizzard? Will I need a coat?" She hesitated. "Skip that. I forgot. Wings."

"We'll use that spell from when it snowed if you get cold."

Snow was as rare as hen's teeth in central Alabama. We got plenty of hail, sleet, and ice. Flurries hit us in late winter edging into spring every other year or so, but accumulation was a major event three or four years in the making.

"Promise to build a snowman with me?" She rubbed her hands together. "We'll need to pack a carrot."

Based on past experience, I wasn't worried about the carrot. First came the rush of enthusiasm, then the stinging pain of frozen hands, followed by soggy regret that ended with me using magic to finish the job.

Glamour might be the bane of supernatural law enforcement, but it was handy when you got lazy.

"Pfft." I waved off her idea. "The guys will be with us."

Understanding brightened her eyes. "Snowball fight."

"Heck yeah." I grinned. "Girls against boys."

Finished with my bag, I pulled out a rolling suitcase I used for Colby on trips, but the safe distracted me. I hadn't gotten the grimoire out since the guys left. That wasn't to say it hadn't gotten itself out. It had. Three or four times. Just, there had been too much to do getting the shop back in shape for me to crack it open for study. But this trip would afford me time to read while we were on the road.

Still, I wavered on whether to bring it.

Some dark artifacts grew a certain sentience that resulted in them toying with their masters. Much like a cat, they wanted to be stroked and admired and treated with reverence. They used their ambient magic to convince you there was a topic you just had to read up on. Right now. This very minute.

Hurry, hurry, hurry.

The resulting adrenaline would convince people to pick up the book, and contact strengthened the compulsion until you ended up whiling away an afternoon doing exactly what the book told you to do.

Protections on the safe shielded the dark artifacts as much as they protected me from their whispers.

That I was eyeballing the safe didn't mean I was in its thrall, but it didn't mean I wasn't either.

A shudder rippled through Colby as she noticed the direction of my stare. "Are you bringing the book?"

"I'm thinking about it." I spelled it out for her. "You'll be safer once I've read it and destroyed it."

Taylor might not have gotten every detail right, but he did his research, and we couldn't afford to ignore a potential source of information on Colby. His obsession spilled across the pages, ten years' worth, but I could admit, to myself, the true reason I kept putting off studying it was the fear I would backslide under its influence. There was a whole lot of ugly in that book, and I was not immune to its lure by any means.

The spells contained within would make any black witch salivate. They would kill to own its knowledge.

To avoid its power falling into the wrong hands, any white witch who stumbled across it would set it on fire, dig holes at the four compass points, divide its ashes and then bury them. Any white witch but...me.

"Yeah, I guess." Her coarser fur stood on end. "That book gives me the creeps."

"Me too." I rested my palm on the safe. "It's a risk, a big risk, taking it outside the wards."

It might explore the house on its own, but I was ninety percent sure it couldn't leave without an escort.

"I'll sleep on it," I decided, rolling our suitcases down the hall. "Let's go pack your bag."

Aside from her teeny pillow and tiny blanket, I had little to pack for her aside from pollen and sugar.

But first, I had a surprise for her.

In the hall closet, hidden at the very bottom, I located a wrapped box. "I bought this for your Mothday."

"It's not my Mothday for two more months."

One of Colby's first requests after she settled in with me was no more celebrating her birthdays. The gap between her mental age and physical age would only grow, and she didn't want the reminder. She was a kid, an eternal one, and I remembered how much it sucked to go from my parents celebrating every milestone to the director only praising me when I sank to new depths of depravity. So, we settled on her having a Mothday every year where she received presents, we partied, and she ate way too much sugar.

"Open the box and then say that again." I set it on the kitchen table. "Hurry, before I change my mind."

No sooner had Colby peeled down one side of the wrapping paper than a sonic squeal burst out of her.

"You bought me a laptop." She sprang from the table into my arms. "Thank you, thank you, thank you."

"You're welcome." I kissed the top of her silky head. "You need something to keep you out of trouble on the road. Plus, I wouldn't want your friends to think you'd died because you weren't online every second of every day."

"You bought it for me because you *looove* me." She cuddled in, her head on my chest. "I love you too."

Throat gone tight, I had to swallow before I could tease her without my eyes leaking in front of the guys.

"Yeah, yeah." I set her back on the box. "Insert mushy feelings here."

"That's a sweet laptop." Clay smiled down at her. "Want me to help with the unboxing?"

"Sure." She finished tearing off the paper. "I can't wait to tell my friends."

Asa gathered the paper and threw it into the trash can, which I appreciated, but Colby didn't thank him. I had lost her and Clay to conversation about the specs and download times for her must-have programs.

Leaving them to geek out together, I walked out onto the front porch and breathed in the night air.

I wasn't surprised when Asa followed. Happy. But not shocked he had taken the hint.

We sat on the steps, under the bright moon, and let the cool wind tickle our cheeks.

Angling his head toward me, Asa studied my profile. "Do you mind if I ask you a question?"

As hard as I had hammered him earlier, I expected he would circle back to me. "Knock yourself out."

"You were thirteen when you were recruited by Black Hat."

"Officially, yes. That was the age I started working cases with a partner. Not Clay, but another witch."

"I've never heard of the Bureau recruiting that young."

"You're not the only special snowflake around here," I teased, but he didn't take the bait, and I sobered "My mother was a white witch, and my father was a black witch." I wasn't sure how much of my past he knew, so I left it at that. "Theirs was an unusual pairing, especially with their combined power threshold, and it made people nervous. Mom's people worried Dad would eat her heart. Dad's people worried Mom would make him weak." I studied the thick clouds. "Then I came along." I pitched my tone like a movie voice-over. "A mongrel with the potential for greatness, destined to bridge the gap between dark and light practitioners, a true power the likes of which no one has ever seen."

He waited, still and quiet, to see what else I would say. Maybe that was why I told him more.

"But I came into those powers early." Or so the director told me. "And...I killed my parents."

A hollow ache rang through my chest, a pain I hadn't let reach me since those earliest days.

"That earned me Black Hat's full attention," I continued, "but my age factored into their ruling." I paused before blurting out the rest. "I was seven, so the Bureau didn't put me down. The director took me in as his ward to keep an eye on me. He trained me himself."

The catastrophic show of power had sparked his interest in me, made him wonder if crossing bloodlines wasn't such a bad idea. But the trauma of my parents' deaths smothered whatever spark had kindled in me. I went on to have an unremarkable childhood, left mostly to my own devices, until puberty hit and unlocked my full potential.

For my thirteenth birthday, I was given a gift. A hunt. I caught and killed my first victim under the moon.

Initiation for Black Hat awaited me the next morning, along with much tutting from the director, as if he hadn't dipped my hands in blood the night before. And lectures, for the sake of those watching his every move, about how I should have been put down as a child. How I lived then and now at his mercy.

"I'm sorry." Asa covered my hand with his warm one. "Rogue magic isn't a criminal offense in children."

Had I been anyone else, I could have gotten off the hook, but I was me, and the director chose to put me in his custody until the day he judged me old enough to take a life with intent, by my own hand, of my own choice, and earn for myself what he wanted for me all along.

Eternal indenture to Black Hat.

"I didn't know that at the time." The director kept me carefully ignorant to instill gratitude for him taking me in. "By the time I did, I had killed in cold blood, and I belonged in the Bureau."

Supernaturals earned a lot of leeway in the *is it murder or dinner* department.

Humans had encroached on many species' ancestral lands, putting them in hunting grounds that, as far as paranormal law went, made them fair game. Black witches, however, didn't have to kill to survive. They did it for power, and more talented practitioners added years from a victim's life to their own.

The leeway shown to other predatory species wasn't awarded to them, which left smart black witches to prey on others with extreme caution. Get sloppy, get dead. You were made an example to remind other black witches to dine in private and clean up after themselves.

Asa slid his fingers through mine, meshing them, offering me his strength. "Rue..."

"I killed my first partner too." The confessions kept coming, pouring out of me, as if I wanted him to hear my sins and judge me for them. "Maimed the second."

"You were too young to control your powers."

"I still wonder about that." I flexed my fingers, enjoying the warmth of his palm against mine. "I was so angry, so lost. I lashed out at everyone around me. I had no real control, and the director encouraged it. He wanted to push me until I tipped over the edge, and I got tired of hanging on by my fingernails."

A low growl poured into the night air, the rumble a comfort that vibrated in my bones.

"Clay was my third partner, and I'm certain he got stuck with me because he's indestructible. Or close to it. The director felt I could grow into my role as an agent with Clay watching over me, minimizing the risk to others." I risked a glance at Asa. "I used to hate Clay for that."

"The director ordered Clay to spy on you and report back."

"Yeah." I tipped my chin up to stare at the moon. "He was nice to me, but I didn't trust him. Not for a long time. Not until I read one of his reports. He told the director I was a bloodthirsty killing machine when the truth was, I had gotten so sick from the carnage of a warg brawl, I threw up on Clay's shoes."

Asa's intense gaze lingered on the side of my face, but I didn't turn to see what his expression would tell me.

"The director broke me into little pieces until I lost so much of myself, I had no idea how much was missing or what I had lost." I risked a glance at Asa. "Clay was the one ready with a bottle of glue, a magnifying glass, and a pair of tweezers. He always fit me back together again."

Over and over and over through years and years and years until mentally I was a patchwork quilt.

"And…" I dropped my face into my hands, "…I can't believe I told you that."

Only the director knew all the gory details of my past. Even Clay had large gaps in his knowledge, despite the director briefing him prior to us partnering. As his earlier outburst proved, the director had left out a *lot*. I don't see why he bothered editing his narrative to suit his audience. Habit, maybe?

As the golem's current master, the director could have ordered him to keep his—and my—secrets.

"I appreciate the gift you've given me," Asa murmured. "I understand how much it cost you."

"It frightens me that I told you," I confessed. "It terrifies me even more that I wanted to do it."

Whatever the reason, I felt compelled to blab my worst qualities, and that left me fragile in my own skin, afraid the next touch might break through the hard shell I had spent a lifetime building to protect myself from feeling too much, from wanting too much.

"The fault might not lie with you." He ducked his head. "Mother told me once that when her people find their mate, their souls recognize their match in each other and forge a connection that facilitates sharing their hopes, their fears, their pasts. Then, if the bond is proven true, that friendship evolves into...more."

A spike of relief stabbed me under the rib cage to hear I hadn't gone soft, that this *thing* with Asa was to blame for me blabbing old secrets to anyone in hearing range tonight.

"You're saying our compatibility is giving me verbal diarrhea?"

Asa choked on a laugh that made me grin. "Perhaps?"

"You've never done this before?" I lifted my wrist and shook the bracelet. "This is your first time?"

"You are my first, yes."

"Ah." Heat rose in my cheeks, and I cleared my throat. "Okay."

With the fingers of his other hand, he traced the curve of my cheek. "Is this your first time?"

"I have never been given a hair bracelet or an emotional laxative, no."

More soft laughter parted his full lips, and my gaze landed on his mouth with a startling hunger.

"You're dae, right?" I tore my focus away from him before I did something stupid. Like kiss him just to see how he tasted. "Who's to say daemon mating rituals are all that matters? Who cares if your daddy is a king? Your mom sounds amazing. Honor your heritage, both sides or neither, in a way that feels authentic to who you are, not who your parents want you to be."

"You have a gift for cutting to the heart of the matter." He grimaced, tightening his fingers as if afraid I would pull away from him. "Forgive my poor choice of words."

"Trust me." The pinch in my chest eased at his earnest apology. "I've heard all the jokes."

A jiggling noise caught my attention, and I spotted Colby in the window, working to open the front door.

"I'm done packing." She flitted out to light on my shoulder. "I have everything I need to kick orc butt."

For a second, I got confused what orcs had to do with zombigos, but I put together she meant her game.

Mystic Realms.

An MMRPG, or massive multiplayer role-playing game.

Her attention shifted to where Asa held my hand, and her antennae quivered with interest.

"Clay and I should be going." Asa rose with fluid grace. "We'll pick you two up first thing."

"Okay." I let his fingers slide out of mine. "We'll be ready."

Heavy footsteps tromped out of the house onto the porch as Clay joined us.

"This kid is brilliant." He gave Colby a miniature high-five with his pointer finger. "She would give the Kellies a run for their money."

Flushed with praise, Colby glowed. Literally. She had been doing that a lot lately. "Thanks."

"I'll send you the files on the wendigo case." Clay patted my head on his way past. "Night."

Colby and I kept our spots while the guys exited the yard and climbed into the SUV.

The wards blipped as they passed through them, sealing us in until morning.

"Want to bake some cranberry-orange scones for breakfast?"

Angling my head toward her, I pursed my lips. "That's an oddly specific request."

With her restricted diet, she didn't much care about baking. It was all pollen and sugar water for her.

"Clay said it wouldn't hurt his feelings if we baked them." She twitched her wings. "So, can we?"

"Why not?" I had a lot to think about and a case file to read. "We need to use the eggs before we go anyway."

While Colby ran her mouth a mile a minute, explaining in great technical detail what she and Clay did to optimize her new laptop, I hummed agreement in the right spots as if I had a clue what any of it meant. I had avoided buying her a laptop for years in order to force her to be present when we went on trips. But I didn't want to risk her inventing her own entertainment while we were on a case in an unfamiliar area.

Clay was right, she was brilliant, and smart kids tended to make trouble when they got bored.

Sadly, I had the feeling none of us would be bored once we got where we were going.

5

Chattanooga was a reasonable distance away, so it made sense for us to drive. That, and it spared Colby from spending hours pretending to be my hair bow on a plane. She sat hip to hip with Clay, both decked out in noise cancelling headphones. Asa drove, as usual, and I rode shotgun.

The platinum-blond wig Clay wore was a perfect match for Colby's soft fuzz. That he wanted to give her a safe perch for when we stopped for gas and food was another example of his thought-fulness.

Plus, it gave him an excuse to buy a new wig. For him, it was a win/win. For us too, really.

The wig promised she could hang with her new BFF in public instead of always being stuck with me.

Once confident little ears wouldn't overhear, I opened the case file, ready to quiz Asa on a few points.

Before crawling into bed, I had read everything Clay sent me, but I preferred the hard copy for skimming.

"The wendigo killed seven people before you arrived. Three after." I flipped through the stack of missing persons reports filed by victims' families at four local police departments. "That qualifies as a massacre."

The director must be working around the clock to suppress the details, given the high-collateral damage. No wonder he called Clay and Asa away so soon after the copycat case. This case had all the earmarks of breaking human news in the making. Wendigo attacks were often blamed on mountain lions, but no one would buy a single cat had eaten ten people without being hunted down with its head mounted by now.

"We have reason to believe there are more victims. We found several caches in various states of decay." He switched lanes as storm clouds rolled in overhead. "There will be hikers from out of state who haven't been reported missing yet. There always are in cases like these."

Chattanooga wasn't our destination, sadly, but we would pass through it to find our remote rental.

Flipping to the photo of the decapitated wendigo, I mused, "There wasn't much blood, was there?"

Lightning illuminated Asa's features as it forked across the sky. "I noticed that too."

"Do you think it was already dead?" I thumbed through more photos. "You just...killed it some more?"

"I'm not sure." Asa switched on the windshield wipers as light drizzle hit us. "It's possible."

A reanimated wendigo would be easier to control, subject to its master's whims, not dissimilar to Clay.

Necromancers were the only supernatural faction able to fashion new life from an existing creature who rose with their own free will. Even then, their vampires were clannish and could be subdued by their own masters. But those masters were vampires, leaders of their clans, not the necromancer who resuscitated them. That autonomy might explain why humans were *resuscitated* but everything else was *reanimated.*

Still mulling that over, I asked him, "Any signs of other wendigos in the area?"

"The scat smelled the same, but that could be credited to a shared food source. The territorial markings, what few we located, were left at identical heights on trees. Only an alpha claiming land for their clan or a loner protecting their cache would scent-mark an area, so it's not unusual for them to be uniform."

Closing the file on my lap, I watched the swish and flick of the wipers. "What did you do with the body?"

"Another team was staying in Chattanooga. We buried the remains, since it's a high-traffic area this time of year, then called in the coordinates to them. They were to cremate it and clean up the noted caches."

Fire was the go-to method for destroying paranormal bodies, evidence, and dangerous objects of power.

Ideally, each team was assigned a witch to reduce documented evidence to ash, eliminating the need for clean up later. Except in cases, like the copycat, where large-scale exposure to humans or para lives were at risk. Then the preservation of evidence became a top priority. This case, thanks to its high body count, was fast becoming the latter.

"*If* it was alive to start," I mused, "the witch could have followed you, dug it up, and reanimated it."

The idea of them following him unnoticed caused his eyes to flash from green to burnt crimson.

"For her to exert control over such a primal creature, she must have spelled it into compliance. *If*, as you say, it was alive when Clay and I arrived. She could have tracked a vestige of her magic to locate it either way." His eyes returned to their natural color. "The traceries would be stronger if it were already dead?"

"The more magic you sink into a person, place, or thing, the stronger your bond to it grows."

The use of mind control magic on sentient creatures was big magic, and a huge no-no.

I skirted the edge with the teas I brewed for the girls. I had learned from my own experience with having memories erased where the line was drawn and how to avoid crossing it. *Thanks, Gramps!* But true mind control magic, where a person's thoughts and actions were wrested away from them, was taboo.

So, of course, black witches had elevated the practice to an artform.

"Let me know if you catch a whiff of black magic." I fiddled with my seat belt where it cut into my throat, uncomfortable with any comparison made between the director and me. "I still have trouble noticing it."

To put it mildly, my own stink from practicing black magic for years clogged up my nose.

"The more practice you get in the field, the easier it will be to identify. You need exposure to other..."

"Pungent practitioners?" I chuckled at his discomfort for any perceived slight. "I'm okay with being ripe." It wasn't like humans could sniff me out that way. "Actually, I'm developing a charm to keep me funky."

"You don't want the other agents to know you've switched disciplines," he realized. "That's smart."

"I stepped on a lot of toes, crushed a lot of hands, kicked a lot of people in the face, to climb the ladder."

And the director patted me on the head like a good girl each time I stabbed a potential ally in the back.

"I debated telling you this earlier." His lips thinned. "I see now I should have as soon as I noticed it."

The muscles in my lower stomach clenched in preparation for bad news. "Oh?"

"Your scent is changing. That night, when you tapped into Colby's magic, you began to smell..."

"You won't hurt my feelings." I had already granted him permission to speak the hard truths. "Tell me."

"You smell like hydrangeas, under the black magic."

Hydrangeas.

A faint memory whispered through the back of my mind, and I swear floral perfume tickled my nose.

Shaking off the peculiar sensation, I asked, "Is that how Colby smells to you?"

"Colby..." He angled his head. "It's hard to put into words. I sense her brightness, her purity."

"You read the goodness in her the way I'm beginning to pick up the stain of darker magics in others."

"Yes," he agreed with relief I understood what he struggled to articulate. "This new scent is you. It's how you would have smelled, had you been a white witch from the start." He adjusted the wipers. "The more you work with Colby, the more taint will burn out of your soul. I can tell you've practiced while Clay and I were away. The impression is stronger now than when I left." He colored slightly beneath my stare. "As a child, I helped Mother in her flower garden. That's why I recognize the scent."

His quick defense of how he came by the knowledge made me wonder who had poked fun at him for being a momma's boy. Had that taunting forced him into the role? Or did his dutiful nature stem from guilt over his conception? And who burdened a kid with that information?

Probably his father, who would have tried driving a wedge between mother and son at a malleable age.

"I can almost remember my mother smelling like flowers," I murmured, poking at my sore spots to avoid his. "I thought it was her perfume."

"Magical scent tones tend to be hereditary. There's every chance she had a floral power signature."

Leaning back, I rubbed the tender skin over my heart. "Thank you."

Eyes on the road, but his focus on me, he spoke softer than the rain. "You're welcome."

To go so long with nothing to remind me of my mother, I had

given up hope of being more than my father's daughter. But to learn that beneath the blight on my soul, I had scraps of her down deep? It reaffirmed my dedication to the path I had chosen to walk, not the one I had been led down as a child.

Closing my eyes against the sting, I breathed in deep, smelling hydrangeas.

I must have fallen asleep, because a ten-pound moth to the gut rocketed me straight out of my dreams.

"What?" I clutched Colby to my chest in a death grip. "Where?"

"Who?" Her muffled response huffed against my shirt. "When?"

The engine snarled as Asa punched it up a steep drive, and it all came back to me. "Smarty fuzz butt."

"You slept the whole trip." She shoved against me to get breathing room. "I was worried about you."

"You couldn't have—I don't know—tapped my shoulder or tickled my ear? You had to cannonball me?"

"I didn't want you to miss the big reveal." She looked mighty innocent when she lied. "A real cabin."

"Safer than a hotel." Clay leaned forward for a better view. "Closer to the action too."

Arms still linked around Colby, I frowned at him. "How close to the action?"

"About twenty minutes. We can hike to the kill zones from here."

The term *kill zone* turned her tiny face solemn. "Where do you want me?"

The fact she asked, instead of demanding to go out with us right off the bat, gave me hope that she was figuring out these cases weren't all fun and games. They were life and death. For us, and for the victims.

"Let's go in and check out the place, then we'll talk strategy."

A fraction of her earlier excitement returned as we pulled into a circular drive before a two-story cabin. I had to admit, it was beautiful with its aged logs and wall of glass windows overlooking what must be the foyer. The landscaping was minimal but tastefully done, blending into the forest that encircled the home without standing apart from it. The glass made me nervous, but I could spell it tinted until we left, to keep anyone from peering inside while we were in residence. I would ward the area too, just to be safe.

No snow on the ground, but that was a lucky break for us. It would have been fun, yes, but it would have also made hunting the zombigo extra brutal. Maybe we could do a boys-versus-girls water balloon fight when we got home. It was chilly here, but there it had been plenty warm enough.

"This is amazing," Colby trilled after we punched in the code the owners texted us. "Look at this ceiling."

We stood in the entryway, watching her soar. There was a small loft set in the peak of the home, and I had no doubt Colby would claim it the second she calmed down enough to spot it. Light and airy was a theme for sure. Skylights peppered the roof, allowing moonlight to filter in through the trees overhead.

"This is a nice place." I patted Clay's shoulder. "Good job."

"There's a hot tub out back." He rubbed his hands together. "I call dibs." He eyeballed Asa and me. "And no shenanigans in the water we're all going to be using."

"This place is a rental," I said slowly, "on a website where anyone can book it. Like honeymooners. Like couples. Like, I don't know, groups of swingers who want to leave their dirty little secrets in the mountains." I hid my smile while he paled. "I wouldn't dip a toe into that DNA pool."

The edge of Asa's lips twitched in the beginning of a smile. "Who knows when it was cleaned last?"

"I hate you both." Clay stormed outside to get his bags then yelled back, "For that, I get the master."

"I can spell it clean," I confided to Asa, tapping a finger on my bottom lip, "but do I want to?"

"You'll cave." He turned to follow Clay out to the SUV. "Eventually."

"Stay put," I called to Colby. "I'll grab our bags and be right back."

She had, as predicted, located the loft, and was busy exploring it. "Mmm-hmm."

Outside, I noticed Asa had claimed our bags while Clay struggled with his hatboxes.

Who needed six—no, seven—wigs to hunt a zombigo in the mountains where no one would see him?

The fact I had that many paperbacks and a new cookbook hidden in my luggage was beside the point.

"Gimme." I bumped my hip against his, already regretting the bruise it would leave. "Let me help."

"How can I trust you?" He clutched his babies to his chest. "You're a monster."

"Yes, well, I'm a monster who can magically sanitize the water. I do it all the time for Colby."

Any time I mixed her sugar water, I started with a sterile base to ensure she only drank the good stuff.

"Oh, really?" His earlier good mood returned in full force, and he grinned wide. "You're forgiven."

Forgiven, but not forgotten, as evidenced by the fact he continued to juggle his boxes solo.

Empty-handed, I turned to fiddling with my bracelet out of habit, drawing Asa's attention like a magnet.

"We paid the owners to stock the fridge and pantry." Asa stilled my hand with his. "You can bake to your heart's content." He bit his bottom lip, revealing a hint of fang I was certain hadn't been there until now. Except in his daemon form. "I should have explained myself before I gave this to you." He lifted his gaze. "I didn't want to risk losing you. To someone like Nolan Laurens, who fits more easily into your new life."

Those fangs were distracting. Sure, the daemon had them, but this was Asa. He made them look *good*.

"I could have said no." I studied his earnest expression, a dangerous man with questionable morals who, for some reason, wanted me enough to get crafty. In more ways than one. The guy had impressive skills, and the credit belonged to his mother, which didn't fit with how she policed his appearance. Unless that had been the point. Making him fae inside and out. Teaching him a lost art in order to hold him up as the ideal fae son, with respect for their heritage. Had she done it to combat his father's daemon influence? No wonder Asa felt torn. His parents' expectations were tearing him down the middle. "I had an inkling of what it meant, and I chose to accept it."

To accept you went unsaid, because I would have choked on those words.

Rolling his thumb over my wrist bone, he soothed the skin beneath the bracelet. "I can remove it."

A twinge in my chest that he would suggest it left me uncertain. "Can we still do...this...without it?"

"Yes." Heat simmered in his gaze when it clashed with mine. "We can do...this...however you like."

"I'll keep it." I had to work to swallow when he looked at me like that. "For now."

Oh, how the bracelet must have laughed as I stood there with the perfect opening to get it removed and turned down the one man capable of taking it off me intact.

Goddess bless, I was a mess.

"I'm glad." He pressed his thumb against my racing pulse. "Let me know if you change your mind."

"You're *sure* rejecting the gift isn't the same as rejecting you?"

"I'm sure." He continued his slow caress up the inside of my arm. "How about I remove it while we're on this case? I can put it back on you, or not, when it's over. Your choice. No pressure. Take the next several days to decide how you feel about wearing it." He hesitated. "And if you want to continue to do so."

Without letting me overthink my decision, he unfastened the bracelet and dropped it into his pocket.

Immediately, my wrist felt naked.

After spending his absence griping about it, picking at it, itching under it, there was no sudden relief.

There was...an emptiness that spread like crackling ice through my chest until my heart stuttered once.

"Are you sure removing the bracelet isn't the same as you rejecting me?"

"This is not a rejection." He brought my bare wrist to his mouth, kissed the raw spot, and chills skated up my arm. "This is how I should have done it on Halloween, but I let the idea of spending weeks or months apart excuse me for a selfish act."

As much as I wanted to blame the sudden flare of separation anxiety setting my pulse hammering on the bracelet, I wasn't wearing it.

A cold sweat broke down my spine. "Does removing the bracelet cause any side effects?"

Magic could spark allergic reactions, withdrawal, nausea, *itchiness*, and tons of other fun symptoms.

A troubled line marred his forehead. "Your heart is racing."

"Yeah." I pressed a palm to my chest. "It's going for Olympic gold in there."

"This shouldn't be possible," he murmured, examining me with a deepening frown.

Afraid I might start blubbering at any moment, I pushed out the words. "What?"

"Are you sure your father was a witch?" He leaned closer, breathing me in. "He couldn't have been...?"

"...a half daemon?" I wanted to laugh. "There's no way." I tried to picture it. "I know my grandfather."

Though my grandmother had never been so much as a whisper

in our family. No big surprise there, since my grandfather hadn't claimed me publicly and never spoke of my father. His son. I wasn't family to him. I was...a well of potential he was content to dip his hands into when his throat went dry, but that was all.

"I know my mother," he countered, "and yet, I'm not fae."

"That's not..." I got tongue-tied realizing I had mentioned Grandfather. "He would have called my dad an abomination and aborted him for the crime of polluting the purity of the bloodline." The words tumbled out before I considered my audience. "I didn't mean... I don't see you as..." I rubbed a hand over my face like it would help with the verbal diarrhea. "Bloodlines are everything to witches. Most of them are bred for greater power, not made with acts of love. They don't tolerate difference. Grandfather in particular."

One of the reasons he kept our relationship secret was my mixed heritage, and that was two pure witch bloodlines.

"A black witch father and a daemon mother would have given your father incredible power."

The idea I might be even more of an outcast overrode my earlier panic and left me numb to the notion.

"Hold on." I folded my arms across my stomach. "Why did we jump to that being the problem?"

"Only those with daemon blood suffer malaise after a potential mate removes their token."

Meaning he hadn't lied to me. I couldn't hold it against him. He just hadn't known...

No.

A daemon grandparent?

There was no way under the sun or the moon Grandfather would have ever...

No, no, no.

Just no.

It must be my mixed blood reacting to his mixed blood and mixing magical signals.

"Maybe I'm just a wimp," I argued, grasping at straws, "and my feelings get hurt easily?"

"We can test my theory." He stuck his hand in his pocket. "Are you up for an experiment?"

"Depends." I cinched my arms tighter around my middle. "What do you have in mind?"

Withdrawing the bracelet, he held it out to me. "Do you accept my fascination with you?"

"Yes," I breathed, fidgety with the nerves I lacked the first time now that I fully understood him.

Just as before, Asa secured the bracelet, and the knot vanished until there was no break in the design.

The weight on my chest, the heaviness in my bones, the sting of my nerves, eased within seconds.

"How do you feel?" He withdrew to give me a moment to settle into wearing it again. "Better?"

"Much." I drew in a deep breath, let it fill my lungs, and exhaled my tension. "The anxiety is gone."

Asa stepped into me, tucked me against his chest, and I breathed in his comforting scents.

Sweet-burning smoke from rich tobacco and the bite of ripe green apples.

"I wouldn't have removed it had I known..." He slid a hand into my hair, his warm palm cupping my skull, and held me tighter than I would have allowed another. "But then, I wouldn't have put it on you either."

"I can't be a quarter daemon." I fisted my hands in the back of his shirt. "I would know, wouldn't I?"

The possibility cast our connection in a new light, a glaring one, and illuminated my peculiar behavior.

Fascinated was a good word for my boundless curiosity when it came to him, but was it real? Had I been as intrigued by him as he appeared to be by me? Or were two sets of rogue daemon hormones at fault?

"There's sympathetic magic between black witches and daemons. It's how they can summon us."

On our first case, he told me the pungent scent of my dark magic reminded him of home.

I just hadn't realized at the time he meant it literally. Neither had he, if he hadn't mentioned it sooner.

"You're responding to me on a wholly different level than I anticipated." Asa worried one of his earrings, a ruby teardrop. "I thought ours was simple compatibility, but it's more."

About to ask for a definition of *more*, I experienced an epiphany. "Clay knew."

Asa opened his mouth, probably to defend his partner, but closed it just as fast. "It's possible."

Eager to get answers, I dialed Clay and asked him to step outside with us to avoid Colby overhearing.

"We need to eat." Clay took the path at a clip. "Then we need to rest. The wendigo hunts at midnight. The witching hour, as they say." His easy pace faltered when he noticed our expressions. "What did I miss?"

Not since the early days had I questioned Clay's loyalty. It hurt to do so now. Much more than it did back then. He was my friend, but this was too much. "Why are you so against my fascination with Asa?"

"Really?" He thinned his lips. "You called me away from a Thanksgiving dessert competition for this?"

"Answer the question," Asa said quietly, his burnt-crimson eyes dark and intense.

"I don't take orders from you, Ace." Clay rumbled, voice like gravel. "I'm the senior agent here."

"I thought you were my friend." I aimed straight for the heart. "I thought you cared about me."

"I am, and I do." His jaw flexed as he took in our united front. "What's really going on here?"

"Asa removed the bracelet." I watched Clay for his reaction. "It was...an unpleasant experience."

The temptation to lie was written clear across his face. I knew him well enough to spot it. But right on its heels came a weary resignation that left my gut hollow.

"Rumors, Rue." He dragged a hand down his face. "That's all I've got."

"I'll take them." I nudged him when he didn't spit it out. "Tell me."

"Your dad was too powerful, too clever, too cruel. His magic didn't smell right. It was blacker than black. There was no spell he couldn't cast, no taboo he wouldn't break, no heart he couldn't claim. There were whispers that the—" he bit off the title that would have told Asa exactly who my grandfather was when I wasn't ready, "—that his father had struck a deal with the proverbial devil to make his son that potent."

A deal with the devil could be construed as a daemon bargain. "Why did I never hear about this?"

"Your grandfather quashed the rumors and made the repercussions clear for repeating them."

"You must have suspected," Asa said quietly, "for you to warn us off each other."

"I wouldn't put anything past her grandfather." Clay exhaled. "I wanted to protect her, and that meant it was in her best interest not to find out the hard way if the gossip was founded via a fucking mating bond to a half daemon in line for a fucking throne."

"A mating what now?" I whipped my head between them. "I thought that wasn't a thing."

"Fated mates aren't a thing," Asa corrected me. "Daemon and fae can both form mate bonds."

"Is that what's wrong with me?" I eyed the bracelet with fresh suspicion. "Are we...mating?"

No amount of emotional laxative could get me over that hump. I wasn't ready for that. At all.

"The bond is a choice." Asa rubbed my back. "One we both get to make."

"Okay." The twist in my chest relaxed. "That's good news then."

"I'm sorry I didn't tell you." Clay dipped his chin. "I honestly thought it was just talk until you met Asa."

But he believed it enough to warn us off each other when it became obvious we couldn't stop ourselves.

I had no doubt he thought he was protecting me. It was what he did best. But the earlier conversation with Asa came flooding back, reminding me of Clay's original purpose. Did he still report to the director? I was sure he did. Did he tell him the truth or what he wanted to hear? I wasn't as certain about that.

Damn his hide for making me question his motives again after all these years.

"I have a lot to process." I stepped away from them both. "I'm going to cook dinner."

Food steadied me, calmed me, and I could use all the Zen I could pan-fry to think this through.

Their eyes bored into my spine as I walked into the cabin, but I didn't look back.

6

Midnight came two seconds after I shut my eyes. That was how it felt, anyway. Rest proved more elusive than usual, thanks to the possibility of my grandmother being a daemon. No. That wasn't quite it. What I couldn't shake was the fact I had never questioned her absence. Never thought to ask who she had been or why she had been erased from our family history.

As a child, living with the director, I assumed she had wronged him or been found unworthy of him. That he refused to so much as give her a name comforted me with the belief someone else been lacking in his estimation. I hadn't thought of her once since joining Black Hat, like I had forgotten my father must have had a mother until Asa mentioned it. Even now, my thoughts jumbled up if I focused on her for too long.

What if the reason she never crossed my mind was the director made sure of it?

Fear trickled down my spine to think his tea might have done more than erase memories of my parents.

What else was I missing from those early years? What other

questions had I never known to ask? Or had they been deleted from my repertoire after being asked one too many times? I didn't suffer from what a doctor would call repressed memories. They weren't hidden, they had been obliterated with dark magic.

They were gone. Erased. There was no retrieving them.

Done wallowing, I sat up and swung my legs over the edge of the bed.

To tint the windows and lay the temporary ward around the cabin had left me with a headache the fitful sleep I managed hadn't cured, but I wanted to avoid pulling on Colby in case we needed fire-power later.

The *ba-bump, ba-bump, ba-bump* of Asa's heartbeat, imprinted on my memory, came from the kitchen.

I rubbed the bracelet on my wrist, worried all over again that I had accidentally mated a daemon prince. I bet the director would *love* that. Then again, if he knocked up a daemoness to produce an heir with untold powers, then he very well might be tickled pink if his granddaughter got crowned the high queen.

Ugh.

Of all the men to tempt me, Asa had to come with more strings attached than a spider minding its web.

After dressing in jeans, boots, and a tee, I palmed my athame and strapped on my spell kit.

The spell kit reminded me of a bulky leather fanny pack, except it buckled like a belt at my waist then fastened around my upper thigh to provide extra stability for potion vials. The overall effect was very steampunkish, but it was an heirloom piece, and its weight comforted me.

Given what the night would bring, I slid my wand into the slim pocket in my pant leg and fastened it shut.

With no busy work left, it was time for me to face the music.

The music, aka Asa, stood with his back to me while he coaxed rich coffee from a complicated machine.

No sign of Clay yet, but I heard him stomping around in his room, a sure sign he was still in a mood.

A pale flash announced Colby as she drifted down to land on my head with a wide yawn.

"Your cell may or may not work, depending on the weather," I reminded her, "but the landline is solid."

That was the first thing I tested before agreeing to let her stay behind in the cabin while we hunted.

"I know, I know." Her wings drooped into my eyes. "If I lose internet, I'll know my cell is dead."

Forget using the cabin's Wi-Fi, though I was sure it worked fine. I wanted her laptop tethered to her cell so she would know the second a spell was cast to cut out our ability to communicate. Any blip in streaming her game would notify her trouble was afoot. It was a better system than even the traffic light I'd rigged for her back home.

"And then what will you do?"

"Call for help on the landline if I can." Her legs twitched. "If I can't, I run—er—fly away."

"Good girl." I patted her butt to keep her from sliding off me altogether. "We'll be back in six hours."

Wendigos were nocturnal. Zombies were too. Black witches were diurnal, but it was safe to assume ours would keep the creature or creatures' schedule. Zombies, if that was what we had, required supervision. Plus, the bad guys loved to work the nightshift. It was this whole thing. We would be home before dawn.

"Okay." She kicked off my eyebrow to get airborne. "See you later."

Outside, I breathed in the crisp night air and did my best to get in the right frame of mind.

"Colby will be fine." Clay halted an arm's length away, which I appreciated, given I was still hurt. "She's a smart kid, and we made an emergency exit while you were asleep."

"You *made* an emergency exit?" I examined what I could see of the cabin. "What does that mean?"

"The bigger skylights in the loft crank open to let in cool night breezes. I cracked the one in the loft a few inches and popped off the mesh screen so she can fly out if she needs a quick escape."

"Good thinking." I kept my tone neutral. "I didn't know they could do that."

"The newer ones do." He cut me a reflexive glance that skated away before I met it. "One of the reasons why I chose this place. I figured she had her pick of exit routes. We just got lucky one was in the loft."

"Thanks."

I was fighting hard to hold on to my mad when he was doing what he always did—looking out for me. He might not go about it how I would like, but he was good down to his bones. Or he would be. If he had any. Which he didn't. Anyway. Not the point. He did his best, but sometimes he got it wrong.

How often had I gotten it wrong and had him shrug it off with a laugh or a hug?

"Rue," he said softly, reading me easily. "I really am sorry I didn't tell you sooner."

"We'll get past this." I shoved him. "Let me stomp around and grumble under my breath for a little while first." I set my expression into serious lines. "I can't let this go. You get that, right? I have to know."

Hunger to know my parents, even with outlandish rumors, left me ravenous for more scraps of their lives.

"Only one person can tell you." Clay dipped his chin. "Asking would give him too much power over you."

As usual, he was right. No one divined the director's twisted motives better than Clay. Except maybe me.

The old coot would use this breadcrumb trail to lure me deeper into the fold, right back to his side.

Daemon blood might explain my ruthlessness and bloodthirstiness when I was high on black magic. I had no daemon form like Asa, but we shared the same instincts. I had recognized his potential for violence the first time we met, and part of me had liked it. A lot. Enough to swap spit muffins with him.

But was that logic talking, or was I looking for an excuse to get me off the hook for my past crimes? "There must be another way."

"If you start picking, I don't know what you'll unravel, but I guarantee he'll tie the threads into a noose."

Too bad I didn't know someone who had been friends with Mom, who might have overheard the rumors about Dad, a person who was out of the director's reach. Someone like...

Megara.

As soon as Asa exited the house, Clay grunted to indicate it was time to go, and I put the topic to bed.

Part of me wondered if Asa was regretting his impulsive act, given his suspicions about my heritage.

To slap a hair bracelet on a witch was one thing. To bind a daemoness was another.

As if reading my mind, he took my hand and laced our fingers.

The friction of his palm sliding across mine twisted my stomach into knots I tried hard to ignore.

And if a tiny smile played around his lips as he watched me squirm from the intimacy, I ignored that too.

Before the twenty minutes were up, Clay jerked to a halt and cranked his head toward the brush.

"Oh goody." He coughed into his fist. "We've got scat."

He knelt beside the human-sized pile of poop and used stick to break it apart, searching for larvae to age the dry mass. It was all I could do to see through the tears streaming from my eyes from the foul stench.

"Less than twenty-four hours old." He covered the waste, sans larvae, with a layer of dirt. "It's still in the area. That's good news."

"How is it even pooping if it's dead?" I pulled up short. "Does that mean vampires poop?"

Taking the question in stride, Clay answered, "The zombie is expelling gristle and bone that—"

The wind changed, causing the stink to follow us, and I gagged as it swirled around us.

"Never mind." I swallowed convulsively. "Forget I asked."

A bone-chilling howl rent the quiet night, unmistakable for a wolf or coyote, and I shivered at its hunger.

Flame ignited on my periphery as Asa embraced his daemon form in response to the threat.

"Close." The daemon flared his wide nostrils. "Smell bad."

"You can say that again."

"Close," he repeated with adorable earnestness. "Smell bad."

That was about the time I noticed we were still holding hands, and mine were aching thanks to the new width of his palm and girth of his fingers. Gently, so as not to hurt his feelings, I released him.

The daemon took no issue with that, happy to trade me a lock of his hair to hold instead.

Because of course he did. The only person more obsessed with his hair than me was him.

We tracked the wendigo four miles before we came to a crevice in a rock face that acted as the entrance to a narrow cave. Details from the copycat case rose in my mind, and I struggled not to pivot on my heel and march right back to the cabin.

Layers of brittle tape curled, as if this mural had been taken down and put up many times over the years and the artist didn't want to risk damaging the paper further. The fae presses had the most extensive coverage, but the major para newspapers—all magicked to appear blank to humans—had run the story.

Candids of Clay and me from those days filled spots here and there on the wall, but the bottom row...

For a moment, my heart forgot how to beat, and my blood turned to ice water in my veins.

Colby was safe.

Safe.

Not every bad thing that happened was an elaborate plot to harm her.

We had a simple case. Track the zombigo, kill it—again—then find the witch responsible for creating it.

That was it.

That was all.

Nothing hinky.

Nothing Colby-y.

Nothing to worry about.

Once I tuned out the annoying pounding of my frantic heart, the guys' too, I detected no other signs of life.

"I'll go in." I moved toward the jagged entrance, eager to burn off my nerves. "You two stand watch."

Clay rolled his shoulders, clearly uneasy with me going in solo, but he couldn't fit through the opening.

The daemon wavered in preparation for a shift, but I put my hand on his arm to stop him.

"I need you both in fighting form if it's in there."

The daemon was unimpressed with my reasoning, but he grunted assent and stood with Clay.

They had to know that I knew that they knew there was no zombigo in there.

Otherwise, they wouldn't stand there and let me walk into certain danger. Still, despite the ding to my pride, I intended to explore in the event there were clues to be found. Poop was nice and all, but its secrets were limited. Or should that be secretions?

To light my way, I slid my wand from its sewn-in pocket in my pant leg and willed the tip to brightness.

A loud crunch underfoot distracted me as I wriggled between the stone slabs barring my way.

Lifting my boot, I identified a jawbone snapped in two from my weight.

A *human* jawbone.

The deeper I traveled, the worse it smelled, until I hit a narrow anteroom stacked to the high ceiling with bones. Some were cracked and yellowed with age, but flesh clung to others, reminding me of ribs from a macabre barbecue joint.

The human remains were easy to spot, but there were animal bones too. A rotting carcass in the corner was the source of the stink, not the wendigo. I got close enough to determine species, but it was only an unlucky bobcat who had been a snack a few weeks ago. Most likely prior to the wendigo's zombification.

Now certain I was alone in the cave, I brought out my phone and allowed for the minor distraction of taking photos to give us an idea of how many humans had gone missing over how many years.

A careful wendigo, a loner, could hide in one spot for decades without being discovered by the locals.

Proximity to Chattanooga promised it a buffet of tourists would hike through its yard every few days.

More evidence this wendigo had an established den, that it wasn't brought here, and its recent murder spree wasn't instinctual behavior. Otherwise, it would have been bagged and tagged long before this.

Necromancy ought to be left to the necromancers, but they only resuscitated the dead for profit.

Black witches tended to be more practical and self-serving. They would hunt the most vicious creatures they could find, kill them, and then resurrect them to ensure their loyalty. Bargain-basement necromancy at its finest.

Working my way backwards, I reached the mouth of the cave and told the guys, "No one's home."

Neither one looked surprised to hear that, confirming my earlier suspicions.

"Can you tell what denned here?" Clay dusted a cobweb off my shoulder. "Animal or creature?"

"Definitely creature. There were more human than animal bones."

"Old den." The daemon flared his nostrils. "Smell like cat too."

"That lovely aroma comes from a bobcat carcass in the late stages of decomp."

"You know," Clay interrupted, "Ace never said more than two words to me after he shifted in all the time we've been partners. Then you come along, and he's always ready with a helpful remark."

"Like Rue." The daemon passed me a handful of silky hair. "Rue pet."

"How sweet." Clay rolled his eyes. "It still would have come in handy on those cases where I would be like 'Hey, Ace. Do they have guns?' and you were like *shrug*. That could have been a one-word answer. And yet you gave me a subtle movement, and not even a helpful one."

Already bored with the conversation, the daemon zoned out, happy for me to simply hold his hair.

"I took photos and logged the coordinates." I checked my bars. "Reception is better than I expected."

There had been no cell coverage gaps since we arrived, and believe me, I would have heard about them. Forget using any blips in service as a warning. Given I had refused to share the cabin Wi-Fi password with Colby, she would have been pouting if nature ruined her raiding plans.

The phone buzzed in my hand, and my heart tripped over itself, but the text was from Arden.

Blowing out a slow breath, I steadied my nerves and reminded myself Colby was fine.

Once I got over my jitters, I turned my attention to Arden and switched gears from para to normal.

Under less hectic circumstances, I would have replied later, but the shop was a priority, and so was she.

Despite the tea, she wasn't sleeping much. Neither was Camber. Since I stayed up late, puttering around in my kitchen, it wasn't unusual for either girl to reach out to me at odd hours for comfort I was happy to provide, case or no case.

>>*Uncle Nolan hopped a plane. He always says he's going to stay, but he never does.*

>>*I don't know why I let it upset me when I know better. Alabama has nothing on Africa.*

>>*I wish he had stayed in Spain. Why come back for like a day and then leave again?*

A twinge of resentment toward Nolan for hurting the girls left me reconsidering my stance on hexes.

>*I wish I could fix this for you.*

>>*Not your fault he's a jerk.*

>*Want me to beat him up the next time I see him?*

>>*Yes, please.*

>*Consider it done. Now, go sleep.*

>>*Fiiine.*

"You're not purpling with rage or sprinting back toward the cabin, so I guess that wasn't about Colby."

For a second, I forgot Clay really didn't know, that he wasn't just being polite.

Unlike calls, which everyone overheard, no matter how awkward, he couldn't hear texts.

"Arden's uncle blew into town the day you arrived and made big promises to the girls he just broke. He's a wildlife photographer who travels all over the world. He came because of what happened to them, or I thought that was the reason, but Arden texted he got itchy feet and decided to walk them off in Africa."

"Then he's a dick." Clay made a disgusted noise. "Arden could use the moral support right now."

The reminder I was on yet another case, instead of supplying that support, didn't sit well with me.

But a deal was a deal. I couldn't break mine with Black Hat. The cost for Colby and me was too high.

Teeth bared, the daemon rumbled, "He ask Rue on date."

"Ah." Clay rubbed his jaw. "I see."

"I doubt it," I muttered, not trusting the look in his eyes.

"The real problem was his *twu wuv* bailed," Clay teased, "so he flew off to nurse his broken heart."

"Not *wuv*," the daemon snarled. "I break his face."

"No, you won't." I yanked on his hair. "Nolan is human. He only asked me out because of the girls, and the girls would have been there the whole time. It was more of a family dinner than a date."

"The plot thickens." Clay's grin spread with delight. "He was bringing you home to meet the family."

"He not family," the daemon roared. "I break *your* face."

"Clay," I warned, "knock it off before I leave you here as a statue for the birds to poop on."

Smudge or erase the *shem*, one of the Names of God written on his forehead, and the flow of his power was disrupted, immobilizing him. He would be stuck as a lump of clay until Asa or I repaired the damage.

Afraid of my threat, or wary of the daemon's temper, Clay decided to behave.

"Rue has never, in all the time I've known her, dated. She's just not wired that way."

"Thanks for that," I grumbled, unhappy at him for highlighting my inability to forge romantic bonds.

"Until she met you, Ace." Clay ignored my death glare. "That's what freaked me out the most. It was like my kid sister discovering boys exist." He tilted his head. "No, that's not quite it." He gave it another shot. "More like she decided they didn't have cooties after all."

"I not have cooties." The daemon puffed out his chest. "Asa have cooties."

A laugh burst out of me that left the daemon grinning from ear to ear, huge fangs on full display.

Which didn't, in any way, remind me of the daintier version Asa had been sporting earlier.

"You share the same body." I hated to break it to him. "That means you share the same cooties."

"Asa have cooties." He jutted out his chin in stubborn refusal. "I not have cooties."

Oh, yeah. There was more self-awareness, more identity, in Asa's daemon side than maybe even he understood.

"Okay, fine. You win. Asa has cooties." I checked with Clay. "Do you want to keep going or circle back?"

We had only the old den to show for our first outing, but dawn was still a few hours away.

"We've come this far." He checked the GPS app on his phone. "There's a waterfall just ahead. The area is a big draw for hikers. The wendigo likely denned here for the water source, and the lure for food. We should clear the area before we head back."

Texting Colby an update, I warned her we might be later than anticipated, but not by much.

To the left, a tree with deep furrows you would expect from a bear marking its territory caught my eye. I crossed to it, examining the bark for signs to help me date it, and the daemon followed me on its tether.

"Hmm." I picked at the beads of sap, but they were all hard. "Can you tell if the zombigo did this?"

A slim chance remained that a mate or small clan was in residence, but it was shrinking all the time. As predators, they would grasp the necessity of moving dens after losing one of their own. I doubt they had any idea what had happened to their brethren, assuming there were more wendigos, but the smells of decay and black magic would have warned them away from it and its hunting grounds.

"Same as cave." He leaned in, sniffed the trunk. "Smell old." He inhaled again. "No cat."

More proof that the wendigo had been native, not brought in with the practitioner.

Wendigos weren't super rare, but they were uncommon in urban areas. Their lack of impulse control and appetites meant they tread the line of exposing supernaturals to humans too often to be allowed to breed freely. They were tracked, monitored, and wiped off the map if they let their hungers rule them.

"The black witch found the wendigo here." I turned it over in my head. "They hunted it, killed it, brought it back, and unleashed it in its territory to cage it within defined parameters. That's why it's retracing its steps. Not instinct. Instruction. Its orders must be to patrol and attack all intruders since it's quit using its den."

But why bother reanimating it? What here was worth the effort? Unless the location itself was the prize? Any predator would rid itself of competition, and black witches were no exception. Coven relocation was rare, but a loner? Maybe the black witch wanted a new territory and thought an enforcer would help them secure it against any other threats. If so, that plan blew up in their faces the moment it began eating townsfolk, alerting Black Hat to the witch's failed attempts to control their henchman.

All of which reminded me of an old practice I hoped the Bureau had kept up since I left.

"Have you asked the Kellies to dig up tags on local supernatural wildlife?" I aimed the question at Clay. "There should be a record of any wendigos or other predatory species around here for culling purposes."

Already, Clay was shaking his head. "This area has no recorded tags."

That tidbit increased the odds it had been a loner. "Then how did the witch know where to find it?"

"Either they're local," Clay said, "or they got lucky."

The Kellies kept tabs on locations with higher-than-average missing persons, deaths, and animal attacks. But so did monster hunters interested in bagging their next big thrill. This witch could have used any number of resources to locate an active zone, one teetering on the edge of intervention, even if they went in blind to what manner of beast or creature called it home.

"Maybe," I murmured, unable to peg why the witch's stroke of luck in finding the wendigo unsettled me.

The trek to the waterfall lasted about fifteen minutes, but the ground was level, the path was well-worn, and the walk scenic. Easy to see why hikers used this route often, even if it meant they were parading in front of the wendigo like contestants sashaying across a pageant stage. Except the winner got a slash instead of a sash.

With that happy thought, we reached a rustic campground, and I held out my arm to bar the daemon.

Two tents set back far enough not to risk contaminating the water supply, their flaps angled toward us.

"Hello?" I listened for hearts beating. Or, as I used to think of it, dinner bells ringing. "Anyone home?"

The lack of heartbeats didn't mean no one was there. Just that no one had been left alive.

A circle of stones created a simple fire pit, complete with a metal grate for grilling, that formed the heart of the camp. A grilled meat tang clotted my nose, but the rich scent wasn't quite right for burgers or brats.

The daemon and Clay exchanged a weighted stare, then Clay jerked his chin at me toward the first tent.

Once again, I got the impression I was being *allowed* to partici-pate in the search. It grated on my nerves, to be coddled by them, but I didn't have that black magic oomph. Without Colby, I was the weakest link.

The second after I unzipped the flap on my designated tent, I knew who pulled the short straw. "Clear."

"Found them," Clay said grimly. "What's left of them."

After I joined him, I counted three rib cages, but the rest was too mangled and strewn for me to identify. The hikers hadn't started to smell, yet, but the air was cooler up here, and the decomp would be slower.

Done waiting for an invitation to join the party, the daemon prowled out and began canvassing the area.

"We'll need to call this in." I entered the tent to examine the bodies. "The cave needs cleaning out too."

The Black Hat Bureau's purpose was protecting the supernatural community from discovery by humans, who outnumbered and often out-violenced us. We weren't policing supernaturals for their sake. We did it for our sake. And if we made the world slightly less terrible in the process, then cool.

But the flip side of that was, if a few humans had to die for our cover to remain intact, then we had more than enough folks on the payroll who wouldn't mind a hot dinner without any pesky legal repercussions. I ought to know. I had cashed in more than my fair share of meal vouchers over the years, though not for humans. Their gamey hearts weren't worth the chew.

"Hear that?" The daemon lifted his head, tilting it to one side. "Someone there."

"Where?" I craned my neck toward him. "Show me."

The final victim rested under a fallen tree, its dirt-caked roots creating a blind for them to hide behind.

A woman, late forties, clutched her abdomen, grappling weakly with her insides to hold them in.

"Hey." I knelt beside her in the soft pine needles. "Can you hear me?"

Fever had turned her eyes bright, and she had trouble focusing on me.

"Monster," she whispered, voice ragged. "Leave...me." She wet her cracked lips. "Go."

No medical degree was required to tell me the woman was dead. She just hadn't finished dying yet. Her trauma was too extensive, and she had been left untreated for too long. She would never make it down the mountain. Even if we got her medevacked, I saw this going one way. And that sucked. Really sucked.

The fever burning her up had warped her sense of time, a small mercy, but her clock was ticking down fast.

"Shh." I took her hand, mine sweaty and unsure, but I let my conscience guide me. "You're okay now."

Shifting my weight, I withdrew my wand and pressed it gently into her side as I began a syphon spell.

The instant her pain hit me, my phantom wounds mirroring her real ones, I grunted from the unbearable burden she had endured since the attack. I jerked my hand back on reflex, desperate to sever our link, but I had underestimated her. She clung to me with more strength than I had credited her, equally desperate for respite.

A soft exhale parted her lips, a surcease of pain that left her weeping with relief, and I found my resolve.

"We'll protect you." I sat down when I started getting woozy from spending so much magic. "Just rest."

"Thank you." Fresh tears cut tracks through the dried blood on her cheeks. "You're an angel of mercy."

No.

I was a stone-cold killer who had developed too many cracks in my psyche to continue with the life.

This was an act of mercy, yes, but it was a calculated one. I could afford to be kind, given we had already decided this was our last stop for the night. Otherwise, I would have put her out of her misery with a cut of my athame across her pale throat. Maybe a quick death, the ultimate mercy, would have been kinder.

For both of us.

Settling on the ground behind me, the daemon ceded control to Asa, who wrapped his arms around me. He couldn't share in the syphon spell, but I could tell he wanted to help, and having his solid presence at my back was the next best thing.

I had gone so long without anyone to lean on, I had trouble relaxing into him, but only for a moment. As always, I couldn't resist what Asa offered, and that easy trust, the eager dependency, scared me spitless.

While he and I held vigil, Clay stood watch to ensure the zombigo didn't circle back to finish the job.

Predators often kept caches of dying prey to finish off at their leisure, and I didn't want to be dessert.

Hours later, as pink and orange clouds streaked across the sky, sunlight hit the woman's cheeks, and she expelled a shuddering breath. A smile of utter contentment bowed her pale lips, and then she was gone.

To witness her end clenched an undefinable thing in my soul that wept knowing she had ascended some place worth smiling about while my parents were both dead and gone. For good. Forever. For always.

One day I would join them in that void of nothingness, the lack of consciousness a blessing in the ether.

Unlike this woman, I doubted I'd die with a smile. Probably a grimace. Or a scream. Hazards of the job.

"You really have gone soft." Clay clucked his tongue to gentle his scolding. "You held vigil for a human."

"We all deserve a hand to hold at the end." I kicked out one leg to pocket my wand. "I might also need a hand now." I slumped back against Asa. "I can't feel my legs."

Behind me, Asa rose with a soft grunt that told me I wasn't the only stiff one. Hooking his hands under my arms, he lifted me onto my feet. Fingers trailing around my waist while I regained my balance, he circled in front of me and drew me into an embrace that squeezed out tears for a woman I hadn't even known.

"Clay is right." I sniffled against his shirt. "I have gone soft."

To model this new identity after humans I respected might have been a step too far.

Full of life, yes, but also full of feelings. Most emotions eluded me, they were too nuanced for my ignorant heart to decipher, but I didn't want them if they left me soggy and puffy.

"To grieve the loss of a life is no small thing." He brushed his lips across my temple. "You offered her comfort in death. You took away her pain." He breathed me in. "You are *becoming*, and I'm honored to witness it."

"I thought I already became." I withdrew to wipe my cheeks. "Growing pains suck."

Black witch to white witch. White witch to...? I had to know what I was to know what I would turn into.

"You're fighting against what you've been taught your whole life. It's changing you, shaping you. More now that you're back on the job. With a familiar." Clay continued to keep watch. "You're engaging in a lifelong battle against yourself, Dollface. Polish up your armor. You're going to need it."

Arms cinched around my middle, I held myself tight. "Things were easier when I ate my feelings."

Clay, trying to get a laugh, winked at me. "You mean hearts."

"Okay, fine, hearts." I had to steel myself against the scent of blood on my skin. "Man, am I hungry."

That outburst was proof positive I wasn't fully rehabilitated, or else I wouldn't be smelling death settle on the human I had eased into her next life while clenching my gut to keep my stomach from rumbling.

The pit of magic in my core, always ravenous, snarled and snapped at my denial. But I was stronger.

That didn't mean I wouldn't practice common sense and move upwind to remove any temptation.

Thankfully, she was human, and her heart held no gain for me. That helped me resist too.

"The Chattanooga team is on their way to clean up this mess," Clay told us. "Ready to head back?"

A nod was all I had the energy for as I accepted the hand Asa offered to lead me to the cabin.

And if I twined our fingers, it was only to give me a firmer grip, not because I couldn't help myself.

7

The sounds of battle greeted us when we entered the cabin. Over the chaos, a confident voice barked an impressive string of orders. I had no idea what they meant, but Colby's friends understood her murder-y shorthand, and soon fresh cries of agony bounced off the walls as the gamers vanquished their enemies.

Seriously, what had those poor orcs done to deserve The Blade of Doom kill formation or the Eyeball Gusher finishing move?

"Potty break," she told them. "Pick off the stragglers. I'll be back in five."

After gliding down from the loft, she lit on my head and leaned over to examine my expression.

"Rough night." I scratched her back. "How was yours?"

"I leveled up, finally beat this stupid orcon, like a dragon and orc combo, that's been guarding a hoard I wanted to plunder, and I stole a new pet off one of the corpses of my enemies. He's adorable. An orange kitten in a suit of armor that came with the expansion pack *someone* wouldn't buy me but everyone else has."

Whoever thought of paying real money for virtual items? Genius. And the bane of parents everywhere.

"You stole a kitten off a corpse." I replayed that in my head. "I don't know if I should be proud or disturbed."

"Proud." She fluttered her wings. "I've almost collected all the expansion pack extras from my kills."

A person like me had no business raising a kid. Colby wasn't a kid, and I wasn't trying to be her mom. More like the fun aunt who let her get away with too much and loved her unconditionally. But I had to wonder if it was a good thing that I had created a cyber serial killer on the prowl for rare treasures.

Colby lived a virtual life in so many aspects, and I fully supported that. It gave her a safe way to connect with others her age or those who shared her passions. All without revealing her nature. Or her location.

But maybe I ought to put on my faux-parenting hat and give her a talk about why serial killing was bad, even if your victims had cool stuff you could pickpocket off their dead bodies.

After all, she had me for a role model. I was, at best, a reformed homicidal maniac.

"I'm going to wash up, and then I'm going to cook breakfast." I twitched my shoulder to send her on her way. "Have you eaten yet?"

"My five minutes are up." She buzzed Clay on her way back to the loft. "I gotta go."

That was not the same as telling me she had eaten her breakfast, but she was old enough to come down and fix herself food when she got hungry. I ought to be thankful she wasn't a teenage boy I had to nag about showers. Moths were tidy creatures.

The bedroom I had chosen stuck with the overall cabin theme. The bed, dresser, and nightstand were made of logs the color of the walls. Without the quilts in gorgeous colors and patterns breaking up the sameness, I wasn't sure I could have navigated the room. It was too much like a funhouse with mirrored walls, floors, and ceilings. The effect of so much wood stained the same color was dizzying.

Aiming for the bathroom, I discovered more of the same. At least the tub/shower combo was white.

Under the hot spray, I washed off the woods and the camper's blood. Forehead resting on the cool tile, I asked myself why I had been moved to sit with her until she passed when I could have expedited her departure and beat the sunrise to the cabin.

The knowledge it was the right thing to do sprung into my head, fully formed, leaving me without doubt.

The right thing to do.

It felt weird to just *know* and not to have to ask for a second opinion or look to others for an example. Maybe my plan to act like a good person until I figured out what that meant for me was manifesting in real changes after a decade of faking it.

That thought bolstered my mood as I dried off and changed into pajamas to cook in, since I planned on retiring to my room as soon as I had a full stomach. Entering the kitchen, I found Colby and Clay with their heads bent together over his phone.

"What's so funny?" I started rooting around the cabinets. "You're both snickering."

"I'm showing Clay some of my favorite kills," she explained, "just the ones I've uploaded to Twitch."

Oh, yeah.

Definitely having the serial killer talk with her.

Once I spotted a bowl full of fruit on the counter, I knew what was on the menu. "Where's Asa?"

"Perimeter check," Clay murmured to me then refocused on his screen. "Shorty, the day *Pacific Rim* becomes our new reality, you are on my team. You and I will pilot a Jaeger together. Catch my Drift?"

Colby burst into laughter then explained to me, the idiot in the room. "The pilot mind link is called Drifting."

"I knew that."

I totally did not know that.

"Mmm-hmm." She shared a glance with Clay. "Rue prefers books to movies." She cut her eyes toward me. "*Romance* novels." Her antennae quivered. "The last one was about a snake shifter and an eagle shifter."

"That explains so much about you and Ace," he said thoughtfully. "So much."

"Very funny." I rolled my eyes. "Both of you. Seriously. You should take your act on the road."

At her mental age, Colby still viewed boys as cootie farms whose main export was, well, cooties.

For that, I was grateful. I would never have to give my little moth the talk about the birds and the bees.

"I'm making quick and dirty bananas Foster pancakes." I thumped Clay's nose. "People who mock my taste in reading, or men, get none."

"From the heart of my bottom, I apologize for any rudeness on my part." He pressed a hand to his chest. "I shouldn't have said what I said about you and Ace. It's not your fault romance novels have led you to believe the reformed bad boy is where it's at."

"Romance novels, which *you* got me hooked on, have taught me valuable life lessons."

Clay rubbed his nape and avoided Colby's smug grin as she filed away that tidbit.

The sword cut both ways, and he better remember it. She had an excellent memory when it suited her.

"Name one." Colby squinted at me. "What have you learned except kissy stuff?"

Put on the spot, I now had to articulate a truth I hadn't realized until Clay teased me.

"How relationships work." I chose a few bananas to slice. "Not the kissy ones, but the rest."

Expression pinched, Colby thought it over. "You read them to figure out how to make friends?"

That made me sound all kinds of sad, didn't it? That I had to turn to fiction to grasp the friendship ideal.

But I was pretty sure that was the reason why Clay hooked me in the first place. He wanted me to read normal relationships, to glimpse normal lives, to experience normal problems. It was a secondhand life, not much different than Colby's virtual one, if less interactive, but it did help me see there was more to living than blood and death. There was also improbable shifter romance, which was my latest addiction.

"I wasn't raised like a normal kid." I pulled down the other ingredients and started measuring and mixing my batter. "I wasn't taught how to socialize or how to interact with others in a casual setting or...how to make friends."

Until Clay took an interest in me, I had no one and nothing.

Except the director.

So, like I said, I had nothing.

"*And.*" I flicked my fingers at her, dusting her in flour. "I like the kissy stuff."

While Colby digested that, Clay went back to his phone, and I started heating a pan on the stove.

A long howl raised the hairs down my nape, and I drifted outside to pinpoint the source in the distance.

The scents of sweet tobacco and juicy green apple filled my head as Asa joined me. "He's up late."

Asa might have leaned against me until our shoulders brushed, and I might have leaned right back.

The innocent contact shouldn't have spread chills down that arm, but even my fingers were tingling.

"Based on the direction," he murmured, "I would guess he's aware we've located his food cache."

The campers, his fresh kills, not the cave, which appeared to be his pre-zombie digs.

"If that got his boxers in a twist, that zombigo has more self-awareness than I would like."

"Zombigo?" He huffed out a soft laugh. "Wendigo zombie?"

Inordinately pleased with him for putting it together, I flashed him a smile. "Exactly."

His gaze snagged on my lips, and I resisted the urge to wet them, as my romance novels suggested I do.

"I made a gift for Colby, but I wanted to show you first." He eased back a step. "To get your approval."

"Color me intrigued." I ignored how my heart turned to mush at his thinking of her. "Whatcha got?"

At the SUV, he opened the rear hatch, hesitated, then pulled out a flat white box. "It's not much."

From his tone, I could tell he believed that. Otherwise, he would have brought it up sooner.

In gifting Colby her laptop early, I must have ruined his surprise, which made me want to kick myself.

"I'm sure she'll love it." I removed the lid while he held the box. "Oh, wow."

A knitted blanket in shades of green sat neatly folded inside. Raised leaves gave a 3D effect to the design that blew my mind. I had no idea knitting could be this intricate, or that he was so gifted at his craft. It fit with her bedroom's forest theme at home, and she would love the velvety soft yarn he used to create it.

"It's gorgeous." I was afraid to lift it from the box, but I could tell it was Colby-sized. "She's going to flip."

"It's not tech, so I wasn't sure she would like it." He frowned into the box, as if he only saw flaws where I only saw beauty. "The thing is..." He put the lid on it. "The throw has a gift I wanted to discuss with you."

"I thought the throw was the gift."

One I would steal for myself in a heartbeat if she neglected it for one single minute.

"I mentioned while you were recovering that I practice Tinkkit." He shrugged it off like mastering ancient fae crafts were no big. Maybe he was embarrassed? Knitting wasn't mainstream for guys.

For daemons? Unheard of. But it fit this dae well. "You were over-whelmed at the time, so you might not remember."

"The sight of you knitting, in glasses, is etched onto my frontal lobe."

That jerked his gaze straight to mine, and his bright eyes burned crimson.

"The yarn was green," I recalled, willing him to forget my lobe. "You were working on this even then?"

Rather than admit it, he fiddled with the lid. "It repels bad dreams."

"Are you serious?" I stood there, mouth hanging open. "How are you not a billionaire?"

If I could imbue that type of magic into a practical piece of art like this, I would be the Queen of Etsy and spend my days Scrooge McDucking through my vault of gold coins. Or maybe not. I always thought that would hurt when I watched the cartoon. I would go with dollar bills. Those I could wad into balls to make my own money vault/ball pit. I bet Colby would love it.

And...I had been fantasizing a beat too long if the concern tight-ening his expression was any indication.

"I don't sell these." He clutched the box against his chest. "The magic only works when freely given."

"I meant no offense." I rested a hand on his arm. "This is incredi-ble. Truly. Thank you."

"Would you mind?" Slowly, as if convincing himself it wouldn't end up on Etsy, he held it out, his request clear. "I'm not sure how she would take it from me."

"I do mind." I hooked my arm through his. "She likes you, and she'll love this."

Dragging his feet, he entered the house behind me, earning us a curious glance from Clay.

"Asa made you a gift." I hauled him over to her. "Want to see?"

"You made it?" Her wide eyes shifted between us. "That's cool."

"You don't have to use it," he said under his breath, "if you don't like it."

He set the box on the counter before her and kept easing away until I had to grab him again to keep him from slinking to his room to escape her reaction. Used to fading into the background, I worried he would disappear under scrutiny. That was the reason why, I told myself, I held on tighter.

Rubbing four hands together, Colby tore off the lid then plastered on the expression every kid who ever asked for a gaming console but received Monopoly instead wore to mask their disappointment. Or so I had been led to believe by the Christmas movie marathons Colby forced me to watch each December.

"It's great, Asa." She injected false cheer into her voice. "Thank you."

"He hasn't told you the best part." I elbowed him in the ribs. "Go on, explain it."

Still not looking at her, shoulders bowing under her expectation, he murmured, "It repels bad dreams."

"Like a dreamcatcher?" Her wings flittered with a rush of excitement. "And it works? For real?"

"Its magic only works for you," he said, peeking up, "so you'll have to test it."

"Ace has never given anyone a bum gift," Clay said in his partner's defense. "It's the real deal."

"It feels..." she lifted it and buried her face in it, "...like a warm hug from Rue."

With a practiced move, she slung it across her shoulders then tugged it up until it covered her head.

"Thanks, Asa." She tucked it around herself. "This is the best present ever."

Only her eyes peered out of the cowl of fabric. Even her antennae were in hiding. Out of the box, I could tell it was a four-by-four square. The perfect size for Colby to carry around with her at home and on any cases that required our assistance to maintain the letter of my bargain with Black Hat.

"You're welcome." Gaze sliding away, he tugged on one of his earrings. "I'm glad you like it."

"Want to see my moves?" She jostled Clay's elbow to get his attention. "Show him."

The two of them settled in to watch her slaying her enemies while I returned to the hot stove, thankful the cabin hadn't burned down around us, and made us all breakfast. I kept sneaking peeks at them while I plated the food, and I couldn't help but feel like this was as close to a family as I'd had since my parents died. As much as it streaked my black heart with rays of much-needed lightness, it cost me my appetite.

To have a family meant I had something to lose.

After everyone had eaten and retired to their rooms to sleep, to binge baking shows, or to battle the orc scourge, I selected the largest mixing bowl from beneath the kitchen counter. I used the deep sink to fill it with water then sloshed to my room.

Cross-legged on the bed, the mattress as fluffy as a down pillow, I sat with the bowl cradled between my thighs. A drop of blood earned me a dial tone, for lack of a better explanation, which I used to call an old friend beyond the veil.

Megara had practiced law in one form or another for three hundred years before she took a silver bullet to the heart after a divorce case turned violent in the courthouse parking lot. I hadn't known her then. I didn't meet her until after my parents died, and she executed their will from the beyond.

Had she survived, I liked to imagine she would have taken me in. Or at least been the Rue to my Colby.

"Megara, I summon thee." I squeezed out another drop. "Megara, I summon thee."

The stubborn wench always refused to show until after I observed every formality, which could probably be blamed on her former occupation. She remained the best lawyer on either side of the veil, but death did impact her business. Her fees were steeper these days, she was harder to contact, and she also required her clients to play secretary for her. There was no way around that when you hired incorporeal legal aid.

"Thrice I bid thee." More crimson plinked into the water. "And thrice I tithe thee."

I ran a fingertip along the edge of the bowl, and the water rippled, darkened, swirled in a mini whirlpool.

"Hear me," I called in a resonant voice. "Arise."

A face appeared wreathed in smoke, not from theatrics, but from the cigarette hanging from her bottom lip.

"Darling." Her yellowed teeth glinted at me. "Two calls in the same year? Why, I'm flattered."

Between her and Clay, they excelled at guilting me about... well...everything.

"I have a question for you." I couldn't peel my gaze from my bloody fingertip. "It's about Dad."

"I didn't know him as well as your mother, but I'll answer as best I can."

"I heard a rumor my paternal grandmother was a daemon."

"Heard a rumor, huh?" She took a long drag. "That dirt clod finally told you, didn't he?"

"*Meg.*"

"I heard the whispers, of course, we all did." She pursed her lips. "Your father was exceptional. You can't begin to imagine the power at his command. I've never seen anything like it. But it was a dark power fed by dark deeds." She tapped her cigarette. "How your sweet, joyful mother found anything to love in that miasma of death, I will never know, but she was like that." She shrugged a frail shoulder. "And, I confess, he was made better by her. He tried. For her sake. He became...not a bad sort, but not her equal."

Given the great divide between us, I felt comfortable confessing, "I have a daemon...acquaintance."

A lascivious spark lit her clever eyes. "Ah."

"I seem to be experiencing some daemonlike reactions to him."

"Like ripping his clothes off and licking him head to toe? Remember the horns, dear, they're sensitive."

Sex with the daemon half of Asa, I could safely say, had never crossed my mind. Horns on Asa, though...

"Um, not quite." I fought not to squirm at the mental picture. "More like an emotional attachment."

"Feelings." Her glee dimmed as she took another drag. "Not my forte."

Lifting my hand, I shook my wrist to show off my bracelet. "We're sort of...fascinated...with each other?"

How I made it sound like a question when I had agreed to it not once but *twice*, I had no idea.

"Jesus, Mary, and Joseph." She coughed until her eyes watered. "Who is he?"

"His name is—"

"No, no, no." She waved the cloud of smoke away. "Who are his people? What is his father's name?"

For a beat, I debated faking interdimensional interference to get off the hook. "Orion Pollux Stavros?"

"Vonda, you would have loved this," she called, as if my mother could hear her. "You've been claimed by a prince of Hael. One of the high princes, no less. They're the only ones who do the hair thing. They are a peculiar caste and very particular about their hair, which I'm sure you've noticed if you're wearing *that*. I can't believe it. I just can't." Her bark of laughter stretched into a long howl of mirth. "It's too delicious."

Cheeks burning from her raucous amusement, I dipped a finger in the water. "You're not helping..."

The ripples broke up her features, and she used the time while they settled to rein herself in.

Leaning forward, she flicked ash off the tip of her cigarette. "Have you test-driven him yet?"

"*No.*"

"You aren't serious." Deep wrinkles did little to hide her disappointment. "You're not still a virgin."

"No." A hard edge honed my voice. "I had sex at thirteen to protect myself."

That encounter had been one part advance planning to one part magical high from my first kill.

The guy was harmless enough, and human to ensure he was clueless as well. I scouted him out weeks earlier. A male witch would have run screaming from the proposition, aware of what I was sacrificing. A human, though? At fifteen, he didn't much care that I was younger. Only that I would take off my pants.

A snarl vibrated through our connection that I felt in my bones as she cursed the director's existence.

Black witches weren't any more or less powerful for being virgins in their day-to-day spellwork, but their willing sacrifice of that last barrier of innocence was a potent boost to any major working. Both men and women saved it for a once-in-a-lifetime spell they otherwise couldn't have cast on their own.

"I'm surprised the bastard explained it to you," Meg snarled. "Then again, I'm sure he had a plan for it."

"I overheard a girl on the grounds bragging about how she planned to seduce a man so she could drain a lake where merfolk hid their gold and gems." I was the only child tutored by the director, but there were others on the property now and again, most of them the children of Black Hat agents come to check in. I think he requested their presence, to socialize me, but I was too shy to warm up to others after an hour. "I never saw her again. I wanted to believe then it meant she had succeeded, maybe bought a new life."

"Sweet child," she sighed. "The girl told someone. That was her first mistake. She let herself be overheard. That was her second mistake. There are no third mistakes for black witches. She was as good as dead the moment she opened her mouth, poor thing."

"Letitia and Maria." I would never forget those names. "Letitia came back, years later, and I asked about Maria. She was flattered I noticed her, I think, and happy to regale me with the details of how she talked Maria into having sex with her older brother. That made it easier for her to follow them to the lake."

Once it was done, her brother called to tip her off when to drive his truck up there to collect the haul.

"After the couple had sex, the brother pretended to leave but actually joined Letitia. Maria drained the lake, stole the mermaids' treasure before the water rushed back in, and the brother and sister were waiting for her. They killed her and shared her heart."

The whole thing had an incestuous vibe that still bothered me, a twisted fairy tale in gossip form.

"That convinced me the best course of action was to pick a guy, rid myself of the potential, and hope I survived my punishment."

The last part had been a near thing. The director was so furious, he beat me within an inch of my life with his cane. But I was older then, around eighteen before he'd decided how best to use me, and my years in Black Hat had hardened me to the pain.

And he wondered why I didn't leap to answer the phone each time it lit with his private number.

"Have you tried again?" Meg broke into my grim thoughts. "Please tell me you didn't quit after that."

"I went through a man-eating phase," I said and left it at that, not wanting to relive those days.

"Good." That satisfied her. "Men are like shoes. You won't know who fits until you try them on."

Uncertain if she meant that literally, I let the topic drop. "So... daemon blood."

"The only way to be certain is to ask your grandfather for your grandmother's identity, and I *will* send a passel of my great-great-grandsons to whoop your tail if you try. That man would charge more than you can afford for the information, and he would keep the salient details to himself to sell to you later."

"That's pretty much what Clay said too."

"He might have rocks for brains, but he's not wrong."

I wasn't clear on the details, but Clay and Meg disliked one another so intensely they refused to speak to each other. All I knew for certain was they met while he was on a case, and she was alive, but the odds were good he put down someone she loved for Black Hat.

"My...friend...is half fae," I found myself confessing. "His mother's people do this thing where—"

Nose mashing against the barrier, she exhaled a wall of smoke. "Do go on."

"Stop being a perv." I twisted my mouth into a disapproving frown. "I'm being serious."

"Oh, fine." She settled back with a huff. "Go on."

"They compel their potential mates to..."

A glint returned to her eyes. "Yes?"

"...talk. About themselves. A lot. I can't shut up around him. I just word vomit all over the place."

"Dear heart, I'm not prone to romantic sentiment, that was your mother's forte, so I won't offer you my relationship advice." She crushed out the glowing tip of her cigarette. "This is all I will say on the matter. You're not a picture book left on a coffee table for just anyone to flip through at their leisure. Far from it. You're a grimoire, kept in a private library, wrapped in a girth of chains, and cinched with a padlock. If Fate decided to arm your beau with a pair of bolt cutters, perhaps she worries you might spend your life waiting on a perfect man with a perfect key to fit your lock when perfect...doesn't exist."

Shades of regret colored her tone, and I wondered if she wished she had taken a chance on a not-quite-Prince Charming of her own.

"Is it real?" That was what I wanted to know. "Or is it biology?"

"When you're with him, does it feel real? Better yet, when you're apart. Does it feel real then?"

"Yes," I decided after considering my answer. "That's what makes it mortifying."

The urge to confide in him felt authentic. He was only half fae. How much of my confessions were simply my awkward attempts at navigating an undeniable attraction to a man whose opinion mattered to me? I wasn't sure how much to blame on his nature versus how much to blame my failure at flirting etiquette.

"There you go." She pinched a fresh cigarette between her lips without lighting it. "Question answered."

"It's not that simple."

"Ah." She gave a slight nod. "You want me to tell you what to do."

"That would be nice."

"As I said, not my forte." She studied me. "Only you can decide what—and who—is right for you."

"We got off topic." I rolled the bracelet between my fingers. "I only meant to ask about my dad."

"This is my parting salvo." She held up a lighter with her initials engraved on the front. "If you didn't care about your daemon, would you still be so curious about having daemon blood? Aside from how this may affect your relationship with him, does it otherwise impact your life? Will that knowledge change who you are?" Her eyes grew shadowed in the flame summoned by a flick of her thumb. "At the end of the day, does it matter?"

The short answer was *no*.

The more complicated one was *yes*.

A knock on the door drew my attention from Meg. "Come in."

Expecting Colby, who had an uncanny radar for when I was talking to Meg, I startled to find Asa.

"Hello," he said slowly. "I heard voices and came to make sure everything was all right."

Given his excellent hearing, I was willing to bet he heard more than that if he had been listening in.

"Who is this delicious morsel?" Meg wet her lips. "You're lucky my biting days are done, tidbit."

Asa slid his questioning gaze to mine in a clear plea for rescue I was reluctant to give.

Meg was fun when she lit into someone. As long as the someone wasn't me.

"Megara Baros, this is Asa Montenegro." I gestured between them. "Asa, this is Meg."

"I'm her godmother." Meg rested her chin on her palm. "You gave Rue the bracelet."

"It's a pleasure to meet you." Asa made an elegant gesture at his waist. "I apologize for intruding."

"I was about to go." Meg faked a yawn. "Why don't you tuck in my darling girl for me?"

Heat splashed my cheeks, and I wished I could reach into the ether and strangle her.

"Good night, Meg." I pulled the plug on our connection then turned to Asa. "Sorry about that."

"I didn't mean to interrupt..." He quirked a brow at the bowl. "What were you doing?"

"Meg was Mom's best friend." I set it aside. "I figured if anyone had the scoop on Dad, it would be her."

Leaning against the doorway, he let his keen interest show. "Did she know anything?"

"No more than Clay." I rolled a shoulder then noticed his hands. "Hey, what does your bowl do?"

Black glaze cupped the base and lightened to a vibrant crimson at the lip. A deep notch pierced its side, shaped like an old-fashioned spit curl, and a noodle was escaping through it. No. Not a noodle. A length of cream-colored yarn.

"It's a yarn bowl." He dipped his chin to hide the flush in his cheeks. "I was about to start a new project."

This was not the next High King of Hael or anywhere else. Sure, he could be terrifying, but it cost him. He was more at home like this, with his yarn bowl cupped in his palm and his glasses hanging from the neck of his dress shirt. I couldn't picture him ruling over a people who relished destruction and chaos, who let their worst impulses act as their conscience, when he preferred creation and quiet.

We were a bad idea. Terrible. I couldn't think of a worse one. For either of us.

So, of course, I waved him in then patted the mattress beside me. "Having trouble sleeping?"

"I always knit before bed." He sat, stiff as a board. "It helps me unwind."

Eyeing him, I decided to ask, "Was that a yarn joke?"

His soft laugh told me I hit the mark with his subtle humor.

"I should go." He didn't budge. "You need your rest."

"Sleep and I aren't on a first-name basis. Or last name." I sawed my teeth over my bottom lip. "I planned to read until my eyes gave up and forced my brain into submission. Want to join me? I read, you knit?"

Asa twisted to see me fully, and his gaze dropped to my mouth, proving romance novels knew what they were talking about.

"In your bed?" His voice lowered to the rumble of distant thunder. "You want that?"

I hopped up like lava had bubbled out of the mattress, snatching the bowl to cover my nerves.

"Leave a metaphysical doorway open, and who knows what might drift through it." I sloshed water onto my toes. "I have to cleanse this first." I inched toward the bathroom door. "Do you need anything?"

Peridot eyes flashed to burnt crimson as he studied my face. "Only you."

Chills raced up my spine, tingling in my scalp, and I hurried to empty the bowl.

"I can do this." I gave myself a pep talk. "It's sharing a hobby. That's it. Nothing wrong with that."

Asa wasn't going to toss his bowl and ravish me the second I entered the bedroom.

And I wasn't going to lick his horns or any other part of him, even if his lips *did* look ridiculously soft.

A flush spread over my body, tightening my skin, and my toes curled against the cold floor.

Whose bright idea was it for me to read steamy shifter romance in a bed with him anyway?

Oh yeah.

Mine.

8

Midnight came between blinks. One minute, I was asking myself if a polar bear shifter and a seal shifter were a great idea. The next, I jolted awake with the scent of pipe tobacco and green apples in my nose.

"Um," a small voice said from the doorway. "It wasn't locked..."

A groan poured out of me as I attempted to roll toward Colby, only to fall off the bed with a solid thump.

"Ouch."

As I lay there, adrenaline dumping into my veins, my hip smarting, I grasped the situation.

I had fallen asleep on top of Asa. Like I starfished over the man. But he hadn't budged from his side of the bed. Which told me it was my fault.

"Rue." Asa slid onto the floor next to me. "Are you all right?"

No.

I was trying very hard to die so he would forget I spent the day clinging to him like his favorite boxers. Surely my memorial would distract him from what a weirdo he had climbed into bed with this morning.

Tilting my head back to see Colby, who was smothering a laugh, I asked, "Give us a minute?"

"Sure." She sped off, snickering on the way. "Hey, Clay, guess what?"

What she said next, I chose to ignore in favor of the gorgeous man leaning over me. "So..."

"So," he agreed, his fingers tracing my cheekbones. "You're a cuddler."

"I guess?" I leaned into his touch. "I've never slept with a man." I blushed. Hard. "Like sleep-slept."

"I know what you mean." He cracked a smile. "I've never sleep-slept with a woman either."

"Really?" I wedged my elbows under me to leverage myself upright, putting me nose to nose with Asa. "You're the love 'em and leave 'em type?"

He hummed low in his throat, which was not an answer, but I forgot that as his warm breath hit my face.

"Which type are you?"

Mind blank, I couldn't see past the heat simmering in his eyes. "What were my choices again?"

"Colby said you..." Clay skidded to a stop behind me. "Well, this is awkward."

"To be continued," I told Asa, resting my forehead against his until my pulse returned to normal.

"I can go," Clay offered, "if you two need another minute."

"That would be nice." I couldn't fight the pull to stay here, with Asa. "As you can see, I'm fine."

"She made it sound like you broke every bone in your body."

"And you believed her," I asked dryly, "that a tumble off a mattress would snap me like a twig?"

Tonight's wig, one with tight black curls that hugged his scalp, didn't budge as he shook his head.

"Ace didn't return to his room last night, so I worried." He folded his arms over his chest. "Sue me."

"I would win." I breathed in Asa one last time. "The law would be on my side."

"We have a wendigo to hunt if you two are done staring meaningfully into one another's eyes."

"We're not." I rubbed my nose against Asa's just to annoy Clay. "We'll press pause, though."

Asa rose to his feet and offered me a hand up then left to dress without another word.

The yarn bowl, he left on the nightstand on his side of the bed, like a promise. Not that he had a side on my bed, but he had spent the night in the same room, on the same mattress, as me. And I was assigning way too much significance into a single night of shared hobbies between insomniacs. This was no different than baking with Clay.

Except Clay had never made me a hair bracelet from his wigs.

He had baked me cupcakes, though. Tons of them, over the years. And cookies, cakes, candies...

Give it up, Rue. You can't rationalize this away. You agreed. Not once, but twice. Now deal with it.

Emotions were hard, dang it, and I didn't know what to do with mine. There were so many these days, a smorgasbord of them. Sure, I'd designed a pattern of behavior to mold myself into a better person. Yeah, I was proud when I hit all the right notes. But this was different. Totally unscripted. Made up on the fly.

That felt dangerous, reckless, foolish. I never should have said yes to him the second time. But it also felt *good*. I didn't know what to do with him, but I wanted to figure it out.

The wanting frightened me. I wasn't the type to hang my hope on another person. It was too dangerous.

"You don't look so hot." Clay pressed the inside of his wrist to my forehead. "Do you have a fever?"

"I don't get sick." I swatted his hand. "I'm freaking out a little."

"You spent the night with Ace." He studied me. "You okay after that?"

"We didn't do anything," I rushed out in a single breath.

"Yeah." A grin overtook his face. "I know."

"What is that supposed to mean?" I squinted at him. "How do you know?"

There had been no time for the guys to talk behind my back, not that either would do that.

"The higher the daemon's caste, the weirder their customs." He laughed at my scowl. "Think on that."

As Meg had warned me, Asa was particular about his hair, but what other idiosyncrasies awaited me?

Pivoting on his heel, Clay aimed for the hall, humming a jaunty tune that made his smile stretch wider.

Meanwhile, I was left to picture that mortifying scene in historical films where a king deflowers his new wife in front of thirty advisors to ensure the marriage was consummated, and that she was a virgin.

"What is that supposed to mean?" I anchored my hands on my hips. "Clay, get your butt back in here."

Clay did not, in fact, get his butt back in there. He went to the kitchen and started the coffee.

Growling low in my throat, I got dressed, handled hygiene, which caused me to cringe after it hit me that I had been all up in Asa's face with morning breath. Night breath? Whatever it was, it wasn't ideal. There was no undoing it, though. He might as well learn early I wasn't princess material before this got serious.

No, no, no.

That made it—*us*—sound like a foregone conclusion.

More like if, *big* if, we got serious.

With more force than necessary, I strapped on my kit, pocketed my wand, and prowled to the kitchen.

Colby sat on Clay's head, bouncing on his springy curls, with her blanket draped around her shoulders.

Now that I thought about it, she had been wearing it when she woke us up earlier.

I wasn't the only one who noticed, based on the pleased crook of Asa's lips as he watched her antics.

"What's the plan?" I helped myself to a cup of coffee. Black. "Do you want to retrace our route?"

The first sip burnt my tongue, but I got it down then passed the mug to Asa, who didn't miss a beat.

There had been a definite wendigo presence in the area, but the bobcat carcass's state of decomp dated the latest activity weeks earlier. Cooler mountain air, and the shelter of the cave, made it difficult to tell.

I figured the black witch we were hunting had killed the wendigo not long after it brought down the cat.

"Thank you," he murmured, sipping after me without a hint of discomfort at the temperature. "Here."

A muffin sat on his palm, a bite missing on one side, a dare bright in his eyes.

As I plucked the offering from his hand, a silly thrill shot through me.

"What did I tell you?" Clay leaned in close. "Spit muffins."

Not even that gross oversimplification stopped me from taking a larger bite out of the one Asa left me.

The peridot of Asa's eyes deepened as he watched me until Clay coughed into his fist.

"There's a child present," he reminded us, nudging Colby back to the loft. "Keep it rated PG."

"PG-13," she yelled down as she settled in for her next battle. "I'm old enough for kissing."

Unable to hold Asa's stare a moment longer, I broke away and called out to her, "Stay inside, and keep your phone close."

"Will do." An evil cackle drifted down to us as she addressed her team. "I see the raid was successful."

"That kid." Clay shook his head as he led the way out the door. "She's something else."

"Bloodthirsty and vengeful," I agreed. "She also holds grudges about expansion packs."

A neat furrow creased Asa's brow, but he didn't contribute. He was plenty computer literate, but not so much on the gamer side of the spectrum. I couldn't blame him. I didn't know much. I picked up the lingo for the sole purpose of communicating with Colby, and I still didn't understand half of what she told me.

"Tonight, we head west," Clay answered my earlier question. "We're walking about a mile parallel to the path from last night."

"Any major campsites in the area?" I fell in step behind him. "Any word on the cleanup?"

"The cleanup is in the books, and the team is standing by in town in case we need them again before it's over." He checked the compass on his phone app. "There are no campsites, but there's a scenic over-look folks gawk at when passing through."

"A patient hunter could make that work for him," Asa said, his breath tickling my ear.

"Nah." I smiled at him over my shoulder. "Too messy."

"Nothing is too messy for a wendigo," he pointed out. "You saw that camp."

A cramp hit my stomach at the reminder when death, even trau-matic death, never used to bother me.

"They would have to hide in the brush under the overlook then snatch people who came to the rail. That's the easy part." They were ambush hunters. "But what about the victims' cars? Would a wendigo know what a car was? Or that it had to be disposed of? The trick would only work a few times if they let empty cars pile up on the side of the road. They could roll them off the mountain, but that would be loud. It would also draw human attention no wendigo would want so near its hunting grounds."

"You've put a *lot* of thought," Clay said, "into wendigos attacking tourists on scenic overlooks."

"Not really." I shifted my attention toward him. "I've just seen a lot of cheesy horror movies."

Genre standards let you puzzle out how any given plot would twist long before the movie got there.

"Since when do you watch those?" He checked our coordinates. "Colby's too young, right?"

"Camber and Arden." I blew out a breath. "Teens these days love their gore."

Granted, I loved gore when I was a teen too, but the blood I spilled hadn't been corn syrup and red dye.

A high-pitched buzzing noise whizzed past my ear, and I swatted at it. "Stupid mosquitos."

A wide palm hit the small of my back and knocked me to the ground as more pests dive-bombed me.

"Not bug," the daemon rumbled from behind me, having claimed Asa's skin. "Bullet."

"A bullet?" I reached down to retrieve my wand. "Clay, you hear that?"

"Yeah." He crouched, hand on my shoulder. "Stay down, Rue."

"I'm not going to eat dirt while you two square off against whoever's out there."

An oily sensation spilled across my skin, a greasy film that coated the air I breathed, sticking in my lungs.

"Black witch," the daemon told me, confirming what I sensed as the presence of dark arts. "Bullet hurt."

"What?" I whipped my head toward him to find dark blood trickling down his torso. "You've been shot?"

A low voice rustled through the leaves overhead, carried to us by magic. "Give me the book."

"Book?" Bile splashed the back of my throat as my mind turned toward the grimoire. "The only book I've got with me has a library stamp on the inside flap. I would show you, but I don't have it on me." I was an old pro at lying with truth. "Also? I'm not going down the mountain without it. You'll have to fight for it."

Ms. Agnes, our librarian and book club organizer, would ban me for life if I didn't return it on time.

Sure, I could buy my own copies, but where was the fun in that? I needed that bond of community, as all witches did. Plus, I got a cheap thrill when I beat the other women to the sign-up sheet for new releases.

Top of the list, baby.

"Give me the book," she demanded, her voice cold and stark, "and I'll let you live."

"You'll have to be a smidge less vague." I pushed up, but the daemon kept me pinned. "How about you put away the gun, and we'll talk like civilized witches?"

What kind of sad excuse for a witch shot people? With bullets? In a gun? It was so...*mundane.*

How embarrassing would it be to die that way? No self-respecting para would put it on their headstone.

"How about I kill you," she countered, "then help myself to the book after your wards die with you?"

This witch had been to the cabin, scoping it out, scoping *us* out, far too close to Colby for my comfort.

"No," the daemon roared, straightening to his full height, making himself an easy target. "No hurt Rue."

"Get back down here." I grabbed his ankle, but he slipped through my fingers. *"Asa."*

9

Head thrown back, silky hair flowing in streamers behind him, the daemon charged the shooter.

"This is going to suck," Clay grumbled, then sprinted after him, leaving me alone with grass in my teeth.

The black witch opened fire again, but she only had so many bullets, and the daemon was *fast*.

As soon as the gunfire fell silent, I popped up to help them, wand at the ready.

Right in time to watch as the daemon planted one hand on the witch's shoulder while palming the top of her skull with the other. He ripped her head clean off, held it up by the bloody ponytail, and yelled in her face in a language I was grateful not to understand, based off the pallor sweeping through Clay as the words registered with him.

Jogging off the beaten path, I closed the gap between the daemon and me, ignoring Clay's subtle gestures to stop.

"Next time, don't kill the bad guy—or girl—until *after* we question them, okay?" I placed a hand on the daemon's muscular forearm. "How badly are you hurt? Do you need to shift? Or get medical attention?"

"For Rue." He presented me with the severed head. "Gift."

"You shouldn't have." I accepted it, grateful for my cast-iron stomach. "Really."

Preening like a peacock while Clay searched the body, the daemon set his hands on his hips. "Rue like?"

"I preferred the cupcake." I bit the inside of my cheek to keep from laughing. "But this is nice too."

"No identification." Clay patted her legs to check for a hidden pocket. "She never drew her wand."

Her faith in the gun had been that absolute, and it troubled me. We were missing something here.

"She used magic to project her voice." I held up her head, studying her features. "I don't recognize her."

That wasn't saying much, given the gap in my *employment* history. Even before then, I had been more of an antisocial butterfly.

Without Clay chipping away at my conditioning, forcing me to wake up and think for myself, I would be a feminine version of the director. And after that nightmarish showdown in the forest with the Silver Stag, I would have wielded untold power without the pesky conscience that burdened me day and night now.

I would have... I couldn't bear to think of what I would have done to Colby had we met any sooner.

"Snap a headshot," I told Clay. "Get the Kellies to try their luck IDing her for us."

He did as requested, firing off an email that would, I hoped, give us insight into the witch's motivation.

"The book." Clay rose with a sigh, leaving the weapon for the incoming team to bag and tag. "Any clue what that was about?"

Oh yeah. I had a pretty good idea what title was worth her life. But I wasn't going to name it out here.

Sidestepping his question, I asked one of my own. "This is the first you're hearing about a book?"

"The original case involved a wendigo." He snorted. "They're not much for reading."

Which meant the witch's purpose had changed, or we had been wrong about their goal from the start.

The daemon shifted his weight, lifting his chin to scent the air, then gave us the all clear.

We were safe.

For now.

"Lovely." I stared down at the corpse. "Am I being paranoid in thinking this was about me?"

By *me*, I meant Colby, whose name I wouldn't utter where the wind could catch it.

"How do you figure?" Clay dropped his gaze back to the woman. "What are you seeing that I don't?"

"A wendigo case brought you out here," I reminded him. "You handled it and left."

"Asa and I," he said, mulling it over. "Not you."

"She determined you only work black witch cases," Asa surmised, "and raised the wendigo as bait."

"Zombigo," I corrected, "but yes."

"She set the trap for you," Asa said, voice rough, "with the belief you would bring this book with you."

A book worth luring me to the middle of nowhere to collect left me little doubt of the title in question.

"That's how I read it." I bobbed my shoulders. "Otherwise, she would have made her demands of you."

Neither a golem nor a dae carried books of power on their persons, aka grimoires, but witches...

Black or white, from charms to herbs to wands, we believed in accessorizing.

I angled my head toward Asa's voice, careful to avoid admiring his bare torso or the dress pants slung low on his hips from his other form stretching the waistband to the breaking point. Okay, fine, so I took it all in. For science. Medical science. He had been shot, after all.

He might need a field medic. I wasn't one, but I did have a poultice or two in my kit that might patch him up until we got back to the cabin.

"You're bleeding," I said, proving my grasp on stating the obvious.

Unconcerned, he kept his stare fixed on me. "This changes things."

Our simple zombie case had blown up in our faces, and we had to dig through the debris for fresh clues.

"We need to head back." I stood before him, fingers running down his taut abdomen, the muscles clenching beneath my examination. "You're hurt, and we need to get your wounds treated."

Sliding one hand behind my neck, he pulled me toward him until I was close enough for him to touch his forehead to mine. "Your concern honors me, but I'll be fine."

"I'm fine too." Clay gripped my arm, hauling me back. "Don't worry about the holes in me, Rue."

The sudden movement caused the daemon to burst from Asa's skin in a flash of fire. *"Mine."*

"Not yours," I reminded him, shoving him back for good measure. "Clay was right to break us apart."

Many times, I had read about the phenomenon of the world shrinking until it only held two people.

That moment, with Asa, was the first time I had experienced the heady rush for myself.

I yelled at those heroines, ready to throw their books at the wall. I called them total idiots for letting their guard down in battle just to smooch their hero. Yet there I had stood, recycling Asa's air, with a dead body a foot away.

I was a total idiot.

"As much as I would love to go back to the cabin, we've created a problem." Clay glanced between us. "If that was the zombigo's— which is still a dumbass name—handler, then we've just unleashed it."

"Any active workings would have died with her," I disagreed, confident in my assessment. "She was too weak to leave a lasting construct."

The zombigo, wherever it had gone, ought to have collapsed where it stood when she died.

Our backup team could track it down, by smell alone, and cremate the remains.

Problem solved.

Case closed.

Go team!

Phone still in hand, Clay puffed out his cheeks. "We've got an ID."

"Really?" I frowned at his reaction. "That was fast."

"The Kellies use facial recognition software to help identify agents killed in the line of duty these days." He flashed his screen at me. "That was Annie Waite."

"A Black Hat black witch," I supplied as I skimmed the bio the Kellies attached from her file. "No way was she powerful enough to reanimate a gnat, let alone a wendigo. Lovely. That means she's got a partner, a more powerful black witch, out here somewhere."

"Rogue agents?" Clay cut his eyes toward the darkened trees. "Anyone else experiencing déjà vu?"

First David Taylor, then Annie Waite, and now a third black witch gone dark side?

The Bureau hit bumps in the road, sure, but that was to be expected when you blackmailed, kidnapped, bought, stole, traded, or threatened agents into service rather than recruiting them through, say, hiring fairs. But this much upheaval? It was dangerous. For humans, for agents, and for the director.

"How much power is required for reanimation?"

Asa was back, his transformations giving me whiplash, and his wounds seeped with fresh blood.

The ironclad grip Clay kept on my arm kept me rooted to the spot as I tuned in Asa's heartbeat.

Ba-bum, babumbabumbabum, ba-bum.

"You can't hold that form." I tuned him out just as fast. "That's why you keep shifting back and forth."

Upon hearing that, Clay released me to inspect his partner's wounds. "The bullets were cold iron."

"Yes," Asa hissed on an exhale, as if giving up the charade of invincibility hurt worse than the injuries.

"Let's get him back to the cabin." I circled them. "We need to make sure he purges those bullets."

"You two go ahead." Clay stared off in the distance. "I'm going to make the circuit, see what I see."

"She came armed for fae." I wedged my shoulder under Asa's armpit to help support him. "That's more proof she knew who and what she was luring here."

A bullet was a bullet as far as witches go. The expensive upgrade had nothing to do with me.

Thanks to my previous dietary habits, and my genes, I would most likely survive anything short of having my heart pulped or my brain scrambled. But cold-iron rounds were specific ammunition for hunting fae.

That witch, whoever she was, had expected Asa and come ready to take him out.

Did that mean she was targeting him? Or simply that she knew Clay was the unstoppable force?

Bullets didn't much matter to golems either. He would repair the damage within hours.

"Call if you run into trouble." Clay kissed my forehead. "Be careful, Dollface."

"You too." I returned my attention to Asa. "You okay to walk back?"

"I can manage," he grunted and pulled away from me. "I shouldn't put so much weight on you."

"I can take it." I tightened my arm around him, forcing him to lean on me, and we set out toward the cabin. "Trust me."

"I do." He rested his chin against my temple for a beat. "Thank you."

"You got shot protecting me. This is the least I can do."

A rustle in the leaves drew my eye toward the branches overhead, and I half expected for Annie to make her demands of me again. About the time I talked down my paranoia, an ominous prickle stung the base of my neck, and a low growl spilled into the cool air. The foul stink hit next, blurring my vision with tears.

Asa was in a bad way, worse than I first thought, if he hadn't clued into the problem yet.

"We're going to take a little break." I eased him to a stop then helped him sit. "Just rest for a minute."

His head lolled against the trunk, his hair tangling in the bark, and he gave no sign of hearing me.

Heck of a time for the team to decide to split up, just when I could have used Clay's muscle to carry Asa.

With Asa leaving a blood trail, the zombigo must have decided we made easy pickings and followed us.

The fact it was tracking us confirmed its maker was still out there, so good news/bad news?

Drawing my wand, I stood over Asa, putting the tree at our backs. I had seconds to gather my intent to ready a spell before the creature burst from the underbrush, drool stringing its jaw as it snapped at my throat. I stabbed the wand tip under its chin, and my simple defensive exploded in white light, the blast far beyond my capabilities.

The beam shot through the top of its skull, straight to the moon. Smoldering leaves rained down over us, and smoke rose from its charred limbs. The zombigo did a stagger-step forward, its claws raking the air, and then it collapsed at my feet in a sizzling heap of rot.

A wave of white-hot fury zinged through me as I scanned the treetops until I spotted a white orb.

"Get your fuzzy butt down here," I snapped out at Colby. "And dim that glow."

The moth did her best to drag her arrival out for as long as possible, until she spotted Asa and cried out.

"Hair bow time." I pointed at my head. "Now." I waited until she lit then turned to Asa. "Still with me?"

With his eyes shut, his head tipped back, lips parted, he could have been sleeping.

Or dead.

Arrowing my senses toward his heartbeat, I listened to its faint but steady thumping.

For once in my life, I wasn't made hungry by the enticement. I was too frantic over his quick decline.

Afraid to take my eyes off Asa, I dictated a text to Clay to let him know what happened then set to work.

"I'm sorry," Colby whispered from the top of my head. "I didn't know he was hurt."

"You promised to stay in the cabin." Fear for them both sharpened my tone. "What were you thinking?"

"The magic called me." She burrowed closer to my scalp. "I was playing my game, and I heard it."

Hooking my hands under Asa's armpits, I heaved with everything in me to get him swaying on his feet.

"The magic spoke to you?" I coaxed him one step, but he was dead weight. "Does it have any advice?"

Huh.

So that was how desperation tasted on the tongue.

I'd never heard of magic talking to a person, but Colby was a singularity. Who was to say magic, her magic, wouldn't respond to her differently? The fact I made her my familiar had nothing to do with her power. I was only able to bond with her because she had it. Where it originated, aside from within her own soul, I had no clue. Her purity, her innocence, upon her death was what magnified that kernel until it exploded.

Air stirred across my scalp as she fluttered her wings, and a fission of excitement sparked in her. "Yes."

"Okay." I leaned him back against the tree. "I'm open to suggestions."

I had lost my mind if I thought, for one second, taking advice from a disembodied voice was smart.

But Asa...wasn't moving. He was barely breathing. His heart had all but given up on him.

I had nothing to lose by thinking outside the magical box.

Except him.

And I couldn't look too closely at why that caused my own heart to break into a panicked sprint.

"We can heal him." She hopped down onto my shoulder. "Maybe?"

"Maybe isn't great for me." I clutched my wand tighter. "I need you to be sure."

Otherwise, we might cook his brain the way I flambéed the zombigo.

"We can..." she tilted her head, "...remove the bullets."

Not without a knife, tweezers, flashlight, and a metal-detecting spell. "We can?"

"Yes." She climbed up onto his shoulder. "Then he'll heal."

His knees buckled at that slight touch, and he slid through my arms to hit the damp earth.

"Asa?" I shoved the hair away from his face. "Can you hear me?"

"We need to do this." Colby scurried onto his chest. "Hurry, Rue."

With no sign of Clay, the only hope I had of getting him to the cabin, I had to side with her.

"Okay." I clamped my eyes shut, my stomach roiling. "I'll try."

Low in her throat, Colby began to hum a tune that struck me as familiar. Her glow increased in time with its cadence, until she was as luminous as the moon on a starless night. When it hurt to look at her, she quit her song. Her brilliance was a balm to my dark soul, and I soaked in her goodness until it filled me.

"Now," she breathed, her voice a vibration on the air. "Do it now."

Wand hot in my hand, I touched it to the puckered edge of the worst of his injuries and shoved power into him until beams of light shone from the bullet holes, piercing the darkness like searchlights. His wounds, they...boiled...the blood foaming as the battered projectiles were ejected in metallic lumps. The raw skin sizzled and hissed as magic cauterized his injuries from the inside out, leaving a burnt-flesh smell behind.

The magic fizzled out of me, and I sank onto my haunches. I put away the wand and smoothed my hands over Asa's chest and abdomen, stunned at the miracle Colby had worked through me with her magic. He would live. Already his heart thumped stronger in my ears, and his lids fluttered as he fought to surface.

Anger drove me to pick up a malformed bullet, and I squeezed it until the metal bit into my palm.

"Rue," he exhaled my name, his voice a thready rasp of sound.

"I'm right here." I clasped hands with him, pocketing the bullet. "I'm not going anywhere."

"We did it." Colby shot for the moon. *"We did it."*

"You mean you didn't know it would work?" I gawped at her. "I told you—"

"I heard a voice in my head, and you decided to listen to it." She spread her hands. "It was fifty-fifty."

As much as I wanted to snap at her, she had me there. I had known the risks and chosen to take them.

Heavy footsteps announced Clay's arrival, and he jerked to a stop beside the charred zombigo.

"What the f—" he spotted Colby, "—fudgesicle happened here?" Then he sniffed. "What's that smell?"

"Asa." I squeezed his hand harder. "Colby healed him."

A long whistle escaped Clay as he took in the proud moth's fading glow. "Impressive, Shorty."

"Can you help me get him back to the cabin?" I stared down at Asa. "He's still out of it."

"I'll handle it." He clamped a hand on my shoulder. "You did good, Dollface."

"All I did was channel Colby." I covered his hand with mine. "It was all her."

"Ammo is no use without a gun." He grimaced. "Okay, poor analogy, but you get me."

"I do." I smiled to show him it was okay. "You go ahead. I'll hang back and finish up here."

"Not happening," he said cheerfully. "Miracle moth or no miracle moth, we're not separating again."

Given there was at least one more witch on the prowl, I couldn't argue with his caution.

"Asa." I traced the curve of his cheek with my free hand. "I'll be right back, okay?"

His fingers tightened on mine, holding me to him, and I almost caved to his silent request for me to stay.

"I'm here now." Clay knelt beside Asa. "I won't let Rue out of my sight." He patted Asa's leg. "Promise."

The vow carried enough weight that Asa let me go, but I didn't venture far. Just to the zombigo's corpse.

"Are we not going to talk about the moth in the room?" Clay shot her a mock glare. "You jailbroke."

Leaving her to explain herself, I snapped several photos for our report before I touched my wand to its leg and pushed enough of my own magic into the body to render it to fine ash I kicked across the earth.

After rejoining Clay and Colby, I gritted my teeth against the urge to help when he lifted Asa in his arms. I had the oddest thought it had something to do with his hair, with some jealous urge to scoop it up and hold it away from Clay so it no longer touched his skin. Clearly, I was losing my mind, but I did wonder.

Curling my itchy fingers into my palms, I asked, "Will you get in trouble for touching his hair?"

"Nah." Clay ruffled Asa's hair to prove his point. "I have no sexual organs, and I can't reproduce."

According to him, the absence of genitalia did not equate a deficit of imagination, skill, or pleasure.

"What does that have to do with anything?" I frowned at him. "And what about Colby?"

"Colby is a child, and an extension of you, so she's fine." His lips pulled to one side. "The rest? Talk to him about it."

That promised to be awkward, so I elected to pretend I hadn't mentioned the hair, he hadn't mentioned the lack of sexual organs, and decided we could never mention any of this again, and I would be happy.

On the trek to the cabin, I watched Clay's back. Colby rode on my head, her legs twitching in my hair.

Pitching her voice low, she leaned over my forehead, curiosity a spark in her eyes. "No sexual organs?"

Trawling my memories, I came up with a decent comparison. "Did you have any Barbie dolls?"

"No," she said slowly, "but I've seen the memes."

Afraid to ask what memes, I plowed ahead, hoping that meant she grasped basic doll anatomy.

"Okay, well, golems are like Ken dolls. They're sculpted from clay into a male form, but without the male parts." Vague was the way to go on that front. Not that I meant front like *that*. And now I had a mental picture of Ken's crotch stuck in my head. "Clay identifies as male, but he's got a friend who identifies as female, and then there's Misha. They work in grounds security at the Black Hat compound, and they identify as neither."

There. Nice and simple. Easy to digest.

A version of the same talk Clay had given me when I finally worked up the nerve to ask him early in our partnership.

"So, Misha is nonbinary?"

And...she left my weak sauce explanation in the dust.

Kids these days.

They had the internet at their fingertips and held the world in the palms of their hands.

"Exactly." I glanced up at her. "How did you get so smart?"

With Colby, I often forgot she wasn't a ten-year-old kid. She was twice that age now. She matured much slower than other kids her mental age, but she would retain her childlike innocence forever. There was a fine line between patronizing her and relating to her, and it moved often. This auntie gig was hard work.

"One of my friends, Max, prefers they/them pronouns. I got curious. The internet isn't *only* for games."

"I must have wax in my ears." I sucked in a gasp. "I can't believe you just said that."

"Rue." Her sigh rustled my eyebrows. "You are so lame."

"Yes, well, I'm old. Old people are allowed to be lame." I hesitated. "Did that answer your question?"

"Yeah." She retreated to settle in. "Do you think they make wigs in my size?"

"If they can make doll wigs, they can make moth wigs." It couldn't be that hard. "We'll ask Clay."

"Nah." Her voice went quiet. "I was just curious."

Obviously, I wasn't the best role model. For literally anyone. But I also hadn't spent much time on what I started to worry might spark a trend with Colby with Clay in her life. Hair, makeup, clothes. That stuff. It hadn't mattered to me. Ever. I trained, I studied, I practiced. That was it.

The director wasn't much into teaching me how to be womanly, so I skated by on the bare minimum.

Lucky for me, I had that youthful glow that required no makeup to enhance, and I let it work for me.

Unlucky for all the owners of the hearts I had consumed to earn this rosy complexion.

And doubly unlucky for me if I had to explain to her my true beauty secret was, well, murder.

10

Back at the cabin, Clay put Asa to bed. In his room. Clay had played nurse for me often enough I trusted him to take care of his partner without me hovering. Asa and I might be swapping spit muffins, but there were rules and traditions and protocols when it came to every aspect of his life and person, it seemed, and I didn't want to misstep.

And *no*, I wasn't tossing out excuses as fast as they came to mind.

Or hiding out in my room because for one heart-stopping moment, I had thought I lost him.

I didn't even have him. Not really. A hair bracelet and a few dozen cupcakes did not a boyfriend make.

"Rue."

I jumped a foot in the air when Clay found me. Pacing. Asa's dried blood still under my nails.

"Hey, now." He hauled me in for a hug. "He's sleeping off the healing, that's all."

"I don't like this." I mashed my face into his chest. "I don't like feelings."

"Yeah, you do." He chuckled and swayed a little with me in his arms. "You're worried about Ace. That's a totally normal reaction."

"Not for me," I grumbled. "I thought he was..."

"Me too." He kissed my temple. "Shorty told me about the voice."

"What do you think it means?" I tipped back my head. "Usually, hearing voices is not a good sign."

"Hearing voices is *never* a good sign." He spun me out in a practiced move and let go of my hand so that I fell onto the mattress. "Do you think she means it literally?" He stretched out on the bed beside me. "Could it be her instincts waking up now that she's getting regular practice with her magic?"

"Literal, as far as I know." I curled on my side against him. "Goddess bless, what a mess."

"We'll figure it out." His wide hand stroked up and down my back. "Don't worry."

"Oh crap." I jerked away from him. "I almost forgot." I thumped my head on the pillow. "The book."

Braced on one arm, he stared down at me. "What about it?"

"The grimoire." I spelled it out for him. "David Taylor's grimoire."

"That has to be what the witch was after." I rubbed my temples. "What else could she have meant?"

The name on the inside cover was Proctor, but there was no record of a Proctor working for Black Hat.

Then again, the copycat had admitted David Taylor was a masque. We had no idea of his true identity.

"I forgot you had that." His lips twisted at one corner. "How much have you read?"

Asa had read it from cover to cover, but Clay wouldn't have forgotten it if he had put his hands on it. The thing pulsed with black magic even I could sense. That was why I put it in the safe. To dampen its pull. At least that was what I told myself to avoid remembering how the thing liked to move around on its own.

"Enough to know I ought to destroy it after I've memorized the parts relevant to Colby."

Most witches had excellent memories, a requirement for spell-work unless you wanted to drag a sack full of reference grimoires with you everywhere you went for the rest of your life. As soon as I got home, the Colby-inspired passages were top of my to-do list. The sooner I committed that research to memory, the sooner I could set fire to the Proctor magnum opus, whoever they may be or might have been.

"You sure that's wise?" He rubbed his jaw. "Might be worth a more in-depth read."

"Tempting me is dangerous." I wiggled my toes. "I don't need help making bad decisions."

"Hey, I warned you off Ace." He chuckled at my scowl. "It doesn't get worse than that."

"Pretty sure there are worse things than crushing on a coworker."

"You mean like crushing on a daemon prince?"

A groan poured out of me, and I shut my eyes. "Why did it have to be him?"

"The hair." He smoothed a hand over his curls. "I blame myself." He struck a pose. "I gave you unrealistic expectations. I was too fabulous. It clearly sank into your tender, young mind and forced a bar to be set that only Asa's flowing locks have reached thus far. He's the only guy I know who spends as much time in front of a mirror as me. Obviously, you find men who take care with their appearance attractive."

"Why does it have to be so complicated?"

"Good hair doesn't just happen..." His lecture on product, which I had heard before, stalled. "Oh." He sat upright. "You mean Ace." He rubbed a hand over his mouth. "I notice you're not in there, hand-holding."

"He was in my room when I woke, back home." I picked at the covers. "How long did he wait for me?"

"The whole time you were out," he admitted. "He knitted, mostly, but he read the grimoire too."

"Do you think he expects me to return the favor?"

"He wouldn't take it personally if you didn't." He grunted as he stood. "There's no rush, Rue. Take all the time you need to be sure. He would rather you come to him when you're ready than out of obligation."

"Thanks." I stared at the ceiling. "I'm going to check in with the girls, see how the shop is coming along."

"You do that." He paused on the threshold. "I'll keep an eye on Ace."

"Thanks." I bit the inside of my cheek. "Again."

With a nod, Clay shut the door behind him and set off down the hall.

Phone in hand, I texted Arden rather than call on the slight chance she might be sleeping. Most times, she and Camber spent their off days together, on a couch, watching horror flicks that lulled me to sleep.

>How are you? How is Camber? How's the shop?

>>Okay. Hungry. Good.

>Are you two not eating while I'm gone?

>>Unlike some people, we don't have boyfriends who send us mountains of daily cupcakes.

>He's not my boyfriend.

And he was lying in his bed, across the hall, recovering from gunshot wounds.

Alone.

>>It's okay to care about a guy, Rue. They're not all dick weasels.

>I don't know what a dick weasel is, and I'm not going to ask. You can't make me.

>>Camber is sleeping over, which is how I know she's hungry. Her stomach is growling. We're watching a Leprechaun marathon. Can you believe someone thought making eight of those was a good idea?

>Order pizza on the shop card.

>>*For real?*

>*No, for fake. What do you think?*

>>*Thank you!*

>*I would tell you not to stay up all night, but you pretty much have, so don't stay up all day too.*

>>*What good are off days if you sleep through them?*

>*Fair point.*

>>*Commercial break is over. I'm going to order that pizza. Talk to you soon.*

About the time we finished our goodbyes, I had a bee in my bonnet to check on Asa.

Those stupidly excessive, ridiculously delicious cupcakes had struck a guilty chord in me.

I swung my legs over the side of the bed, a twitch in my calves propelling me forward, and I flung my cell on top of the covers. When I gripped the doorknob, I jerked back as a powerful vibration filled my palm.

The wards held strong, I would have known the instant that changed, so whatever was out there...

Asa.

A bone-deep certainty filled me as I opened the door slowly to reveal the daemon curled up on the floor. It hadn't been a growl I felt, but deep snores that rattled through his chest like wet purrs.

He had come to me for comfort when I didn't go to him, but he had left the door as a barrier between us to respect my privacy. Poor guy must have been exhausted to conk out so fast after Clay left.

Standing there, I felt six inches tall. No. Less. Three inches. Maybe two. One started to feel like a stretch.

"Hey." I crouched beside him and placed my hand on his shoulder. "How are you feeling?"

"Rue," he mumbled, his lids fluttering open. "Good."

Smoothing a thumb across his fever-hot skin, I asked, "Do you want me to walk you back to your room?"

"No." He nestled against the planks. "Stay here."

His answer didn't surprise me one whit. "Can I talk to Asa?"

"Sleeping." He yawned. "Healing."

Cold iron targeted the fae side of Asa, so it made sense the daemon half of him would be less affected.

"Come on." I hooked a hand under his arm. "I'm not leaving you out here all day."

"Tired." He curled tighter. "Sleep now."

"You'll sleep as soon as I get you in my bed." I tugged on his arm. "I'll throw my back out moving you."

Grunting through his teeth, proving he was feeling the hurt too, he rose to his full height.

"You can take my spot." I led him into my room and shoved him onto the bed. "I don't sleep much."

"Hurts," he murmured, snuggling down with his face in my pillow. "Rue make better."

"You're still in pain?" I sat on the edge of the mattress. "Want me to get Colby? We can—"

"No." He fixed his burnt-crimson stare on me. "Rue." He curled around me. "Rue make better."

Tears pricked the backs of my eyes as what he meant sank in. Just being here, with him, made it better.

"Let me get my..." I attempted to rise, but he yanked me down again. "Can I get my book, please?"

"Rue come back?" He studied me. "Not trick?"

"The book is right there." I pointed it out to him. "How about you hand it over instead?"

The daemon palmed it with ease and brought it to his face. *"Bearly His Mate?"*

You can read almost popped out of my mouth, but I shut it in time.

"Yes." I snatched it out of his hand. "Thank you."

"Read." He snuggled back in, curling around me tighter. "Like voice."

To read shifter romance to the daemon or not to read shifter romance to the daemon.

Ha.

Like I entertained that notion for a hot second. I did *not* want Asa to know what I read before bed. There was nothing wrong with reading romance. No matter how spicy. There was nothing wrong with loving to read romance. Even if it scorched off your eyebrows. But people tended to judge you for it. Harshly. And I was doing my best not to hex people for being stupid. Not that I expected Asa to judge me for my taste in books. I just...didn't want him thinking I was fetishizing shifters. Even if he technically wasn't one?

I also might be worried after Meg's throwaway comment about horn licking that the daemon might get, well, invested in the story-line? No matter what Clay said, I couldn't view Asa and the daemon as one person. I responded to them differently, as if they were individuals, and they each reacted to me in their own distinct ways.

"You know what?" I faked a stretch. "That spell really took it out of me." I yawned. "I think I'll sleep too."

"With me?" His delight lit up his face. "I make room."

The daemon's version of making room for me was to scoot to the edge of the mattress, which might have worked had he not taken up the whole thing in the first place. Even on his side, I had maybe a foot of space to wedge myself into if I wanted to make good on my lie.

Reading the situation, he shoved up on his elbow. "I sleep on floor."

"No." I pushed him down and wiggled in. "You sleep here."

Careful not to invade my personal space more than necessary, he kept his hands to himself and his body on his half of an invisible line he seemed to have drawn across the mattress. I didn't have to wait long to experience the door phenomenon up close and personal as the whole bed shook with his deep snores. It made slinking onto the floor simple, and I stood over the daemon with a fond smile. He was cute with his feet hanging off the end of the bed, one horn stabbing his—well, my—pillow, and his lips motorboating.

Unwilling to leave his side, I took my book and curled up with it in the corner of the room. I didn't have a chair, but the mountain of blankets made a comfy sitting area. I snuggled in, cracked my book, and read.

A text chime on my phone woke me, and I jolted awake in bed, confused how I got there.

"Everything okay?" Asa's soft voice made me bounce on the squishy mattress. "Rue?"

"Just disoriented." I wiped a hand over my face. "This is not where I fell asleep."

"You were on the floor when I woke." He sat in my book nook. "It couldn't have been comfortable."

"You were shot. Multiple times. You're the one who needed to be comfortable. I was too wired to sleep. That's why I gave your daemon the bed. He was tired and..." I wasn't sure how much he recalled, but the least I could do was tell him. "I found him asleep outside my door. I couldn't leave him out there."

"Him?" A hint of a smile shadowed his mouth. "Or me?"

A flush exploded up the back of my neck into my already red face. "Both?"

The faintest glimmer of pleasure sparked across his features before he dipped his chin.

"I apologize for interrupting your rest." He toyed with the blankets. "I didn't mean to come to you."

"You took bullets for me. You can pajama party with me any time."

"I'll remember that." He peeked up at me through his lashes. "Do you need privacy?"

"We've already slept together," I joked, then bit the inside of my cheek. "You meant my phone."

His soft chuckles spread through me, erasing the worst of my embarrassment.

"You're fine," I assured him. "Aside from you and Clay, I only get messages from the girls. And Colby."

Sad how I didn't have to break a sweat to make my social life sound pathetic. I was lucky to have Camber and Arden. It was hard to make friends when so much of my life was a lie. Mentoring went over easier. It was a classic case of *do as I say, not as I do*. I pretended with the girls a lot too. I stuck to script for years.

Until genuine affection blossomed, and I began to understand why witches thrived in communities.

Maybe that was the problem with Asa and me. I didn't have to act. I didn't need a script. I was just...me.

And he *liked* it.

"Not this again." I frowned at the notification. "A camera on the edge of the property caught motion."

"Anything to be concerned about?" He rose with a blanket around his waist. "Can you check the wards?"

"I'm too far away to feel them." I pulled up an interior camera. "But I did get smart about it this time."

Patting the mattress beside me, I kept scrolling until I found the angle I wanted, then I showed it to him.

"The traffic light." He smiled at me. "Very clever."

The wards had a few different indicators I rigged for Colby, who couldn't feel them the way I did. The most common was a blink, which meant that a person or object had made contact. I had the sensitivity dialed all the way up while I was away, which meant anything bigger than a chipmunk would trigger one.

The blink itself was conveyed via a decorative traffic light I'd mounted on the wall above Colby's monitor. I fixed it so brief contact with the wards would flash yellow for caution. Prolonged contact turned it red. If all was well, it remained green.

"We're green." I closed the app. "That means we're good."

"It's thirty minutes until midnight." He noticed the time on my phone. "We might as well stay awake."

"We have another black witch to catch." I huffed out a breath. "You can stay here with—"

"No."

"You're hurt." I kept my newfound fear in check. "You don't have anything to prove."

"I *was* hurt." He smoothed a hand down his defined chest, inviting me to look my fill. "You healed me."

Without permission from my brain, my hand shot out to trace each puckered scar. "Colby healed you."

"She is the arrow." He captured my hand and pressed it over his heart. "You are the archer."

"And you were a target." A sour taste flooded my mouth. "Because of me."

Laughter shook his shoulders, and he kissed my fingers. "You forget who I am."

"Do you use that tone on all peasants, or am I special?"

"You are special, and I don't address the horde. They, however, have Father's express permission, and his encouragement, to repay what I attempted to do to him tenfold. I have been a target since the day I was born, and I will remain one until the day I die."

There was so much to unpack in that statement. "Your father put out a hit on you?"

"His successor must be worthy of his legacy," he mocked. "Or a new one will be appointed."

"How are you so chill about this? Does Clay know? Does the Bureau?"

"I've had a lifetime to accept death is inevitable." He glanced away. "And yes, they're both aware."

For a good three seconds, I debated strangling him, which would make his dire prophecy come true.

"How is the director okay with this?" I couldn't put two and two together to get four, not with Asa's birthright. "He just lets it happen?"

"White witches are hunted from birth by their dark counterparts," he reasoned. "No one stops that."

"That doesn't make it right." I balled my hands into fists. "Not all cultural practices are great ideas."

A knowing warmth softened his expression. "You see the problem."

Goddess bless, I walked right into that one.

"Cultural practices," I grumbled, unhappy in the extreme that no one had told me. "How does it work?"

"They don't interfere on cases, if that's what concerns you. They challenge me on my own time."

"Yes, Asa, that's exactly what concerns me." I rolled my eyes. "Not that you might die, or that you sound fine with it, but that it might impede an ongoing investigation. What else would I care about?"

Springing to my feet, I was done sharing space with him and all these *feelings*.

Hearts were good for one thing.

Dinner.

I should have remembered that.

"Rue."

Ignoring him, I yanked on the doorknob until it yielded to my temper, but Asa reached over my head and slammed it shut before I could escape into the hall. His warm front pressed against my back, and his chin came to rest on my shoulder, his breath hot on my skin as he nuzzled under my ear.

Purring, he brushed his lips over the column of my throat. "I didn't mean to upset you."

The casual defeat in his acceptance of his fate reminded me too much of how I always pictured my end. I had known my own legend within the Bureau only made other black witches salivate in my proximity. All of them viewed me in much the way as I had seen them: as a treat I might one day pop into my mouth.

"Why bother with the bracelet if you've already given up?" Forehead pressed against the cool wood, I called myself ten kinds of fool for not forcing him to let go.

"I didn't have a reason to fight." He took my earlobe between his teeth. "I didn't have a reason to care."

Voice as tight as my lower stomach, I asked, "Has that changed?"

Oh, yeah.

I should have sunk an elbow in his gut and bolted before he gave an answer I couldn't escape.

"What do you think?" He leaned in slowly, pressing my hips flush against the door, letting me feel every inch of him. Every *hard* inch of him. And there were a lot of them. "Do you think I would give up on this? On you?"

"I should have my head examined." I shivered as his fingers traced the bracelet. "You're a lot to handle."

"You can handle me any time you want," he breathed against my jaw. "I'm not going anywhere."

"Don't make promises you can't keep."

"I don't." He tugged the bracelet to make his point. "I won't."

About to combust, I yelped and sprang backward when a single hard knock landed on the opposite side of the door, right between my eyes.

I hit Asa just right, and he fell. His arms came around me, hauling me down with him. I landed on his lap with a grunt, unable to hold in a manic laugh when he hissed between his teeth as I squashed his, um, *mood*, flat.

The thud brought Clay into the room, fists clenched, ready for battle. That made me laugh even harder.

"I have regrets," Clay said, after assessing the situation. "So many regrets."

I attempted to roll off Asa, but he held firm, using me to hide the hardness poking me in the butt.

"You two look like turtles who got stuck on their backs." Clay offered me a hand. "Don't let the kid see."

"Thaaanks." I smothered another laugh at Asa's expense. "Can you maybe distract her for a minute?"

One of his eyebrows popped into the hairline of his blue-black comb-over. "Only a minute?"

Heat flooded me in a scalding rush, but Asa had it easy. He just hid behind and beneath me, a chuckle shaking me through him. "Long enough for him to sneak back to his room without flashing Colby."

Strange, I didn't recall the daemon showing up naked, and that was the kind of thing one noticed.

"One minute." Clay shook his head at us. "The clock starts...*now*."

After he closed the door behind him, I broke Asa's grip and slid onto the floor next to him, attempting to keep my eyes above his waist. He remained flat on his back, the quilt riding low. His hipbones proved an unexpected temptation, confirming he wasn't wearing his usual boxer briefs, and proving I couldn't keep my eyes to myself.

"We have a witch to catch." I forced a businesslike tone. "We should both get ready."

Not bothering to gather the fabric at his waist, he stood, allowing it to pool at his feet. "I agree."

Jaw scraping the floor, I did my best not to stare at what bobbed right in front of me. I managed, mostly, thanks to my shock. His butt, though? I studied it as he walked out like there would be an exam later.

As I sat there with my mouth hanging open, a question fell out. "What changed?"

Hand holding was as intimate as we had gotten, despite sharing a bed once, unless you counted hugs.

"You protected me from the zombigo when I was too weak to defend myself. You healed my wounds, and the cold-iron sickness that would have killed me if left untreated. You gave me your bed while you slept on the floor." He glanced back in time to catch me giving his butt the third degree instead of the back of, I don't know, his head or some other socially acceptable real estate. "You care about me."

"Let a guy dry hump you against a door," I mumbled, "and he starts getting ideas."

Fingers digging into the doorframe, he hesitated on the threshold. "Do you regret it?"

An open-ended question like that could have alluded to any number of things. Did I regret the first time I swapped spit muffins with him, setting us on this twisty path? Did I regret accepting the bracelet? *Twice.* Did I regret saving him? That one was a no-brainer. Did I regret that I...cared?

That last one cut the deepest, so it must be what he meant.

While I might not appreciate being put on the spot, I wouldn't lie about it. "No."

His gaze traced over the door where I had been pinned moments ago. "You're okay with this?"

"Yeah." I rubbed my cheeks, which did nothing to cool the sting. "I'm good with door humping."

A smile broke across his lips, traveling up until it sparkled in his eyes. "Good."

He left, and I sat there, wondering why it sounded like I had agreed to something.

11

"Rue."

Zooming for all she was worth, Colby shot into my room and made wide laps around the ceiling.

Dizzy from the acrobatics, I dropped my gaze. "How much sugar have you had today, ma'am?"

For her to be this hyped, she must have stayed awake all day, probably raiding and pillaging.

Ignoring the question, which was answer enough, she asked, "I get to go with you, right?"

"Last night wasn't exciting enough?" I made up my bed. "You need more adventure?"

"Yep." She brandished a silver rod in one hand. "I'm ready for action."

"What's that in your hand?" I squinted, then wished I hadn't noticed. "Who gave you a sword?"

"Clay and I did arts and crafts on the porch."

"Please don't poke an eye out, yours or anyone else's."

"I make no promises."

"Scoot." I dug through my luggage. "I need to dress."

"Okay." She swooped so close, she could have parted my hair with her art project. "Later."

Alone at last, I rushed through my hygiene routine, pulled on fresh clothes, and strapped on my kit.

Pulse kicking up at the prospect of facing Asa, I joined the others in the kitchen for breakfast.

Sadly, the kind that didn't taste much different from the box you poured it from. There had simply been no time to bake, and I hadn't been in a mood for it with Asa recovering. Now we all had to suffer.

The remaining black witch had lost their partner, and their zombigo. They would come for us. Tonight. We needed to be ready when it happened, and that meant we had to eat and get out there.

A wig box sat next to Clay's elbow, its lid covered in silver moth footprints and its sides full of holes.

Leaning on the counter, I studied Clay. "Who thought giving Colby a sword was a good idea?"

"You're always telling the kid to unplug." He twirled his spoon. "What's the problem?"

"You weaponized her." I leaned in close. "Do you know how dangerous that is?"

"The edges are dull." Asa moved in behind me, almost touching. "There's not much of a point either."

As nice as it felt having his warmth at my back, I had to keep my wits about me. "You made it?"

"I whittled her sword, yes. On the drive here." He reached around me, caging me in his arms, and poured cereal into bowls. "I also carved her a shield, and other items relevant to her interests, to occupy her if the internet went down."

"I'll teach her how to use her new arsenal," Clay promised. "I haven't used a sword in years, but it's like riding a bike. It comes back to you."

About to address the issue of an arsenal, and a battle-trained moth, I opened my mouth only to have a spoon shoved into it as Clay leaned across the counter.

A subtle growl rose over my shoulder, and Asa froze halfway to filling our bowls with milk.

"You taste that?" Clay's lips pulled to one side. "It's like fu—" He cleared his throat. "It's like cardboard."

Crunching the cinnamon-sugar mouthful, I shrugged. "What do you expect from a box?"

"Please bake for me." He made his eyes big and liquid. "I can't work under these conditions."

"Not so long ago, I recall a cranberry-orange scone incident."

Despite the fact I had lost sleep baking them, he had eaten every single one in the box.

Clay ate nine scones while Asa and I were packing Colby and my things into the SUV the morning we left Samford. A tenth had hung from his lip when we confronted him in the kitchen. He inhaled the eleventh, an extra fluffy one, to spare us from fighting over the last one, or so he claimed.

The twelfth never made it in the box. It was the cost of doing business. I had eaten it for dinner.

"Pump the brakes." He held up his hands. "Colby gave those to me, as a gift."

"Mmm-hmm." I finished the task of making cereal for Asa and me. "You didn't share, so why should I?"

"You love me." He fluttered his lashes. "I'm your favorite."

"That's only half true." I rolled my eyes at him. "Fine." I huffed, secretly pleased. "I'll bake."

Turning in the circle of Asa's arms, I pressed a bowl into his chest, which he studied warily.

"Have you never had cereal?"

"That is sugar pressed flat, cut into squares, and sprinkled with cinnamon."

Apparently, Clay wasn't the only breakfast snob around here.

Too bad for Asa, I knew how to push his buttons.

"Mmm." I stole his spoon, piled it high, and stuck it in my mouth. "Sugary."

The way he fixated on my mouth almost caused me to choke, but I managed to swallow with dignity.

A battle warred across Asa's face as he fought his instinct to taste my food after me.

"If you're not interested..." I took another bite, crunching noisily, "...I'll finish this myself."

The next time I loaded my spoon, I teased him a heartbeat too long, and he swooped in to devour it.

"That's cheating." I tapped the end of his nose with the spoon then shoveled in another bite. "How rude."

"How are you feeling?" He leaned into my space, his hips pinning mine against the counter. "Hungry?"

Now that he mentioned it, I was experiencing a rumble in my tummy. "I'm always hungry."

Behind me, Clay snorted but didn't say a word as I attempted to work out what I had done this time.

"You spit muffined my cereal." I stared into the bowl while Asa smiled down at me. "That's why it tastes better." I took another mouthful. "No. I was wrong. It doesn't taste better. I just want it more."

After the bedroom door incident—*ahem*—cereal wasn't the only thing I wanted more.

"Can I bring my sword?" Colby buzzed me. "I've always wanted to know how it feels to stab an eyeball."

Tipping my head back, I had to wonder where I went wrong. Probably the whole black witch thing, come back to haunt me in the form of a moth who was weirdly bloodthirsty for someone whose diet subsisted of pollen granules and sugar water.

Busy swashbuckling midair, Colby didn't notice Asa's and my close quarters, and he eased back before she got an eyeful of this thing unfurling between us. He was considerate of her, and I liked that about him. It helped that his brain worked better around me than mine did around him.

"Leave the sword at home tonight." I ate the rest of our shared bowl of cereal. "You need to be focused when you're in the field. You also need to think first with your magic and not with your body's reflexes."

As fierce as her spirit was, magic or not, she had to learn to think like a familiar in battle.

Landing on Clay's head, she quivered her antennae. "So, tomorrow is a maybe?"

"We'll see." I pointed to the counter, and she flitted down to ditch her weapon. "Are you ready to go?"

"Yeah." She cast one last, longing glance at the sword. "I'm ready."

"Asa?" I noticed he hadn't touched the other bowl of cereal. "Aren't you hungry?"

"Yes." His gaze touched on my lips. "But I can wait."

The excuse might have fooled Colby, who wrinkled her nose in solidarity, but I knew better. I could put a spoonful of it in my mouth, and he would devour it. And I...wouldn't mind watching the show.

This fascination thing was downright bizarre. I had all these weird food-based impulses around Asa that would have earned a hard *no* if anyone else tried it with me. I did *not* eat after people. Or drink after people. But I—from a purely symbolic point—couldn't put enough of him in my mouth.

The thing about black witches was they didn't suffer romantic inclinations. They married, yeah, to form alliances. Aside from deflowering, sure, they had sex. Mostly to procreate. Or to enhance a spell. Sex magic was a thing, and it was gross. Feed me beating hearts over swapping bodily fluids with some rando guy any day of the week.

Mom and Dad had loved each other, which made them an odder couple than just their opposing magical practices. I don't recall how my parents behaved with each other, or me. The director had cost me those comforting scraps, robbed me of those hazy childhood recollections.

Thanks to Meg, I knew Mom had been obsessed with Dad from

the first moment she saw him. Mom had been a bit of a rebel in her circles, I knew that from Meg too, but no one had expected her to fall for the baddest bad boy on the market.

Certainly not the director, who had a black witch from a nice family all lined up for Dad to marry.

Nice as in evil, vile, and wicked, but you know. All the qualities the director prized above all others.

The arranged marriage angle made me wonder if Stavros had a nice daemon bride lined up for Asa.

On the heels of that unpleasant thought, I wondered if my bracelet could double as a garrote.

"They're doing it again," Colby murmured out of the side of her mouth.

"Can you two please stop pretending you're alone?" Clay threw in with Colby. "We need to get to work."

"They spend so much time staring at each other." Colby twitched her wings. "Why is that?"

Scooping her up, he set her on his shoulder, and they started toward the door, leaving us to follow.

"You know how you go to the grocery store," he said, "and you see cookies in the bakery?"

"Yeah."

"They look delicious, right? You want to buy them based on looks alone." He held up a finger. "But there is no way they taste as good as they look. They never do. Homemade is better. Always. Then you'll know what's in the dough." He glanced at her. "See what I mean?"

"Rue thinks Asa looks good, but she's not sure he tastes good?"

A laugh spluttered out of me, and Asa plucked at one golden arrow earring while mashing his lips together.

"Uh, no. That analogy got away from me." He tried again. "How about this? Asa is like a cookie. Rue has to decide if she likes his ingredients before she..." Giving up, he slashed a hand through the air. "Scratch that. Forget cookies."

"Let's all forget it," I volunteered. "Clay, where are we headed?"

"We're going to continue to sweep the area, working clockwise. We'll go a little farther tonight, since we have Colby with us. Whoever's pulling the strings around here knows where to find us, I'm sure. When it comes time to play hardball, they'll come to us if we don't find them first. Meanwhile, our orders remain the same—hunt down the black witch responsible for the zombigo."

"Aye, aye." I cut him a mock salute. "Colby, stick close to Clay and keep as quiet and still as you can."

"I'm a pro hair bow." She climbed on top of his head and hunkered down in his hair. "I got this."

We spent a few hours hiking through beautiful woodland without incident, which put Colby to sleep.

Asa walked beside me, but I missed the intimacy of our laced fingers. The moonlight, the scenic route, all made it easy to pretend, just for a second, we were on a midnight stroll for two. But the fact he kept our hands free meant he expected us to see action. I did too, but I dreaded it, considering Colby had a front row seat.

Flame engulfed Asa as his change overtook him with brutal quickness, and I marveled he didn't burn me.

"Smell bad." He crowded me then pointed through the trees. "That way."

"Smell bad as in...?" I drew my wand from my pocket. "Black magic?"

Nostrils flaring, he nodded once. "Death."

Clay had precious cargo to defend, so I set out with the daemon to guide me.

The thrill of the hunt sang through my blood, the daemon's fangs gleaming in a smile next to me. I tuned in to pick up on any heartbeats in the area but found no unfamiliar cadences. The daemon proved to me his sense of smell was stronger than my hearing. No surprise there. I learned early in my career that my extra senses were precise only when stalking food in close range. It wasn't a distance talent.

Arm out to hold me back, the daemon cocked his head and filled his lungs, his forehead wrinkling.

"The book," a paper-thin voice rustled from the darkness. "Give me the book."

Leaning forward, I strained to see the final black witch. "What book?"

"The book," she, and it was female, repeated in her reedy tone. "Give me the book."

"That can't be..." I stepped around the daemon's reach to gawk. "Annie Waite?"

If it was the same woman, her mantra hadn't changed, and that meant we had a run-of-the-mill zombie.

Less exotic, but equally gross, and just as deadly if we underestimated its threat.

Not glancing back, I pitched my voice to carry to Clay. "Have you heard from the other team?"

"No." Clay, and therefore Colby, sounded closer than I would have liked. "That's not unusual, though."

Any team running secondary to one with me on it tended to cut a wide berth to avoid crossing my path. But it wasn't like them not to text a warning the body they had been dispatched to retrieve the night before was missing.

A chill swept down my arms, a premonition I wouldn't like the answers I was about to get.

"I can't tell if she's armed." I nudged the daemon back. "Stay behind me until we know for certain."

Far from being a zombie expert, I didn't want to find out the hard way they were handy with a gun.

"No," the daemon growled, prowling beside me. "Rue get hurt."

Cold-iron poisoning nearly took out Asa, and the daemon with him. I wasn't hiding where it was safe this time.

As much as it pained me to think of her as a weapon, I had Colby. Her power would protect us. All of us.

"Book, book, book." Garbled words poured into the air. "Book, book, book."

"Anyone else think that makes her sound like a chicken?"

Bawk-bawk-bawk.

"Chicken?" The daemon licked his lips. "Crunchy."

For the sake of my mental health, I chose to believe he meant fried chicken skin, not bone-in live bird.

Death wasn't a squeamish topic for me. Neither was a raw diet or even cannibalism. Hello? Heart eater. But there were perfectly good chicken tenders in the fridge back at the cabin, just waiting to be breaded and fried.

A mop of dirty hair plastered to the side of a head that faced off center in a way that wasn't natural rose from the shadows as the zombie lumbered into the path ahead of us. The witch's corpse lacked the fluid motions of the zombigo, and its coordination. She had been slapped together without care on a deadline.

Her uninspired shuffling ramped up when she set rheumy eyes on us, and she wet her lips.

"Stay back," I warned the daemon again, since I still couldn't see her hands. "She might be armed."

Reanimated corpses had no agency of their own, but they followed simple instruction well.

Point and shoot was easy, too easy, and I couldn't let her get close enough to the daemon to try her aim.

"No." He nudged me aside. "Protect Rue."

"I'm sorry about this." I let him get a smidge ahead of me then tapped his shoulder with my wand. He hit the ground like a ton of bricks, and his eyes promised vengeance. "It'll wear off in five minutes." I leapt a clumsy swipe of his arm. "Okay, so probably more like two."

With Clay and Colby on the scene, the daemon was safe as houses, freeing me up to focus on the threat.

"You're a bibliophile, huh?" I blocked her punch, grunting, but grateful she had no magic. "Me too."

Any power left in her body, and she hadn't much to start, was spent keeping her upright and in motion.

"Book," she growled. "Give me the book."

"What book?" I let her get close then spun out and kicked her knee. "Hit me with a blurb or something."

Whoever was up here, sewing together zombies for funsies, I wasn't sharing my card catalog with them.

A prickle coasted over my skin, raising gooseflesh into stinging bumps that ached with irritation.

"The ward," I breathed in recognition. "We need to get to the cabin."

This zombie was a limited conversationalist, a distraction, and a darn good one.

Murmuring a spell under my breath, I ramped up the power I funneled into my wand until its tip shone. I grunted when Colby joined her magic with mine, lighting me up inside, burning me like a shot of tequila.

The zombie tripped over a limb and face-planted, too dumb to do more than wiggle its arms and legs.

"Next time," I said, easing closer to get in range, "come at me with an ISBN or something."

Light encased her when I touched the wand to her skin, and she burned to ash in a blink.

We didn't need the body, since we had already identified her and logged that intel with the Kellies.

Hot breath hit the back of my neck when I stood, and my short hairs stood on end.

Slowly, I turned to face this new threat, but it was too late.

12

The daemon bent, fit his shoulder to my squishy gut, then stood with a growl that brooked no argument.

As tempted as I was to zap him, and the urge was strong, I had already hit him with one spell tonight.

For his own good.

Something told me any argument I made would fall on deaf ears, so I hung there, fuming, longing for the days when people cowered before me rather than slung me over their shoulders like a bag of rocks. It was a rude awakening to go from revered to manhandled—daemonhandled?—on the job.

I reminded myself the lack of fear from the residents of Samford was a good thing, and it was reaffirming to be accepted on my own magicless merit (mostly magicless), but it was fast becoming as plain as the button nose on my face that I hadn't thought I would return to action as a white witch.

I entered this lifestyle on the run, and the trade-offs were worth-while, until danger stalked those I loved and forced me to admit I was much less than I used to be.

The grimoire was looking better and better, and that was how I knew it was time to read it and burn it.

Temptation always started as an easy solution to a thorny problem that wouldn't hurt anyone, or a hit of instant gratification that couldn't be bad when it felt good and harmed none. Then it escalated. Slowly, a trail of chocolate cake crumbs that led to scrumptious damnation with the best intentions.

"Zombies," the daemon rumbled, then set me down gently before frowning at me. "Careful, Rue."

"That goes double for you." I frowned right back. "You see a gun, you run."

"Rue like me." He preened, chest out and fangs sharp. "Rue care."

All that kept him from offering me a hank of his hair was the knowledge we needed our hands free.

"Yeah, yeah." I shoved him aside. "Rent a billboard, why don't you?"

On Colby duty, Clay kept a step behind, but we were almost back to the cabin, and things looked grim.

"I want you in the air," I told her. "Stay high, stay safe."

"Will do." She shot into the cloudless sky, words trailing behind her. "I could help if I had my sword."

Sliding Clay a glare that ought to have singed his wig's roots, I said, "Thank you for that."

"Just wait until you see her wee daggers." He shook out his arms. "They're adorable."

Colby was dangerous all on her own. Tiny weapons didn't make her more lethal. They put my eyeballs at risk, but that was about it. As we crept down the path, I decided my problem was I didn't want the teeny sword to become her Excalibur, or whatever they killed orcs with these days, or for it give her a false sense of safety.

A low moan drew me from my worries and focused me on a tall man dressed in a familiar black suit.

He was handsome enough, until he turned his head and flashed us gray matter seeping from what skull he had left on the far side. I didn't recognize him, but that wasn't saying much. Clay probably knew him.

What mattered wasn't who he was, or what he was, but who he had been.

Black Hat.

The black witch orchestrating this zombie fest wasn't afraid of the Bureau. That wasn't a comforting thought. A witch with that kind of power, who wanted more? Pfft. Who was I kidding? Any witch with a drop of magic wanted it to manifest into a well. But why target this one specific grimoire? How did they even know that Taylor had it? Or that Asa had given it to me for safekeeping?

The grimoire hadn't been entered into evidence. Black Hat didn't know, officially, that it existed, let alone who possessed it. That meant someone with access to the evidence logs had noticed its absence and decided one of the primary agents on the case had found it and kept it.

I was the logical choice, as the witch on our team.

But only one subject within its pages lent it more value than any other grimoire.

The information on Colby.

More than ever, I was grateful to have left it at home.

Even if someone was testing the wards. Someone I hoped was a bunny or a chipmunk or a squirrel.

"That's Joe Brunswick," Clay said from beside me. "Sonofa—" he made a fist, "—biscuit."

Three more bodies dressed in expensive suits shambled toward us, classic zombies, drawn by the first agent's moaning. This must be the rest of his team. Or maybe Asa and I smelled like fresh meat. Fresh brains? I wasn't clear if that part was lore. Also? I did not want to find out. Firsthand or ever.

Glass shattered in the direction of the cabin, and I crossed my fingers they didn't reach the loft and trash Colby's custom gear. Tiny tech carried huge price tags. As for the poor cabin, well, its repairs fell to Black Hat and the homeowner's insurance company. Maybe the owners would believe bears were at fault?

"Can you handle these shamblers?" I watched them another second. "I'll take the daemon with me."

Eyebrow cocked, he quizzed me. "You mean Ace?"

"Yeah. Sure." I was more and more convinced they were separate entities sharing one body, like shifters and their animal souls, but now wasn't the time to have a semi-theological debate. "Let's go, buddy."

The daemon fell into an easy lope, aiming for the action, and I struggled to keep pace with him.

His lengthy strides would leave me in the dust before long. No doubt, that was part of his plan.

Ditch me, secure the residence, then allow me to walk in over dead intruders while he puffed his chest.

Asa did a fair job of letting me do my thing. Even though I was figuring out how much of my thing I could do in my present circumstances. Especially when my power shot through the roof when I tapped Colby through our familiar bond. If I wanted to survive this consultation gig, I had to get a handle on my base power level *and* my supercharged magical threshold. Otherwise, one day, I might get us all killed.

Since I couldn't outrun him, I had to get sneaky. I let him pull ahead, let him feel good about himself, let him hear me huffing with feigned exhaustion. Then I cut hard to the right, away from the chaos that beckoned to him, a smile on my lips as he sprinted on toward the zombies. Me? I hit the front door, found it unlocked, and entered the rental with my wand at the ready.

A silver blur caught the edge of my vision, faster and sleeker than the zombies out front.

No heartbeats in the house.

Whatever it was, it wasn't alive, and it was made better than even the zombigo to move like that.

"I hear you're looking to borrow a book," I called to it. "Swear not to dog-ear the pages?"

A serpentine hiss poured from the darkest corner. Not the most promising response.

"The Proctor Family Grimoire."

Head cocked, I couldn't decide if it had spoken or if the voice had projected from that vicinity by design. The old *look at my left hand while my right punches through your chest and rips out your heart* trick was a true classic. Very popular with the dark magic set.

"I'll have to check my shelves." I pushed to see what answers I could get. "Why do you want it?"

The sibilant warning drifted to my left, but I hadn't seen the creature budge. Its master was throwing their voice to trick me into thinking I was surrounded by creatures.

"Give me the book, or I will kill the people in your town, one by one, until you concede victory to me."

Not *in town* or *in this town* but *in your town.*

It meant Samford.

My town.

My home.

My *people.*

"Threats are not the way to get what you want from me."

A boom shook the house, and more glass exploded as the daemon fell through a skylight to the floor. He held a severed arm in one hand and a leg bone in the other. As the creature shot out to attack, the daemon used the limbs as clubs to batter it away from him.

"Rue *mine*" was his battle cry, which was equal parts cute and cringy.

The *thing* was a giant silver worm with a bullet-shaped head. The scales and unusual color had thrown me. So had the fact its head unzipped down the middle, revealing jaws with needlelike teeth jutting up like the world's deadliest pincushion.

Goddess bless, what a mess.

I only prayed the creature was this much of a nightmare before the witch got ahold of it. I was hardly an authority on oddities of the magical world. There were simply too many. New ones born every day. I just hoped this one was natural. We did *not* need an enemy this creative. Or gross.

Silvery coils tightening, the worm readied to spring at the daemon's head, jaws wide open.

The daemon let it come, and he punched it in the face. Except it had no face. Just mouth. His arm shot down its throat, there was a meaty wrenching sound, and the daemon pulled back a handful of organs.

The nightmare worm thrashed on the warm oak floor, its blood tinting the planks a milky pink.

I tore my focus from the spectacle to check for a second worm, but I saw and heard nothing, proving the creative witch had been creating the sound effects to distract me.

"Smell bad." The daemon dropped the vitals onto the floor. "Long dead thing."

Unsure if he meant it was a long and also dead thing or a thing that had been dead a long time, I let it go to avoid asking. Mostly because I didn't want to open my mouth and taste the air in this place. The room was downright foul from the ripe bodies the daemon had torn into pieces to reach me.

"Reminds me of those dancing tube things at car dealerships." Clay stepped beside me. "What was it?"

The daemon didn't answer, so I gagged as I told Clay, "A giant worm with a head zipper."

"I'll grab some pics for our records, but you need to ash him quick."

"Why?" I brought up my wand. "The mess is made."

"Some worms can regrow bodies from their heads and heads from their bodies if you cut them in two."

"I...did not know that." I cranked my head toward him. "Have you seen one of these before?"

"A contestant on *Spooky House Delights* got fined for using store-bought gummy worms to decorate their Halloween gingerbread house. He mentioned the tidbit about the worm, and it was so freaky I had to look it up, but it didn't do him any good. The ruling stood, and he lost. Pity too. It was an impressive feat of cookie construction."

"Halloween gingerbread is a thing?"

Phone in hand, he recorded the worm thrashing then took snaps for good measure. "Yup."

"Learn something new every day," I mumbled, staring in morbid fascination at the worm.

"I could drop a word in the mayor's ear, see if she might want to add a gingerbread competition to those holiday festivities coming up in December." His expression was delightfully evil. "I might offer to judge."

"Give that woman any more ideas, and I will mold you into a birdbath for Mrs. Gleason's backyard."

Mrs. Gleason was eighty pounds soaking wet, with a beehive hairdo that added a foot onto her height. A good neighbor and a better friend, I was lucky to have her watching the house while I was away. Her and her shotgun, Bam-Bam, who wore matching outfits. Yeah. It was a whole thing.

That said, she had also shot Clay in the butt the first time she spied him sneaking around my property.

"That woman has fine aim." He rubbed his left cheek. "I was impressed by how steady she held the gun."

"We're clear." Asa joined us in his ratty slacks and bare feet. "The horde is dead." He frowned. "Again."

"We need headshots of the zombies to send the Kellies. Failing that, we need fingerprint scans." I wrinkled my nose at the task. "Families need to be notified. So does the director."

"I'll get on it," Clay volunteered, pulling out his cell. "I'll give Colby the all clear while I'm at it."

Alone with Asa and a whole lot of dead zombies, I raked my gaze over him slowly, checking to ensure he hadn't taken any new damage. If a hipbone caught my eye and snagged it, it wasn't my fault. His pants, I decided, definitely had elastic, but the waistband had been stretched to its limit.

"I like the way you look at me," he rumbled, his eyes burnt crimson.

"Like I'm worried you might have fresh holes I need to plug?"

"Like my pants are in your way, and you're considering sliding them off my hips with your teeth."

The smile I gave him would have sent any other man running, back in the day, but he only purred as he let the threat stoke some inner fire until his eyes shone with desire.

Potential daemon heritage or not, I could tell Asa and I were turning a corner.

Fast.

Sharp.

Hard.

Sweat drenched my spine as I held his gaze, and I couldn't decide if I wanted to run to or away from him.

The sensible thing would be for me to stop feeding him, if I wanted time and room to think this through.

But since when was I a sensible person where Asa was concerned?

A streak of white light zipped up and over my head, landing in the loft. "Thank Baldr, my stuff is safe."

Clay ducked his head in, letting me know I was on Colby duty. "Who's Baldr?"

"Not sure," I muttered, "but I bet he hates orcs."

Knowing Colby, Baldr was a deity in her game. To be on the safe side, I would Google it later.

The name rang a distant bell, and the last thing I needed was to discover he was a real god, that her prayers were going somewhere. Most of the gods in this world had given up on us and left, but their selective hearing kicked in when someone praised them. Given she was a bright soul given form, I didn't want her to risk catching celestial interest.

Sheesh.

This auntie gig was exhausting.

"Off to snag those pics." He saluted me. "You starting cleanup?"

"Yeah." That was more moth appropriate than ogling Asa. "I'll start with the worm."

"I'll drag the bodies down." Asa's lips pulled to one side. "I tried to be careful with the heads."

For thoroughness's sake, I would catalog the parts before dusting them in case Clay missed any.

"Stay put," I called up to Colby. "You don't want to get worm ash in your eyes."

"Gross."

A few seconds later, I heard the familiar sounds of battle and knew she wasn't budging for a while.

Nothing like a real-life battle to get your heart pumping for virtual slaughter, I guess.

On silent feet, Asa slipped away and began dragging bodies down to me while I vaporized the worm.

One by one, I snapped a picture of each zombie then reduced it to ash until gray dust lapped my ankles.

With Colby nearby, I drew as needed from her to finish the job, but it left me groggy and weak.

"That's all of them." Asa slid his arm around my waist, holding me upright. "Go shower and get in bed."

"This is like sleeping inside a charcoal grill that's never been cleaned." I shook my head. "I can't do it."

"Your room is untouched." He nudged me toward the hall. "You can rest there."

As good as a hot shower sounded right about now, I couldn't get my feet on board. "What about you?"

"Clay and I have cleaning to do." He hit the closet for a broom and dustpan. "Let us handle this."

"Are you sure...?" I shifted my weight back and forth. "I can stay, help out."

"You've expended enough energy." He began sweeping. "I'll be right here if you need me."

The domesticity of the moment struck a chord with me, and I found my feet glued to the floor.

The broom stilled, and Asa caught me staring. It was like we had swallowed magnets that fought to snap us together whenever we got too close. He might be well versed in his heritage, but I had nothing. There couldn't be that much daemon blood in me. A quarter daemon wasn't a lot. Like my arms and one of my legs were pure witch. One piddly leg was daemon. How could one leg's worth of daemon cause all this?

"Shower." He pointed the broom at me. "Or I'll bathe you myself."

"*Shh.*" I fanned my cheeks a beat too late to pretend I hadn't considered letting him. "Colby might hear you."

He flicked a glance up at the loft, and I had to concede she was too enmeshed in her game to listen in.

"I'll shower." I straightened my shoulders. "By myself."

A teasing light entered his eyes that almost derailed me again.

Fast.

Too fast.

He was speeding toward me, and I was too dumb to step out of the road.

I might as well hold out my arms and make an even bigger target for him to crash into.

Our collision, when it happened, *if* it happened, would be heard for miles.

13

I left gray powdery footprints behind as I padded into the bathroom and cranked the shower to boiling. I let the steam clean my lungs and scrubbed the zombie off my skin and from my hair. Then I stood there, an ungoddessly amount of time, just trying to screw my head on straight.

It almost worked. I nearly found my Zen. But then a black mass scuttled across the shower curtain, and I screamed bloody murder, flinging a spell to zap the holy Hael out of whatever zombie critter had found me. I didn't want to touch it, so it wasn't much, but the creature screamed and slammed against the cabinet.

A cold breeze swept into the room as someone wrenched the door open, banging the knob off the wall.

"Zombie," I yelped, expecting Clay to be my savior. "Where did it go?"

"It's not a zombie," Asa assured me. "It also shouldn't be in here."

He snapped out a command in a language that hurt my ears, and scuttling noises clicked on the tile.

Curtain fisted in my hand, I leaned around the edge and watched as a black...thing...made its exit.

"What is that?" I cringed from the sight of it. "What was it doing in here?"

"It was *crisht'na*." He scanned the room, minus the shower, giving me my privacy. "They're like crabs."

"*They?*" The fabric crinkled in my hand. "There are more of them?"

"I counted three." He kept his gaze away from me. "They're a common species of subdaemons."

"And they're in here because...?"

"They smelled the gore." He backed through the doorway. "And a challenger is in the woods."

"Hold up." I cut off the water. "I thought they didn't bother you on cases."

"They're free to challenge me at any time, but they know I won't retaliate on the clock."

"You're meeting with them?" I grabbed my towel and started drying. "Now?"

Sure, his wounds had healed, but Asa wasn't fully recovered from his ordeal. That would take days.

Attention on the knob in his palm, he began to shut the door. "Yes."

Desperate to keep him talking, I raked fingers through my wet hair. "How often does this happen?"

"Once or twice a week."

Once or twice...a *week*? "How have I never noticed a strange daemon lurking in the woods?"

A wry twist found his lips. "There's a reason why I handle perimeter checks alone."

"You're making yourself an easy target."

"The first meet is an introduction," he countered. "They challenge me, I accept, they leave."

"When do you honor your agreement?"

"Once a case is done, I summon my challengers and clear the board before the next assignment."

BLACK ARTS, WHITE CRAFT

Wrapping the towel around my torso, I stepped out. "What happens to your challengers?"

Averting his gaze, Asa entered the bedroom then faced the door to the hall. The fact he had pressed me against that door earlier left me flushed from more than the steam.

But crabs.

Daemon crabs.

In the bathroom.

With me.

I was *not* okay with that.

However, I was fine with Asa guarding the door while I tugged fresh clothes on in a rush.

"Asa?" I stomped on my boots after turning them upside down and giving them a good shake to be sure I wasn't about to get my toes pinched. "What happens to your challengers?"

"The fight is to the death." He rested his forehead against the wood. "Does that bother you?"

Walking up behind him, I pressed my palm to the center of his back. "Only if you lose."

The supernatural world had rules. Most were common sense laws. Some were more colorful. Either you followed them, or you died horribly. Dominance fights were essential to establishing hierarchy in all shifter cultures. Most of the time, those brawls ended in submission, but death was always a possibility.

From the sound of it, daemon culture wasn't so different from gwyllgi and wargs in that respect.

"I won't lose." He glanced over his shoulder, eyes burnt crimson and ravenous. "Not for a long while yet. Not for centuries. Not for millennia." He twisted until his back hit the wood. He faced me then, my hand on his chest. Gripping my wrist, he placed my open palm over his heart. "I would fight for you...forever."

"You have no brakes, do you?" Unable to tune out his heart, I was drugged by its quickening beat. "You just keep stomping on the gas."

"I'm old." He stroked his thumb up the inside of my wrist. "Older than you might realize."

"Is this the part where you tell me you've waited for me your whole life?"

"You just did it for me."

"You don't even know me." I laughed, and yeah, it sounded a bit crazed. "How can you be so sure?"

As drawn as I was to him, I imagined the moth to a flame phrase was coined for idiots like us.

Fire bad. Danger ahead! Do not pass go. Here be dragons.

And yet—I smelled smoke. I was dancing so close to the flame I was working on my tan.

"The more time we spend together, the more certain I am."

All I knew for sure was I didn't want him to die, and I probably would lick his horns if he asked me.

"I should go." He stepped into my space to reach the knob behind him. "This won't take long."

"I'm going with you."

He blinked at me, I blinked at him. He hadn't expected me to say that, clearly. Well, neither had I. So, ha!

"Your presence signifies we are fascinated with each other. Word will spread." Muscles in his jaw flexed. "My father will hear of it."

"I hate to break it to you, Hairnado, but if your father goes around chopping off hands that touch your pretty, pretty hair, then he already knows about us. I would be willing to bet that played into why you slapped a bracelet on me so fast. You wanted me to be able to play with your hair without repercussions. I appreciate that, by the way. I'm attached to my hands, and yes, I do mean that literally." I stared up at him, challenging him. "If he knows that much, he knows I'm invested in you not kicking the bucket." That last part made his expression go soft. "I have a haircare line to perfect, and you're my guinea pig, okay?" I got back on track. "I'm going with you, and you can't stop me."

"So fierce." He brushed my cheek with his fingertips. "There's no coming back from this."

The bracelet was his declaration of intent, but this...this would be mine. "I'm good with that."

Even if we went nowhere as a couple, or whatever, I didn't want to see him get hurt. He was a good guy, a good agent. And his hair was *so* pretty. No one with hair that pretty deserved to die.

Reaching behind him, I palmed his hand where it rested on the knob and opened the door. "After you."

A smile twitching his lips, he dipped his head and entered the hall. I trailed behind him, texting Colby a heads-up I would be doing a perimeter check with Asa. Clay, I could hear, was in the living room.

When I moved to follow Asa outside, Clay gripped my arm to stop me. "Think hard about this."

Dipping a hand into my pocket, I worried the dented cold iron bullet I hadn't disposed of yet. "I have."

"All right." He released me. "I hope you know what you're doing, Dollface."

"That makes two of us." I quirked him a smile. "We'll be right back."

"I'll be here." He resumed his sweeping. "This sh—" He glanced toward the loft. "It gets everywhere."

I did a visual check on Colby, who was bundled up in her blanket, headphones on, antennae alert, and I couldn't decide if I was glad the carnage hadn't fazed her or disturbed by how she took it in stride. The kid had been through a lot, and I was worse about hanging on to who and what she used to be than she had ever been. The harder she worked to shed her past and embrace her present, the more left behind I felt.

Maybe because my parents' beliefs and values hadn't shaped me. They died before leaving their marks on me. Maybe because the director was the defining figure for me? He molded me, shaped me, groomed me. Or maybe it was because she decided to forget her life, but the director had robbed me of the choice. I kept nudging Colby toward her past, her parents, because she had one. I had...fragments.

"Rue?" Asa touched my elbow. "Are you sure you want to do this?"

Another side effect of Asa peeling back my layers was I spent more time looking back instead of forward. I couldn't change the past. No one held that power. All my history contained was the same old pain and a yawning void where my childhood should have been. I was better off keeping my eyes on the horizon.

"I'm good." I patted his arm. "I got distracted, that's all."

Without saying a word, he warned me that distractions could get me killed. "All right."

Focused on Asa and the woods around us, I kept an eye out for the challenger. I didn't have to search hard to spot him. The gorgeous turquoise skin made him stand out from the greens and browns around us. At first, I thought he assumed we couldn't see him. He wasn't moving. Not even blinking. Barely breathing.

I grasped the situation when he hit one knee, dipped his chin, and pounded a mighty fist with webbed fingers over his heart.

"You may rise." Asa gave silk a run for its money with his smooth voice. "Speak your piece, then leave."

"My lord, Astaroth." As the challenger rose, he flexed open thick red slits on his neck. *Gills.* "I humbly challenge you for your seat."

Astaroth to Asa. I filed that away. Yet another example of him folding himself to fit inside a box.

"Challenge accepted." Undaunted, Asa flicked his wrist to hurry him along. "You are aware of the rules?"

"I am." The daemon lifted his gaze to me, his eyes black from corner to corner, and then grinned at Asa. "You are fascinated with her."

Jutting out my chin, I dared Asa to deny it with the force of my glare. "He better be."

"Oh." Asa fit his hand to the front of my throat and stroked my carotid with his thumb. "I am."

"It was nice meeting you." Unable to tear my gaze away from the molten heat in Asa's eyes, I addressed the challenger. "Enjoy your final days."

A rumbling laugh poured from the challenger. "Are you so certain of him?"

"Yeah." I didn't have to think about it. "I am."

"Then perhaps I made a mistake." His gills flared as he laughed. "Or perhaps the fates will favor me."

"Fate favors no one. Gods take credit for all good things while they ignore the bad that happens on their watches. Faith is for suckers. You have to make your own luck." I shrugged. "That's my *humble* opinion."

"Thank you for your time. I am grateful you have accepted my challenge. I look forward to our battle."

"As do I," Asa said, never taking his focus off me.

The daemon retreated into the woods. Hard to miss him, even on my periphery, with that skin tone. I did my best to ignore the crunching of leaves as legs scuttled over the forest floor, leaving with their master.

"He seems nice." I cut my eyes left, but he was gone. "Pretty skin." I considered him. "Aquatic daemon?"

"Yes."

"Are you fitting me for a necklace?" I pressed against his hold. "Or are you thinking about choking me?"

"Neither."

"Do you think you could let go then?"

"Am I hurting you?"

"No." I covered his hand with mine. "Just curious."

"Aedan was interested in you. You can tell by the way he flared his gills. It's mating behavior, an attempt to lure you in with bright colors. I had to show him that you're mine, that you submit only to me. The fact you didn't glance his way again proved the fascination goes both ways. He won't try tempting you a second time."

"Huh." I let him get his possessiveness under control. "I won't lie. The gills freaked me out."

Asa tilted his head, a frown knitting his brow. "You don't mind my daemon form."

"No." A flush rode my thankfully already pink cheeks. "I don't mind him at all."

That confession unlocked his grip, loose as it had been, and he lowered his arm. "Horns and all."

"Horns and all." I rolled a shoulder then set off toward the cabin. "Meg told me licking horns was a thing the other night. Have any experience in that department? Or was she pulling my leg?"

Noticing I was walking solo, I checked behind me to find Asa glowing red as a tomato fresh off the vine.

"Most horned species enjoy...horn play...but I..." He shook his head. "I've never..."

"You look like you could use a glass of water." I reached back and grabbed his hand. "*Cold* water."

Dumped down the front of his pants. A gallon or two ought to do it. Heavy on the ice cubes.

In a daze, he allowed me to lead him back to the cabin. "You would do that?"

The question pulled me up short, just shy of the porch. "Lick your horns?"

His Adam's apple bobbed as he swallowed hard, but all he managed was a nod.

"I don't see your daemon that way," I admitted, hoping I didn't hurt his feelings. "He's friend-zoned."

As I spent more time with that side of him, I began to appreciate the facets of that personality. Innocent, almost, which was odd for a daemon. He was quick to claim me, but I didn't pick up any flirty/sexy vibes.

For all I knew, he liked having me around for the sole purpose I had security clearance for his hair.

A blur of reality, a crackle of flame, and familiar thick black horns curved over Asa's head.

"You're not serious." I did what I would never had done with the daemon. I reached up and touched one with a long slide of my finger down its slight ridges. "You can just mix and match parts at will?"

The *plop* my brain made as it fell into the gutter could probably be heard for miles.

"No." A shiver coasted through his limbs. "These are part of my natural appearance, but I blend in better without them. People are less afraid of me than when they can identify my species at a distance."

Horns or no horns, Asa still had the effect of sending other, lesser predators running. Cowering, at least.

"What else are you hiding?" I plucked his shirt. "Wings? A tail?" I narrowed my eyes. "It's a tail, right?"

The night his daemon crawled in my bed, I'd missed a golden opportunity to discover extra appendages.

"Mother concealed my daemonic traits for me when I was a child, and I kept up the practice." His breath punched from his lungs, reminding me I was still fondling him. "She never made a fuss over the horns, or my fangs, but fae are cruel and vain creatures." Voice ragged, he fought to calm his pulse. "Those are my only abnormalities in this form."

Except, she wouldn't have erased them if she accepted him. In magicking away the reminder of what he was, she had taught him to hide a part of himself as well. I would have pointed it out, but the conscience I was growing in fits and starts warned me it was cruel and pointless. The past was past. The trick had served him well then and now. I had no right to accuse his mother of assassinating his self-acceptance.

"You're not abnormal." I fisted his shirt. "You're you." I flicked my attention back to his horns. "I like it."

"Thank you," he rasped, his palm cupping my cheek. "That means a lot, coming from you."

By gesturing toward his horns, I avoided fielding his compliment. "Will you keep them?"

"No." He dipped his chin. "Without them, I can pretend, for a little while, that I'm someone else."

Halloween night came rushing back to me, along with his eagerness to dress up and trick-or-treat with us in town. I suspected then that he craved a sense of acceptance, of belonging, and this confirmed it as far as I was concerned. So, I didn't push him the way I nudged Colby toward realizations colored by my past.

I questioned if his unwillingness to accept himself had splintered his personality until he and his daemon were two separate entities sharing one body. But I was learning, slowly, to pull back when I sensed a tender spot and not to exploit it as I had been raised to do.

The door swung open, and Clay stood there with a broom. "Everything good?"

"Yep." I noticed he had removed his wig to prevent ruining it. "How's cleaning?"

"As disgusting as you might expect." He frowned at his ashy clothes. "We need to move to a hotel."

Human witnesses would cut down on the likelihood the black witch would send more zombies after us. I wasn't a fan of courting discovery—this witch didn't seem to care about the rules—but I was also tired and hungry and ready to palm my forehead for not considering an undead creature could slip past my wards.

"Okay." I eased past him. "I'll start packing."

"I'll call..." Asa pulled out his phone then paused. "Make that the Kellies."

Our backup was in the trash bags Clay was setting on the porch. Secondary teams often contained junior agents about to get their first taste of the life via cleaning up after primary teams. Poor suckers. I got the golden ticket on that front. Nepotism saved me from drudgework. Depending on how many agents were assigned to this area, we might have hours, or days to wait for help.

"I'm almost done with the worst of it." Clay sneezed into his shoulder. "I put Colby on hotel detail. She's probably got something by now." He called up to the loft. "Status report."

"Two suites booked at Rosemont Inn. They have a four-point-five-star rating, they're thirty minutes from our present location, *and* they have high-speed internet." She leaned over the edge. "Good enough?"

"Perfect, Shorty." He gave her a thumbs-up, and she returned to her computer. "She's like having a personal Kelly on the team. She's a wiz." He lowered his voice. "She gets to feel like an active member of the team while keeping her out of immediate danger. It's a win/win, am I right?"

The idea of using her as tech support hadn't occurred to me. It was brilliant. The best of both worlds.

"How is she paying for that?" I'd had her memorize my credit card number for emergency purchases, but I hoped she wasn't using it. The insurance money hadn't come in yet, and shop repairs were draining my balance dry. "As you might recall, my shop hasn't reopened yet, so money is tight."

"I gave her access to my black card." He shrugged. "I'm not going to make you pay out of pocket."

Black Hat agents got black cards from a witch-owned bank on a private paranormal finance network. The funds weren't limitless, but they did fit the company aesthetic.

"Good." I patted my hip. "There seems to be a hole in it."

Chuckling, Clay got back to work, and I pitched in with Asa to do the best we could without proper supplies.

Since Colby had put on her headphones again, I texted her to tell her to pack it up, that she had an hour. Then I returned to my room to begin packing for the move to a—hopefully—more secure location.

A foul sensation overtook me as I opened the door, and the spit dried in my mouth.

On the bed, propped against the pillow, sat the Proctor grimoire.

14

The grimoire reclined against my pillow as if it had been given the best seat in the house, and chills tickled my spine like fingers of ice. Its power was a blight upon the air, a foulness I felt down to my toes. It hadn't been this repellent to me when we were at home, but it was downright repugnant now.

Reflecting on what Asa had told me, about the scent of my magic altering, I had a pretty good idea why.

"Hey," I called out, unable to wrench my gaze from the book. "Colby, can I see you for a minute?"

Even unplugged from her game, she tended to listen to music in her downtime. She might not hear me.

A crinkling noise filled the hall, and she hung a quick right into my room. "What's up?"

"Did you bring this with us?" I pointed out my pillow pal. "It's okay if you did."

"No way." Her recoil bumped her into the wall. "I hate that thing."

"Maybe don't antagonize it," I said out of the side of my mouth, "if it followed us here."

A sentient book of dark magic wasn't anything we needed to insult or give agency. *More* agency.

The commotion brought Clay to the door, and he noticed the book right off the bat.

"I thought you left it." He didn't come into the room. "Did you have it warded or...?"

"Obviously." It must have hitchhiked in my suitcase to get past them. "Not cool, man. Not cool."

Drawn by the commotion, Asa drifted in and mulled over the problem with a pensive expression.

"How did it get here?" Clay came in to help Colby wrestle a giant zip-top bag. "Don't say magic."

"It moves around on its own when we're at home. That's why I keep it—" I bit my tongue so hard I tasted blood. I had almost mentioned my safe of horrors, which only Colby knew I kept. "I lock it up."

The slip didn't go unnoticed by, well, anyone. But the book was the immediate problem.

"We should have sensed it, but none of us did." Asa pursed his lips. "This grimoire can cloak itself."

Learning it could stow away on adventures *and* camouflage itself from our senses?

Big problem. *Really* big problem. Big with a capital B-I-G.

"That's not the best news I've ever heard." Clay glared at it. "I don't trust it appearing just as the zombie army announces it's their target."

"Like to like," Asa murmured. "Objects of power gain a sentience, given enough time. They want to be used. They want to wreak havoc. They seek out masters who will allow them to embrace their full potential."

A lightning strike of possibility hit me with such force, I staggered back a step, almost tripping.

"What's wrong?" Asa was there in a blink, cupping my elbow, steadying me. "Did the book hurt you?"

"Colby has been hearing a voice. She says it's magic, speaking to her." I wanted to vomit thinking about it. "Our familiar bond is so new, I wasn't sure if she was mistaking instinct for instruction or if her magic worked in an all-new way. I'm no expert on light magic, not by a long shot, but what if it was the grimoire whispering in her ear?"

Colby recovered the fastest, and the spark of curiosity in her eyes did my stomach no favors.

"The voice was nice, though." Colby lit on my head. "The book isn't."

"That's how they get you." Clay frowned at her. "Don't try to talk to it and find out, okay?"

"I won't." She nestled down on my head. "*And* I'll let you know if it tries to talk to me."

"Good girl." I reached up to scratch her fuzzy head. "Done packing?"

"Almost." She poked her legs into my scalp. "Someone called me away."

"Get back to it." I anchored my hands on my hips. "I need to ward this before we leave."

With a glance back at the bed, she zipped off to the loft with her antennae quivering in thought.

"She's going to try to talk to the book." I stated the obvious. "We need to keep an eye on her."

"She's a kid," Clay agreed. "Kids get curious."

"Can you ward it on your own?" Asa toyed with his earring. "There's a chance, if you borrow from Colby, she can manipulate the magic." He dropped his arm. "The grimoire must not be allowed to forge a bond with her."

"I'll have to dig deep." I rubbed my fingertips together. "I'll need a spotter."

"I'll do it." Clay moved behind me. "I can't let you do this alone, Dollface."

"Asa is here," I pointed out. "I'm not alone."

"He's as likely to use this opportunity to cop a feel as to protect you. He's not a great multitasker."

The dig might have insulted someone who didn't know Clay well enough to tell he meant no insult. He was indulging in a freak-out session. The book had him unnerved in a major way. That made two of us.

"I'll finish packing." Asa eased from the room. "Call if you need help."

Reaching for my kit, I pulled out my small athame. "This is going to suck."

"How did it go?" Clay cut through my mutterings. "With the challenger?"

The distraction from the book, and what it might be doing to Colby, was welcome.

"That happens a lot?" I pulled the herbs required, sprinkled them around the book, careful to close the circle. "Does he ever just check a perimeter?"

"It does, and he does." He watched me work. "I was surprised he let you go with him."

Why I accepted that Clay took those threats to his partner lying down, I don't know. "He won't let you?"

"I killed the first three I bumped into in the woods." He chuckled. "Then I had to pay a blood price to their families, like the challengers weren't going to die anyway. I mean, paternity aside, Ace is a beast. No one is going to take him out. You haven't seen him fight until you've seen him in a free-for-all."

The vote of confidence buoyed me as I finished my preparations, until my brain snagged on that last detail. "You *watch* the challenges?"

"Not only is it great entertainment," he said haughtily, "but do you really think I would let my partner go into hostile territory alone?"

"I wasn't aware it was a spectator sport is all."

With a grimace, I sliced open my palm and christened the circle with blood. I pushed magic into it while I murmured the most powerful ward I could set on the spot with what I had on hand. The power zipped in a loop, enclosing the grimoire, and the oily sensation from the black magic snuffed out with a hiss of displeasure.

"Well?" The room blurred around the edges, and I blinked to clear my vision. "Can you smell it?"

"No." He slapped me on the back. "You never cease to amaze, Dollface."

The weight of his hand was all it took to tip me forward into a fall that would have mashed my face into the newly warded grimoire had he not looped his thick arms around my waist then scooped me against him.

"I'm a wimp." My head lolled onto his chest. "Total...wimp..."

"Hush." He kissed my forehead. "You're good people, Rue. You always have been."

Pretty sure that's what he said, anyway. I couldn't hold my eyes open another second.

The air exploded from my lungs, and I blinked awake with sympathy for any dinosaurs who had attempted to sleep through a world-ending meteor shower.

"Colby?" Asa flicked his gaze to the rearview mirror. "Are you all right?"

"She's fine," I wheezed. "I caught her with my stomach rolls."

Beside me, Clay snorted out a laugh and scooped her off me. I pushed upright while the SUV cut in and out of lanes, and a hard bump jostled me. I banged my head on the ceiling and hurried to strap on my seat belt.

"What's wrong?" I wiped the back of my hand across my mouth to check for drool. "Do we have a flat?"

"Ten points," Colby crowed, pumping her fist. "You're up to thirty."

"Points?" I leaned forward, noticing the crimson smears on the windshield. "Oh crap."

The headlights illuminated a staggering zombie congo line crossing the road ahead of us. There was no way to avoid them. They weren't organized. They were tied together. With rope. Which made them that much worse as they pulled and tugged to get away from one another.

"Any idea who they used to be?" I sat back, bracing for impact with a hand on the back of Asa's seat. "They look human."

"That's my guess." Clay held Colby tight. "Easier to hunt and to reanimate."

"And there are a lot more of them."

The word *disposable* came to mind, but that was how black witches saw humans. As less than. Unworthy of notice. They put the *human* in *human sacrifice*. That was the only use black witches had for them.

Tires screamed as Asa hit the brakes, and my head bounced off the window when he cut the wheel hard.

"Ouch." I rubbed my temple. "Anyone else feeling like Humpty Dumpty?"

No wonder I had ended up with a gut full of moth. His evasive maneuvers had slung her into me.

"Come here." Clay gripped my elbow, hauled me as close as the seat belt allowed, then locked his strong arm around my shoulders to anchor me against his side. "You gotta protect that noggin, Dollface."

"You gotta crack a few eggs to make an omelet," I said lamely, happy to use him as my shield.

"I think you broke her," he teased Asa on a laugh. "Colby, can you sense brain damage?"

Her airy intake of breath wedged a blade in my heart, and I reached up for her.

"He's joking." I snuggled down with her against his side. "I got my teeth rattled, but I'm fine."

"How far are we from town?" Clay settled in to brace us better. "We must be halfway there."

"Lights ahead." Tension rode Asa's voice as he worked to keep us on the road. "Won't be long now."

"Who is crazy enough to throw zombies at us on the highway so close to town?"

"Not crazy." Clay squeezed me tighter. "Desperate."

A buzz in my pocket had me reaching for my cell and hoping momentum didn't jerk it out of my hand.

>>*I shot a trespasser.*

"Oh no," I breathed, recognizing the number. "Mrs. Gleason shot someone."

>*On your land or on mine?*

>>*Ha! With your police friends? Like I would tell you if it was on my land.*

"I have a funny feeling I live next to a graveyard." I exhaled. "She is one hardcore lady."

>*Where is he now?*

>>*I lost sight of him. He ran mighty fast for someone with extra holes in his arse.*

>*Thanks for the update. I owe you a month's worth of tea.*

>>*I'm your neighbor and your friend. You don't owe me anything.*

A fist of emotion tightened around my throat, and I missed Samford like crazy.

Without me realizing it, I had faked making it my home until it had become one.

>>*The Yard Birds are here to help me celebrate. I'll let you know if I see him again. Or find his body.*

The Yard Birds were our neighbors, and a few of her friends. They were our unofficial neighborhood watch and met every Sunday after church. Usually, they drank their weight in margaritas and ended up passed out on the porch and in the driveway, so I wasn't sure how much watching they got done, but they always came through in a pinch.

>*Thanks.*

I was momentarily at a loss for words.

>*I would appreciate that.*

"Well?" Clay kept his attention on the road ahead. "What's the word?"

"She shot a trespasser, has no idea where he went, and she's having friends over to celebrate."

"I wish I had met her twenty years ago," Clay said softly. "What a woman."

"Twenty years ago, her husband was alive. She would have shot you for putting the moves on her."

"I say again..." A smile split his cheeks from ear to ear. "What a woman."

Unwilling to touch that with a ten-foot pole, I pulled up the exterior security feeds. With a sinking feeling in my gut, I realized I had gotten notifications, but I had slept through them while recovering from magic burnout.

"This makes no sense." I shoved upright, still leaning against Clay. "That's Nolan Laurens."

From this angle, I could tell sandlike grains sprinkled from his hand onto the grass. Salt?

What else could it be? What was he doing? What did that make him?

A witch? A masque? Something worse?

"Camber's uncle?" He leaned over to get a look. "The date guy, right?"

"Arden's uncle, but same difference. Yeah. And he invited me *and* the girls to dinner. It wasn't a date."

The sensation of being watched prompted me to flick my gaze up to the rearview mirror.

Asa smiled, a twitch of his cheek, but he didn't say a word about Nolan.

Then again, the daemon had said it all for him.

"I need to call Arden," I muttered, already dreading it, "but it can wait until we're settled at the hotel."

"We're clear," Asa announced. "The zombies won't venture this close to town."

"We hope." I sat up, but Colby stuck with Clay. "Otherwise, this will be an incident with a capital *I*."

David Taylor had knocked down the first domino in a line I had no hope of stopping, now that they were falling. I fooled myself into believing he would keep what he knew about Colby to himself. Black witches weren't in the habit of sharing their power, and knowledge was power. But maybe I had it wrong.

Without knowing Taylor's true name, I couldn't ask the Kellies to ferret out any links to other witches in the Bureau. An official inquiry might tip off what I was beginning to suspect must be an entire rogue coven operating within Black Hat's ranks. One with a sole target, and I had painted it on Colby's back the night I saved her from the Silver Stag.

Too bad we had reduced Taylor to ash. I would have loved to have this witch bring him back so I could kill him all over again for ruining the good thing Colby and I had going.

15

Colby had booked two suites, which worked in our favor. It gave us one big table for her to commandeer for her laptop and other essentials and us a place to work in a separate room, away from tiny moth ears.

The guys had a narrow balcony, just enough to step onto, but it overlooked the parking lot entrance. The cabin view had been lovely. This? Not so much. They would pay for the view with exhaust fumes wafting up through their open sliding door. And the noise. Yeah. They could keep it.

"Backup is forty-five minutes out," Asa reported. "The Kellies advise us to sit tight until they arrive."

"Works for me." I stretched. "I'll see what I can do about food."

The only place open at this hour was a squat Italian restaurant that smelled like onions. We hadn't eaten in ten forevers, so I placed a delivery order for three and hoped for the best.

"He could sense the ward." Clay watched the security footage I'd sent him. "See that? He held up his hand to feel the magic. He must not have much if he had to trace its path like that."

"There's witch blood in that family." I paced the floor in front of the small kitchen. "I chose Arden for the latent power in her. Camber's family has magic too. That's probably why they're friends. Witches crave a coven. Their bonds, as well as those with their families, fulfilled that need. Until I arrived. Young witches gravitate toward powerful mentors. That was why they came to me asking for odd jobs until I took them under my wing. That's why they satisfy that same drive in me—to belong to a community and better it."

"That's white witch logic." Asa set down his phone after viewing the same link. "Black witches are loners until they require extra hands, blood, or power for spells."

"Yes and no." I turned his comment into a teachable moment, since that was my job description. "There are familial groups, multi-generational covens who live together their whole lives. They tend to perform sacrificial magic. On each other. They often sacrifice their own children. Infants, mostly. They get pregnant for the sole purpose of fulfilling a ritual and then spend the next nine months planning it."

Aside from the obvious, that I was in the habit of throwing the worst of myself at people to force them a step back, I wasn't sure why I felt the need to share that tidbit. Or watch while he absorbed it as if it might reveal some flaw in his character I could capitalize on. But that wasn't me. Not anymore.

I was flawed, broken, ruined.

I was cruel, bitter, hopeless.

But I was trying. I was growing. I was learning.

I was closer to embodying that person I saw in my mind when I meditated on who I wanted to be.

Given my own struggles, I wasn't going to shine light on his or anyone else's until the glare blinded them to my faults. That was petty and small and wrong. *Wrong.* A concept that was beginning to take on new dimension for me.

A tentative knock on the door sent Clay sprinting for the food. I couldn't tell if he was that hungry or that eager to escape the topic, but I wish he hadn't left me alone to face the conversational fallout with Asa.

"You expect me to curl my lip or spit on you." He kept his seat. "You know who my father is, what I am."

"You aren't your father, and being a daemon doesn't make you a monster. Your choices determine that."

"You're willing to pardon me, but you can't forgive yourself?"

"I've done horrible things," I said softly. "I was a terrible person."

"Your choices say otherwise."

"You can't use my words against me." I glowered at him. "That's not fair."

"You haven't sacrificed any babies." He rose with fluid grace. "You never would have either."

"You can't know what I would have done. I was high on black magic. I had no moral compass."

"The needle might have spun a bit, but you had one. Otherwise, you and I wouldn't be here now."

Asa crossed to me, took one of my wrists in each of his hands, and unfolded my arms from where I had cinched them across my stomach. That habit was damning in the wrong company. Any sign of weakness could get you killed in our line of work. I had to shed the tics living among humans had allowed me.

"You don't know that." I stood there, shackled by him and not minding it. "I might have enlisted aid from a daemon prince to help me conquer the Earth." I bounced a shoulder. "If he wasn't too busy ruling Hael to pen me onto his schedule."

"I don't want to rule." His thumbs caressed my inner wrists. "Though I might not mind *being* ruled."

"Eww." Clay lumbered in, burdened with bags of food. "I don't want to know Rue's kinks. Or yours."

Heat flashed through me, and Asa smiled, his thumbs telling him exactly how my heart had leapt.

Goddess bless, I was still thinking about his horns. Clearly, I had problems. Two of them. A matched set.

"What are you thinking about now?" Asa murmured. "Your pulse keeps jumping."

"That lasagna is turning me on," I lied, jerking out of his grip. "Parmesan really does it for me."

"Literally just said no kinks." Clay spread out the food on the table and tossed me a plastic fork. "Keep them to yourself."

"I was talking about food."

"What did I tell you about daemons and food?"

"That food fights are foreplay." I stabbed a meatball in Clay's spaghetti and bit down. "Oh, baby."

Asa moved in behind me, leaned over me, and took the fork from my fingers. His growl vibrated through my spine to rattle my teeth. I didn't enjoy having my food taken from me, so I pinched another meatball in my fingers and popped the whole thing in my mouth, giving myself ultra-sexy chipmunk cheeks. Twisting to see over my shoulder, I dared Asa with a look as I chewed, swallowed, then smacked my lips.

"Don't tempt me." He ate the meatball off my fork. "You won't like what happens."

That was the whole problem. I was pretty sure I *would* like it. I might even ask him to do it again.

"Can you two fight over something besides my balls?" Clay snatched the fork. "Seriously. Not cool."

A second knock on the door raised my eyebrows, and I checked with Clay. "You order dessert?"

Asa shrank back, giving me space, and fitted himself into the kitchen, as far from the door as possible.

After wiping my mouth clean of sauce, I scooted around the counter. "I'll get it, I guess."

I glanced back to check on him, but he was doing his invisible man impersonation. He must have scented the people on the other side of the door and recognized them. Black Hat. Must be. And they were early.

The zombified team could have called in an SOS before the witch took them out. That would account for a fresh secondary team arriving ahead of schedule. But the Kellies handled dispatch for all active agents.

They would have known.

They would have told us.

And that meant, whoever our guests were, they weren't our backup team.

Tuning in, I picked out four heartbeats, but that was all I could tell. The door opened under my palm and revealed four agents dressed in their Black Hat best. I greeted them with an expression I used to wear as easy as I smiled these days. Total lack of interest meets an utter willingness for violence. "You have ID?"

The agent on point, a gorgeous redhead with an athletic figure, reached into her suit jacket and pulled out standard Black Hat-issued ID.

"Melissa Rivers," I said loud enough for my voice to carry over the crunch of garlic bread to Clay's ears.

"Hey, Lis." He joined me at the door. "RJ, good to see you. Timothy, looking good. Vanessa, hey."

"The director sent us." Melissa made no move to cross the threshold. "He explained your problem."

Her face didn't ring any bells, but her voice struck me as familiar. I couldn't place it, though.

"Come in." He slung an arm around my shoulders and hauled me back. "Guys, this is Rue Hollis."

"Any friend of Clay's..." Melissa said to me while smiling at him. "It's good to see you."

The other three were less chatty, but I wasn't sure if the problem was me or if they had noticed Asa.

How he managed to make himself smaller, less threatening, was a feat to behold, but it made me twitch how he put himself into a box and shut the lid around others to make them more comfortable. Maybe it made him a better person than me. He wouldn't have to try hard to win that title. But I didn't like how it made me feel. Which just proved that, yeah. He was a better person than me to put others' comfort first.

"Asa," Vanessa said softly, the only one to address him. "It's good to see you again."

"Vanessa." He kept his gaze on his feet. "Always a pleasure."

"It could have been," RJ quipped, "if you had called her back. She's been pining after you for months."

A delicate flush turned her pale cheeks rosy, and she found her shoes of sudden interest too.

Me?

I considered using my athame to peel her boots like apples then feed them to her, soles first.

"Aww hell," Clay breathed. "Vanessa, you might want to step back. RJ, shut the ever-loving fuck up."

Interestingly, Timothy got the memo I was the immediate threat over Asa. He hit his knees, quick, then slid into a bow that resulted with his forehead pressing against the floor. He murmured a prayer or the next best thing, and he didn't budge. He barely breathed. The others watched him with tight frowns.

"Asa is fascinated by Rue." Clay put it out there. "You might not want to give Rue an excuse to kill you."

"I'm not going to kill you," I assured Vanessa blandly. "Keep looking at him, and you might wish I had."

The shift of the mood in the room tingled along my skin as Asa lifted his head fully for the first time since our guests arrived. A smile twitched in his cheek, and he rubbed a hand over his mouth, failing to hide it.

"Let's all cool down." Melissa fell in beside Clay. "Haven't enough agents lost their lives?"

The truth of that sobered me, and I retracted my claws, even if the urge to rake them down Vanessa's all-too-beautiful face still twitched in my fingertips. Which were tinted red with sauce. A reminder how easy it was to reach in and pluck a tastier off-menu item from her chest. I should have felt ashamed, but I was too irritated with myself for how I was behaving.

Asa wasn't the last fry in the bag or the last slice of cake in the fridge or the last cookie in the jar.

He also wasn't food, but that was beside the point. I wasn't fighting with anyone over him.

Moving slowly, as if afraid I might startle, Asa approached me. He stood beside me, our sides flush, and I pushed out an exhale as the coil of anger toward Vanessa relaxed into the chill vibe I had been struggling to manage on my own.

"Now that we've got that out of the way." Clay clapped his hands, and everyone jumped at the shock of noise. "Melissa, you said you guys are here to help with the zombie problem?"

"Zombies?" Her eyes widened to cartoon proportions. "There are zombies?"

"If you didn't know about them," Asa said, twining our fingers, "why are you here?"

And how did she know agents had died working this case, if she had no idea what killed them?

The Kellies would have briefed her, had they sent her, to prepare her team for battling the undead.

"The director told us a black witch was causing problems up this way. That you had seized a grimoire." A wrinkle creased her forehead. "We were ordered to collect it and transport it to the compound while you hunted down the witch."

Except we hadn't told anyone about the grimoire.

Crap, crap, crap.

We had found our second black witch, or she had found us, but what about the others?

Would her team stand with her or against her? Did they know the truth? Or were they following orders? Had we identified our rogue coven and its leader? The questions kept churning, turning my thoughts this way and that, attempting to make sense of all the peculiarities of this case. Hard to do with an audience.

One probably sent to kill Asa, disable Clay, capture me, then ferret out the grimoire and locate Colby.

A subtle tension pinched Clay's shoulders, proof the wheels of his brain were spinning hard and fast too, but he turned the twitch into a sweeping gesture toward the table.

"Oh good." Clay winked at her. "We're just about to sit down to dinner. Care to join us?"

A slow smile crept across Melissa's face, and she reached for her wand. "What gave me away?"

The other agents mimicked her, drawing their wands and sinking into ready positions.

Friends or foes? I couldn't tell yet. They might only be guilty of following her lead.

I didn't want to kill them if I could avoid it, a blip of conscience, if you will. But given the sheer volume of zombies we had dusted so far, a proficient coven made more sense than a gifted solo practitioner with a Frankenstein fetish. Many hands make light work, and all.

"Tell me mine," Clay teased, hoping to deescalate, "and I'll tell you yours."

"You offered to share food with us." She shook her head. "You're selective about your dining partners."

That wasn't strictly true. Clay showed affection through food, yes, and he taught me to do the same. But he also showed respect for his fellow agents when he brought them coffee or treats he baked.

For her to believe otherwise spoke volumes about his read on her character. Whatever their past relationship, he hadn't shown her those same courtesies, which told me all I needed to know about her.

With a polite nod, he fulfilled his end of the bargain. "No one knows about the grimoire."

"More people than you know are aware of its existence." Regret shadowed her features, eclipsed by her determination. "Give me the book, Clay, for old times' sake. Don't make me hurt them."

A prickle stung the base of my spine, and magic hummed under my skin.

Colby.

Her magic friend must be whispering in her ear again, warning her I was in danger, since the familiar bond didn't work like that.

"We don't have a book." I drew her attention from Clay. "Sorry for any confusion."

"Oh?" Her eyes glittered. "What's that on the table?"

Before I could cut my eyes in its direction, the foul presence of black magic slid over my skin in a rush.

That grimoire was going to be the death of us if we didn't figure out how to lock it up tight.

"You don't have to die today, Rue." Her voice softened. "Let us have the book, and we'll go."

"You're an accomplished liar." I smirked with every ounce of arrogance in me, which caused her façade to crack. "How many people have you killed to herd us into this trap?"

This whole case smacked of premeditation, in hindsight. The rogue coven members accepted they might die in the attempt to retrieve the book, and they were okay with that. They felt it was a worthwhile sacrifice, their lives or ours, and that kind of zeal never ended well for the opposition.

"Your wards were too strong at the cabin." She pursed her lips. "The revenants could cross, but all living things were rebuffed."

That explained why I was alerted to the ward breach. It hadn't been the zombies but one of them attempting to break in that tripped the magic. There had been too much chaos at the cabin for me to think twice about it. No doubt, that had been their plan.

"You killed those quicker than anticipated," she continued. "We were forced to create zombies, because of time constraints, and I don't have to tell you how lacking they are when it comes to even the simplest orders."

The zombigo and the zipper-head worm had been fancier than the shamblers for sure.

Revenants sounded witchier than *fancy zombies,* so I filed away the difference to read up on later.

As much as I had studied, the director felt necromancy was beneath us. That if a witch required a sack of animated meat to defend their claim to a territory, or to perform other menial tasks for them, they were unworthy adversaries.

"You killed fellow agents to have enough bodies to throw at us." Clay kept his tone even. "What in that book could be worth the loss of so much life?"

Understanding dawned in her expression, and her gaze skipped to me. "You haven't read it."

Bobbing a shoulder, I lied through my teeth. "There was nothing earth-shattering in it."

"Then you haven't truly read it." Her lips kicked up in a grin. "The book chooses who it reveals itself to."

Given what I suspected, that it was whispering in Colby's ear, I wasn't sure how picky it was about insinuating itself with potential vessels. But that link—that *possible* link—was one I would have to investigate after we got home.

"You're saying—" I forced my face into confused lines, "—it gave me the CliffsNotes version?"

"You're not powerful enough." She jerked her chin up a notch. "You couldn't comprehend it if you tried."

No one in my entire life had ever accused me of being the least powerful witch in the room. From when I was a child, I was treated as a future power. Then I had become one. Granted, I had changed my diet, but Colby's magic was beyond me on my best day. Make that my *worst* day.

For her to be so clueless, Asa must be right.

I was losing that cultivated black witch stink the more I tapped into the familiar bond I shared with Colby. She was burning the darkness right out of me, and I couldn't decide if it was a good thing or if her stripping away my best defense against my coworkers with every spell we cast together would leave me a sitting duck.

Bending over, bracing his hands on his thighs, Clay burst into deep guffaws that left him wheezing.

"It's not that funny." I nudged him with my foot. "Breathe, or you're going to pass out."

"Okay, okay." He lifted his hands. "I've got it under control."

Spurred on by his outburst, Melissa gave me a closer look. "Who are you?"

"Rue Hollis."

"That's an alias." She dismissed the name out of hand. "What's your birthname?"

No way in Hael was she getting that out of me. No one living, aside from the director, knew it. I aimed to keep it that way. The infamy attached to me was anchored in the name he had created for me to hide our relationship. I always assumed it was because he was ashamed of my white witch blood, but maybe, and it was a long shot, he was protecting me from the whispered rumors of daemon stigma.

More than likely, he kept me anonymous so no one would suspect the weapon he spent decades honing until it was aimed at them. Unleashed, I had no conscience, no shame, no morals. I had only the hunger.

"The name you're looking for is Elspeth." I allowed a cold smile to mold my lips. "Báthory."

"That's not possible." She took an unconscious step back before she locked her knees. "She's dead."

"Retired, in the Black Hat business, usually does mean dead. I'll give you that. But I'm alive and well."

"Suppressing your power?" She reclaimed that step. "Or did you lose it during your...sabbatical?"

This right here was what frightened me, that others would pick up on the change in my scent and mistake it for weakness. That was before Colby. I had made myself a target by choosing the path of light, but she ensured I would survive it. Let them think me weak. They had no idea.

"Keep pushing me, and you'll find out."

"Give me the book."

"Not happening."

"Fine." Her magic tickled me as she assessed my power. "Just as I thought." She smirked, but the relief in her posture called out her bravado. "Vanessa, collect the book."

As the weakest of the four, she made as good a sacrificial lamb as anyone, and she didn't seem to mind.

I understood the cause of her glee a moment later, when she sashayed up to Asa, picked up a braid, and slid it through her hand until she reached the end. She twirled that around her finger then heaved a sigh when his eyes flashed burnt crimson in response.

It was the weirdest thing.

One second, Vanessa stood there playing with his hair while I looked on as rage churned in my gut.

The next, her severed hand hit the floor with a thud, spilling crimson stains across the tacky carpet.

Nothing happened, as far as I could see. Except, of course, for her hand popping off her arm.

And then the screaming began.

16

"When you told me that would happen..." I began, while Vanessa wailed, "...I didn't believe it."

Blood pumping from her stump of a wrist, she wobbled back to Melissa, who cauterized it with a spell.

"Father takes infractions quite seriously." He rubbed his thumb across my cheek. "Never doubt that."

"You weren't lying." Melissa glanced between us then to Clay. "They're in fascination with each other."

"Did ignoring clear and present danger to stare into one another's eyes clue you in?"

"Kill them." Vanessa wept in RJ's arms. "Kill them all."

"I told you to collect the book," Melissa said archly, "not grope the daemon."

"Give us the book." Timothy stepped forward, hands out in front of him. "Then we'll go."

"You're going to kill us and then burn this place to the ground to cover your tracks. Try to, anyway. It's what I would do. Good luck with that." I chuckled at Melissa's pinched expression. "The director doesn't know you're here, or why you're here, or who you're threatening, and—make no mistake—he will gut you when he finds out if we don't do it for him."

Rumors of my death had been greatly exaggerated, with good reason. Black Hats didn't retire. We died, or we killed ourselves. That was the only escape. I was an exception, and she would have been smart to wonder why. The director wouldn't kill me, until he determined I was a lost cause. He had indulged me, up to a point, before shepherding me back under his purview. Until I proved to him I was a white witch, he would treat my dietary changes as teenage rebellion he could stamp out given enough time.

"The director has leashed us for too long." Melissa thinned her lips. "You might be happy to wear a collar, but I'm done letting him choke me."

If there was ever an opening for Clay's *I don't want to know about your kinks* line, it was this one.

"Seriously." I stared at Clay. "You're not going to say it?" I huffed. "She left the door wide open."

"We had sex." He shrugged. "I know her kinks. I can't unknow them for the sake of a punchline."

A memory of the time I dropped an oversized wig box that exploded in nipple clamps, dildos, and flavored lube had me agreeing with him. Some things, you can't forget. No matter how hard you try.

The absence of genitalia did not equate a deficit of imagination.

"There's a reason the director has successfully chained us for so long," Asa said quietly. "He's a power."

"And a politician," I added. "The other factions are thrilled to let him handle their problems for them."

The director leveraged their goodwill to expand his powerbase, lengthening his precious Bureau's reach.

"Do you have any idea how many failed coups the director has crushed?" Clay puffed out his cheeks. "As a creature destined for eternal servitude, I get it. The control chafes. You want to strike out at the establishment, kill your master. You'll risk anything—everything—to be free."

Grief welled in me to hear his impassioned speech, the truth in it, and to know my grandfather was to blame.

"Yes," she hissed. "We all deserve our freedom."

"Black Hat exists," I countered, "because people like us ruin freedom for everyone else."

We lied, cheated, stole, killed, and worse. We were monsters by any metric. Irredeemable, some would claim. But we had a healthy sense of self-preservation. That was why the director recruited some problems but killed others.

"We have a weapon unlike any who have come before us." Melissa smiled. "We have the book."

The book, among other things, was a how-to manual for tapping into Colby's power.

These witches couldn't be allowed to learn that knowledge, or it would spread, as secrets did in the end.

When her speech earned firm nods from her team, I no longer had any doubt they were full participants.

That would make what came next that much easier for my conscience to bear.

"You'll die in chains," Vanessa snarled. "We might too, but we'll be chewing on them."

"That would break your teeth," I pointed out. "Points for determination, though."

"Why did you choose her over me?" Vanessa waved her stump at us. "She's nothing."

The slur in her words told me RJ had taken pity on her and hit her with a spell to numb her pain.

"I beg to differ." Asa squeezed my hand. "She's fast becoming my everything."

A gagging noise brought my attention back to Clay, saving me from replying to Asa.

"Really?" I kicked his shin. "Now you've got an opinion?"

The door opened behind them, and a wiry man with a weathered face joined the group.

"Reinforcements are thirty minutes out," he warned. "We need to wrap this up and go."

Well, that was good news. I worried Melissa had killed them too. I was glad that wasn't the case.

"This is your last chance." Melissa turned her beseeching gaze on Clay. "Please, be reasonable."

"I hate to end things like this," he said, "but I've got a policy about not negotiating with psycho ex-girlfriends."

"All right." She flicked her wrist at Timothy. "You've made your choice."

Timothy swept his arm down in an arc, aiming his wand at the nearest target. Clay blocked the strike, then punched Timothy under his chin. His head cracked back from the force, his spine broken, and he collapsed on the floor in a twitching heap.

On the edge of my vision, flame engulfed Asa, and his daemon form sprung at a screaming Vanessa.

"Rue mine!" he roared as he twisted her head off like a bottlecap then yelled at it. *"Mine."*

Meanwhile, I palmed my face, embarrassed by his favorite battle cry. Seriously, we had to work on that.

Through my fingers, I spied RJ sliding along the wall, attempting to reach the table and the grimoire.

Colby was nearby. Not in the hall. In the vents? I could tell by the rush of power illuminating my skin and the bright-white sparks my wand shed onto the carpet. I never stuck to punishments with that kid, but so help me, this time I really was going to pull her internet for a week.

Keeping my face shielded, as if the gory scene was too much, I lured RJ into completing his suicide run.

Sure enough, he swooped in and brushed his fingers across the cover, attempting to find purchase.

I struck out, whacked his knuckles to do the director proud, and he dropped into a tidy pile of ash.

"Who are you?" Melissa's mouth dropped open. "What are you?"

Allowing my hand to fall, I flashed her a feral smile, but we were out of time for games. We were making too much noise. Human authorities would be called to investigate soon, if they hadn't already been, and I wasn't in the mood for interdepartmental cooperation. We needed to wrap up, clean up, and go.

The last man standing, the late arrival, skidded as he took in RJ's remains, but momentum carried him to Clay, who lifted him and snapped his spine over his thigh. The *crack* reverberated throughout the room.

That left us with Melissa, who I really wanted to turn in to the director to earn brownie points.

Okay, fine, so he would torture her horribly, until she begged for a death he wouldn't grant. Not much of a white witch thing to do, but it was the least she deserved after killing all those people to sink her claws into Colby. But, sadly, she would be thrilled to chat with the director to avoid said torture.

She would spill her guts about how I had stolen a grimoire from a case and kept it instead of following protocol by logging it into evidence. Then she would enlighten him as to the reason why. He knew Colby existed, and that was damning enough. He didn't need to know more.

Clay must have come to the same conclusion. He charged Melissa, colliding with her, knocking her back, and pinned her against the door. I wasn't sure why he didn't kill her outright. Sentimentality? He really was a big softie. But his flash of conscience or regret, whatever was going through his head, it cost him.

Wheezing through the impact, she swiped out her arm and clawed his forehead, raking furrows in his *shem*.

The life drained out of him, and he became a lump of clay in a good suit.

Beside me, the daemon tipped back his head and roared until my ears rang.

Fury ignited in my veins until it singed the hair on my arms. The smell left me praying I wasn't cooking from the inside out. Even the ends of my hair carried embers. I opened my mouth to cry out and choked on smoke climbing the back of my throat.

The grate overhead burst open, and my heart stopped as Colby swooped down to land on my head. I coughed and gasped, trying to breathe, but she didn't pay me a lick of attention. Her sole focus was on Clay. Even when a charred smell, like leaves burning, hit my nose.

"Book." I shook and hit my knees. "Book."

Now I sounded like a zombie. I hoped it wasn't catching.

The daemon stomped over to the table, palmed the book, then gripped the cover, half in each hand.

"Stop," he snarled at the insidious tome. "Kill Rue, I kill you."

The pain roared through me in an endless wave, and I sank onto the floor.

"Stop." The daemon pulled until a ripping noise filled the room. "Rue *mine*."

Tension mounted while the daemon and the book engaged in their standoff, but the book caved first.

Colby blasted off once free of its control, her eyes pinwheeling as she absorbed her surroundings. Rough sobs shook her as she cradled her poor hands, which were scorched black from the power roasting me like a turkey.

When she spun back, her eyes were bright with tears when they lit on me, reminding me so much of the night I bound her to me that my black heart cracked down the middle. *"Rue."*

With a grunt of disgust, the daemon slapped the grimoire closed then tossed it onto the bloody floor. He stomped on its cover as he pivoted on his heel, then marched to Melissa. He lifted her over his immobile partner and planted her right in front of me.

"Purge magic." He poked her with a finger, miming how I incinerated people. *"Now."*

Easier said than done, but with Colby cognizant of her surroundings, and her powers, I ought to be okay. Through the stinging ache, I fought to lift my hand toward Melissa. I reached the mucky toe of her boot.

The power within me lashed out in a blazing arc of burning light that forced my eyes shut.

Relief spread through me a heartbeat later, the critical discharge of excess magic sparing my life.

I sucked in my first full breath in minutes and gulped down a mouthful of the ash raining around me, too grateful for the oxygen to complain about its flavor or its texture.

"I'm *so* sorry." Colby lit on my shoulder, and I screamed. "I'm sorry, I'm sorry, I'm sorry."

"Not..." I wet my lips, tasting my blood, "...your...fault."

The grimoire had sunk its hooks in her, there was no doubt of it now, but I would pry her loose and torch the cursed thing.

"Dollface." Clay knelt beside me. "I hate to do it, but I've got to move you."

I must have lost time. Not good. But there was no other excuse for how fast Clay had been reanimated.

"Let's...not." I gulped down more grimy air. "Say...we did."

"Your little explosion set the rug on fire. And the curtains. And the bed." He touched my arm, wincing as tears formed in my eyes. "It's magic. There's no putting it out until it's run its course. Not without you."

Fried to a golden crisp, I wasn't working more magic any time soon. "'kay."

"Look on the bright side." He kept up his cheery façade. "You can add psychic to your resume." With loving care, he lifted me while I wept silent tears that dripped into my ear. "You predicted this place would go up in smoke."

"Self...fulfilling...prophecy." I kept my eyes open by sheer force of will. "Asa?"

"He's rescuing our stuff and locking down the book." He leaned over me. "Come on, Shorty. We're out."

Shrinking to her smallest size, the tiniest she had ever been, she nestled into Clay's hair without a peep.

"Asa would have lost himself to his daemon when he inevitably hurt you, and that's not wise in a human establishment," Clay explained, saving me from asking. "I offered to help, and he granted me permission to assist, but I gave him busywork. He's less likely to rampage if we keep him away until you're settled."

Since I had no recollection of that exchange either, I must have blacked out longer than a second or two. I was still irked Clay asked Asa's permission instead of mine. Though, if I was unconscious, I couldn't have answered him either way. But it was the principle of the thing.

"Colby, when we get to the car, you're on phone detail. Call the hotel office, the cops, and the tip line."

Use of the tip line would preserve Colby's anonymity while directing the real Black Hats to our location.

"Okay," she said softly. "On the pink phone?"

"Yes." He took the stairs at a clip, hit the parking lot, and rushed me to the SUV. "That one."

Had he bought her a new phone? I had no idea. My brain was too crunchy. "Pink?"

"It's untraceable." He grinned down at me. "I put a flaming-hot-pink case on it to make sure we knew which cell was the emergency line. I'm proud to say, we've yet to make an anonymous call by accident."

Back in my day, we didn't have emergency phones. We also didn't have cellphones, there at the start.

"The hotel is empty," Asa said from nearby. "Not a single room was occupied."

That was bad, but I was fuzzy on why that was so unnerving, thanks to the smoke pouring from my ears.

The back passenger side door on the SUV opened before we

reached it, and I glimpsed Asa over Clay's shoulder. Either he had changed and packed with superhuman speed, which was unlikely, or I had lost more time. That probably wasn't a good thing. There were limits to what magic could heal, and brains topped the list of repaired organs that didn't function as well as the factory model.

"Can you heal her?" Asa locked gazes with Colby. "There's a white witch three towns over, but…"

"No," she whispered, shame thick in her voice. "I might hurt her again."

Heartbroken for her, I threw my weight in with Asa. "You won't."

Antennae wilting, she shook her head. "You don't know that."

"Didn't you hear Clay?" I swallowed a cough to put on a brave face. "I'm psychic."

As much as I wished she didn't have to use magic at all, she'd used it to save me at Tadpole Swim. Our bond was cemented. There was no going back. She would die if she didn't use her magic now that her body was producing a surplus for me to harvest what I needed to cast heavy-duty spells. This was a setback she couldn't afford. One mistake couldn't define her, not with that vile book whispering to her.

"We believe in you, Shorty," Clay threw in too. "We know now any buildup can be spent in a burst."

With her in control, I wouldn't be left to cook. Worst case scenario, I could hobble over to the hotel and expel a blast where the damage was already done.

Straightening her wings, she shook off her doubts. "Okay."

Colby glided from Clay's head onto my chest, retaining her small form to keep the pressure on me at a minimum. Eyes squished closed, she began to glow, her magic humming in a soothing cadence. She let her power seep into me, the same as we had done to Asa, and light blasted from my pores, turning the inside of the SUV into a miraculous disco.

This time, as her magic peaked, I experienced no pain. Quite the opposite. She was healing me, and my body melted into a puddle of radiant goo as the agony within me tapered to a bearable twinge and then into nothing.

"Thanks," I slurred, my throat parched but unhurt. "I'm just gonna..."

The lights went out, and I fell deep into a healing sleep.

17

"Morning, Dollface."

The smell of hot coffee and fresh donuts hit my nose, and I cranked open my eyes. "Food."

Clay snorted then sat beside me on the bed in yet another hotel room. "How are you feeling?"

"Hungry." I made grabby hands at his offerings. "Feed me."

A rumbling noise poured into the hall behind him, and a flicker of hesitation crossed his features.

Holding up a finger, he said, "Be right back."

Faster than a speeding bullet, he bolted out of the room, taking my reasons for living with him.

"The food," I called after him. "Bring it back."

"It's back." Asa entered the room, hands full, and kicked the door shut behind him. "Good morning."

"Before you ask how I'm feeling," I cut in, "I demand you hand over the coffee and the donuts."

"You might want to sit up first." He stood over me, smelling better than any man had a right to, and I don't mean the food in his hands. Though that was amazing too. "Unless you plan on absorbing the caffeine through your skin after you dump it down your shirt."

"I like you better when you play the strong, silent type." I sat up with a grunt. "Now gimme."

That was a total and complete lie. I hated how he shrank into himself for others' comfort, but I was getting hangry. Food now. Lectures about him accepting himself later. As if I had any room to talk.

"There's your milk." He passed me a mug and a large dinner plate piled high. "There are your donuts."

"Milk?" I perked and took a sip. "Aww." I set the drink aside. "Clay even warmed it."

The coffee must have been Asa's usual breakfast brew. Served black, I was sure.

"No, that was Colby."

"Oh Goddess. Are we dead? We are, aren't we? She used the microwave and blew us to smithereens."

"Clay supervised." A soft laugh huffed out of him. "Does this mean your ideal afterlife includes me?"

"If black witches had afterlives, and we don't, I wouldn't be offended by the scenery." I wiggled my toes. "Are you going to sit or just stand over me like a creeper?"

"I didn't want to presume." He sat with a contented smile. "How are you feeling?"

"Curious."

Arching an eyebrow, he awarded me his full attention. "Oh?"

"Vanessa."

"She gave me her number, but I never called her, as you heard."

"Not that." I shoved a cakey pumpkin spice donut with thick glaze into my mouth. "That's fine."

"That's...fine?" A line bisected his brow. "You don't mind if other women proposition me?"

"That was in the past, so not really my business. Plus, she's dead." I chugged my milk. "I win."

"You win indeed." His shoulders shook with laughter. "So, what was your question?"

"Her hand." I crammed a blueberry donut in my mouth. "It just like, I don't know, popped off her wrist."

Camber and Arden would have squealed with delight at the fountain of spraying blood. Except for the fact it was, you know, real.

"Not quite." His lips pulled to one side. "A *y'nai* was responsible. They're too fast for me to see when they attack. That's why Father chose them to shadow me. I have to focus, and even then, I hear and smell them more than see them."

"That's not comforting." I bit into my third donut, a classic glazed one, having no regrets. "How did it know so quickly?"

"They can glamour themselves invisible," he continued adding to my nightmare fodder. "It must have been in the room to act without hesitation directly after the infraction."

"Yeah. No." I shuddered. "Invisible hand-chopper-offers don't need to be in my space."

"They can't harm you."

"That doesn't make it any less creepy." I bit into my fourth donut then passed him the rest. "Seriously."

With chit-chat out of the way, and his territorial urges sated, I asked the hard question. "How is Colby?"

"Her hands were healed in the process of helping you. There's not so much as a smudge on them."

Had her magic taken it upon itself to repair the damage? Was this yet another facet of our unique bond? Or had the book stuck its nose where it didn't belong with a seemingly harmless suggestion Colby took?

With the grimoire forefront in my mind, I hated to ask, "How is she bookwise?"

"We've caught her talking to herself once or twice, but she claims she was praying."

"I've never known her to pray," I mused, "but then she's never hurt me like that either."

"It could be guilt," he agreed, sounding unconvinced. "Or the book. It was in bed with her when I woke."

Milk gushed out my nose, cementing my title as sexiest woman alive, and I almost coughed up a lung.

"She slept with it?" I used my comforter to wipe my face. "Tell me she didn't do it on purpose."

"I locked it in the hotel safe before I went to sleep. Its aura bothers me less than it does Clay. That's why he brought you breakfast. I was returning the book to the safe after its little adventure." He cut his eyes toward me. "Colby screamed when she woke up, that's how I knew to go to her. She couldn't get out of her room fast enough."

"That book has to be my top priority when I get home."

"I agree."

"How did the hotel fare?"

"The center of the building caved in, and there's extensive smoke damage to the rest. The fire department is blaming it on bad wiring."

"Did anyone die?"

"No one was there."

A vague memory of him telling me that surfaced, but I had been in too much pain to care at the time.

"The lot was full." I folded my legs under me. "How were all the rooms empty?"

Then it hit me. Those congo zombies had to come from somewhere. From our hotel and its staff, apparently.

"There were several hotels." I chewed my bottom lip. "How did Melissa know we'd pick that one?"

"Colby did her research, using Clay's parameters. Melissa couldn't know we would choose the one she selected, but she must have figured her chances were good. She ticked all the boxes. Clay or I would have chosen the same one based on the information available on the other three hotels. And, there's also the fact she knew Clay, intimately, meaning they've spent some time together at hotels."

Black Hats rarely liaised at their own homes. Few bothered with them. Most used hotels as apartments.

On that depressing note, I hoped for good news on some front. "Did the backup make it safely?"

"They're at the hotel. Three teams. A fourth is en route." He paused. "There were a lot of bodies."

That sparked an excellent question. "Where are we?"

"At the hotel nearest our previous one. I checked us in and kept watch over you and Colby while Clay waited for the cavalry to arrive."

Alrighty then, so maybe I shouldn't use the word *spark* in context to our room, even in my head. "Where does that leave us?"

"Our job here is done." He smiled at my surprise. "We followed our orders to the letter."

But the case was far from closed, and we both knew it. The Proctor grimoire had a following, apparently.

"We hunted the zombigo, put it down." He laid it out as he would in our report. "Access to the body allowed us to confirm it was a reanimated corpse. We tracked down its maker, a black witch, and the confrontation ended with her death, as well as that of her cohorts, and their creations."

Neat and tidy, on paper, but the director would expect a full accounting. "What's the official line?"

"Melissa arranged a coup, which happens every few decades, and she failed."

"And if the director asks why an entire team went rogue?"

"Then we tell him the truth, but not everything. They wanted more power, and to be free."

"The fae in you pops up at the most unexpected times." I don't know why I did it, but I tore off a piece of donut and tossed it at him, laughing when he caught it in his mouth. "It sounds like you've got it figured out."

"Not all of it." He caught another piece, cementing my new

favorite game. "We still need to determine what Nolan Laurens was doing at your house."

Last I checked, he was still there, camped out on my land like he had a right to be there.

"Agreed." I cackled with glee when he caught another. "That's a problem for Samford."

A quick review of my cameras proved Nolan hadn't budged an inch since the last time I looked in on him.

Sadly, that meant I was holding my cell when a notification flashed to warn me the director was calling.

Enjoy your all-expenses-paid vacation straight to my voicemail, Gramps.

"You're not worried he's a zombie too?"

"Zombies don't howl and clutch their butts when they get shot. He's alive. Maybe a masque, but alive."

David Taylor had worn other people's faces to conceal his identity, meaning Nolan might not be Nolan. He might be another member of the rogue coven, one who got stationed at my home to hedge their bets.

All the same, I prayed to the gods and goddesses that had forsaken me that Nolan was himself. That there was a reasonable explanation for his actions, and an association with me wasn't about to cost the girls more than they had already paid for their friendship with me.

"We're almost done here." He stole the donut, pinched off a bite, and tossed it at me. "Maybe four more hours, and this case will be officially closed." He chuckled when I missed. "We can go home."

Home.

The emphasis on the word caused me to miss his second throw too, though, let's be honest. I wasn't going to catch it. I was never going to be one of those people who could toss popcorn in the air and ring their open mouth with it. Donuts appeared to be doomed to the same fate.

Careful not to place any emphasis on the word, I dusted crumbs out of my hair. "Home?"

"Samford for you." He rolled a shoulder. "A hotel for us."

"You could always stay with me. *Us*. You and Clay," I blurted, then cursed my impulsivity. "If you want."

"You wouldn't mind having two houseguests underfoot?"

"Clay is like a brother to me, and you're..." I dusted off my shirt. "You're you."

"I'll ask him." Asa shifted his attention to the door. "We ought to have a week off, after working two cases back-to-back. That's in the regs."

"You would be there for Thanksgiving," I realized, delight winging through me. "Clay could help me cook a full spread." It had been years since I bothered. I usually joined the girls with their parents and brought dessert in trade. "He can make me corn fritters." I kicked my feet and squealed. "I always screw up those."

The door burst open, and the golem in question stuck his head in the door. "Everything okay in here?"

His gaze traveled over me, the empty plate, and the bedful of crumbs.

"Pretend I didn't ask." He eased the door almost shut. "I don't want to know."

"Wait." I swung my legs over the bed. "Asa said you're off for a week as soon as the paperwork clears."

"Hopefully." He nudged it back open. "You know how that goes."

Sometimes, the regs were the absolute law in Black Hat. Other times, they were more of a guideline.

"Will you stay with Colby and me?" I knotted my fingers in my lap. "It's Thanksgiving, and you're..." my throat got tight, "...you're family."

"I don't know." He rubbed his jaw. "I had plans to binge *The Essence of Emeril* and fantasize about his Cajun-injected spicy turkey with grilled polenta, balsamic roasted carrots, andouille cornbread dressing, and fig mille-feuille with balsamic drizzle." He struck a thoughtful pose. "Do I want to eat actual food instead of licking my phone's screen and crying inside?"

"Yes." Colby bulldozed into the back of his head, knocking him forward a step with the force of her hug. "Please, Clay. Will you stay? I'll be on my best behavior. Promise. You can sleep on the rock in my room."

"A rock of my very own?" He patted her back, ruffling his blond buzzcut. "How can I refuse an offer like that?"

Chances were good he knew the rock was a gray beanbag, but I wasn't going to ruin her fun.

"Ace?" Clay checked with his partner. "What do you think?"

The daemon burst from his skin in a lick of flame and scooped me off the bed into his arms.

"Stay with Rue." He turned his head so that his hair slid over his shoulder. "Rue pet."

"I can see from your expression," Clay said smugly, "that you didn't think your invitation through."

The daemon wilted on the spot, a question in his eyes, and I sensed the disappointment in him.

Twirling a lock of the daemon's hair around my finger, I couldn't hurt his feelings. "Sure, I did."

Teeth bared in a huge grin, the daemon flashed his thick fangs at Clay in a clear *I told you so.*

"If I'm going to move into production," I told him, "I need a test subject for my haircare line."

That got the daemon's attention. "Rue brush hair?"

"Brush, wash, comb, braid. All of it. If you let me use you to test my new products."

A growl pumped through his chest. "I like Thanksgiving."

Smothering a laugh, I began to explain. "Thanksgiving is—"

"Brush, wash, comb, braid." He dumped more hair in my lap. "All of it."

"Close enough." I patted his shoulder. "Can you put me down now?"

His grip tightened before it loosened, but he grumbled then placed me back on the bed.

"I'm starting to see what you mean." Clay frowned at his partner. "The daemon is...different...with you."

From the corner of my eye, I watched Asa reclaim control. The absence of shirt didn't bother me one bit.

"The daemon wants to ensure Rue cares for him too." Asa proved he'd heard the tail end of our conversation. "He's more likely to assume control without warning during the fascination."

"You're doing it too." Clay tilted his head to one side. "Referring to your other form as another person."

A faint smile twitched in his cheek. "Am I?"

His nonanswer only served to make me more curious about him. *Fascination* was a good word for it. My thirst for all things Asa was only growing as we spent more time together. I would have cracked open his skull and peeked at his brain to learn all his secrets. If that was a thing. And if it wouldn't kill him. It was this side of creepy too. Best keep that thought to myself.

Clearly, I had spent too much time around zombies to have brains on the, well, brain.

"They're so weird." Colby twitched her wings. "Do all grownups act that strange when they're dating?"

"Yes." Clay backed from the room. "You got it right, staying a kid. I would go back in time if I could, and I was never a child. I would just like to erase some of the things I learned as I got old."

Only the tightness in his lips hinted there were other things he would like to undo. He was such a good man. The best. But he was at his master's disposal. Always. When he was ordered to act, no matter the atrocity, he had no choice but to commit it. To fight it was impossible. The magic animating him would seize control of his body and force him to fulfill the order to the letter. I had seen it for myself.

"I bet there's a spell for that," Colby said thoughtfully as they left. "We should Google."

Alone with Asa, I couldn't stop my pulse from skipping at his proximity.

"I need to touch base with the girls," I said, "let them know I'm coming home."

"Are you sure that's wise?"

"They expect me to obsess over the shop details," I reasoned, "and Nolan is supposed to be in Africa."

"Are you certain the girls don't know?" He kept his tone neutral. "That they don't remember?"

The details of the night they were abducted had been blurred enough for them to heal. Their trauma stemmed more from the fear they were forgetting details than what they recalled. It was the lesser of two evils, I knew that, but it was horrible to cause them to doubt, to wonder, to dread.

"I trust them." I gathered clean clothes. "They would come to me with any concerns."

Jaw tight, he let it go. I could tell he didn't want to, but I couldn't entertain the possibility I would lose two members of my makeshift coven.

No.

They were more than that.

Much more.

Like Clay, they were *family*.

"All right." He mulled it over. "We'll confront Nolan, see what he has to say for himself."

"We have video evidence we can use to pressure him into a confession."

"What about the footage of Mrs. Gleason shooting him?"

Expression blank, I studied him. "What footage?"

Rough laughter rumbled through him, an understanding I would never supply evidence that might be used against her one day. Though she was careful to stick to trespassers, she did have a reputation for an itchy trigger finger.

"We have to figure out if he's Nolan first." I shooed Asa toward the door. "Leverage only works if we have the right type."

"Have you caught him on film since the incident?"

"He's camping on the property." I shook my phone to explain that was what I had been doing earlier. "I've got *hours* of him sitting in a tree, staring at my house."

The odd behavior was one of the reasons why I was okay with waiting until I got home to see what he was about. Surely, if he was coven, he would have bolted after the failed mini coup at the hotel. The radio silence would have told him all he needed to know about whether Melissa emerged victorious.

Once I nudged Asa out into the hall, a little disappointed he let me, I changed and did the hygiene thing.

Since he said we had time, I packed my bag too. Everything smelled like smoke, but at least it was clean.

When I joined the others, all on their laptops at the table, I noticed Colby was paying her screen extra attention. That made me realize she hadn't asked how I was feeling or otherwise acknowledged me since I woke.

Not gonna lie.

It hurt.

But I had a good idea why she was acting like I was invisible, and I decided to let it go.

For now.

"I'm going to step out on the balcony." I hooked my thumb toward the door. "I need to make a call."

Asa watched me go, but Clay frowned at Colby, who pretended hard not to hear me.

Outside, I slid the glass door shut behind me and leaned over the railing as I dialed Arden. "Hey."

"Hey yourself." A giddy quality in her voice made me pause. "What's up?"

"I just wanted to let you know I'm heading home." I was twitchy to go just thinking about it. "How are things?"

"We're right on schedule, boss. The shop looks better now than it did for our first grand opening."

"I'm glad to hear it." I wrinkled my nose when the wind shifted, blowing smoke toward me. "Anything else to report? How are you and Camber?"

"Now that the AC is repaired, we might have to start wearing cardigans to work."

"Or you could just turn down the thermostat and save me money on the cooling bill."

"It's like you don't know me at all."

"Keep it above seventy, please."

"Oh," she gushed, totally ignoring me, as usual. "We could get the shop logo embroidered on a few."

Dollar signs danced behind my eyes. "I don't know if—"

"Mrs. Talbot-Gray has a fancy embroidery machine. She makes a killing stitching names on cheerleaders' bloomers for the local schools. She did ours when we were in pee-wee cheer squad. It won't cost us but a few dollars each. Maybe we could even have some polos done? Oh! Or shirts we could sell in the store?"

"Let's get through the grand reopening first." I rubbed my forehead. "We'll talk merch after that."

"See you tomorrow," she said, sounding certain she had argued and won her case. "Safe travels."

When I started coughing, I trudged in, my mind a million miles away. The guys were MIA, and Colby had a deer in the headlights look, as if they had vanished into thin air, and she had no idea how it happened.

"I'm going to read." I waved. "I have a snake shifter and mouse shifter romance calling my name."

Before I could shut the door to my room, Colby cleared her throat. "Rue?"

"Hmm?" I flopped onto the mattress on my stomach and reached for my book. "What's on your mind?"

Using her butt, she pushed the door closed then landed on the mattress beside me. "Are you mad?"

"Why would I be?" I rested my chin on my fist. "What's going on in that head of yours?"

"Magic isn't whispering to me, is it?"

"A type of magic is, yeah." I didn't touch her to comfort her, as I usually would have, not when I worried a wrong move would lengthen the distance between us. "The grimoire is giving you ideas. Some are good ideas. They're not bad or wrong." I debated how to handle the next bit. "The problem is, when a book like that wants to use you, it has to be smart about it. It can't tell you to, say, stab someone with your sword. You know right from wrong, and you would tell it no. But, if you were playing with Clay, for example, the book could tell you it was okay to stab him. That it would be fine, because Clay is hard to hurt and pretty much impossible to kill."

"He's my friend." She worried her hands. "I wouldn't do that to him."

"You say that now, but the book might convince you." I couldn't resist the impulse to rub her fuzzy cheek. "And once you did it to Clay, the book might give you another idea. It might say, 'See? Your friend is fine. I bet you could stab so-and-so with your sword, and they would be fine too. Do you want to try?' And if you listened to the book for long enough, you might not think it was a bad idea anymore. You might do it, and you might hurt someone for real. Or kill them." I took a moment to remind her, "Swords are not toys. Even toy swords are not toys."

"I don't want that." She shook her head. "I don't want to hear the voice anymore."

"Don't worry. We're going to figure it out. You and me."

"I'm sorry I didn't check on you."

"Don't sweat it."

A bit of her usual sass returned. "Moths don't sweat."

"Smarty fuzz butt."

"Can I stay in here with you?" Her antennae perked. "You can read. I won't look."

Steamy romance was not appropriate for ten-year-old moths, but I suspected she peeked when I was too engrossed in the story to notice.

"How about we pull up your Twitch channel and watch your latest kills instead?"

"Really?" She flitted onto my head. "I've got a lot more than the last time we watched, thanks to Clay."

With Colby leaning over my forehead, her legs propped on my eyebrows, we settled in to watch orcs die horribly so that their gold, pets, and potions could be looted off their corpses. I didn't get the same thrill from virtual violence as Colby, I had seen too much of the real thing for that, but I was happy she had made such good friends. I loved listening to them chatter, how they synced dinner like they were eating together, and how every holiday her crew exchanged gifts.

It gave me hope I was doing right by her, as much as I could, given the circumstances.

This life would be enough for her, I reassured myself.

It had to be.

18

T he dream of leaving for the mountains in four hours turned out as mythical to us as Bigfoot, who preferred to go by Sasquatch, was to humans. The paperwork took forever, so did the repetitive questioning, and I was glad to sign a lengthy statement if it meant returning to my hotel room to check on Colby, who I had been forced to leave alone with the grimoire. Even with exacting Bureau formalities observed, I doubted we had heard the end of this, given our last two cases had involved rogue agents who hadn't survived to speak for themselves. Those were the reasons we gave for deciding to leave for Samford in the morning.

Rather than the coffee shop down the street, which participated in a local farm-to-table program.

Thick-cut pepper-crusted bacon, free-range eggs, and creamy chèvre were calling my name. All served on flaky croissants baked each morning, with a glass of fresh-squeezed orange juice or a mug of hot coffee.

Clay had been in real danger of licking the screen as we skimmed the menu, and I wasn't far behind him.

That was how we spent our night, just like the good ol' days, plotting our route home via food stops.

That was after Colby and Asa fell asleep on the couch watching *Pacific Rim* on the boys' side of the hall.

Left to our own insomniac devices, Clay and I retreated to the girls' side to binge his all-time favorite—*The French Chef.* The last episode was going off when Colby zipped through the door, Asa on her heels.

"Good morning." Asa slid his fingers through my hair. "I see you two entertained each other last night."

The way he scratched my scalp with his blunt nails had me ready to purr for him.

"We watched ten hours of Julia Child," I said, sinking into his touch, "in preparation for breakfast."

"Oh, *oh*, oh." Colby landed on my shoulder. "Can I get a shot of salted caramel syrup when we stop?"

With her looking on, the pleasant warmth pooling low in my belly froze hard enough to skate on.

"Sure thing." I scratched her back. "Play your cards right, and I might even get you cinnamon sugar too."

We had a long drive ahead of us, so it wasn't spoiling her to pick up her version of a to-go meal.

Much.

A sign if there ever was one that I shouldn't be a parent. I was so happy when we made up after a spat, I had a bad habit of smoothing things over by indulging her more than usual. I know, I know, but that was more reason why I was auntie material.

I was all about the instant gratification. Not the long-term repercussions.

Huh.

Framed like that, the big picture of how I dealt with problems in my life came into focus more than I would have liked to admit. Like blocking calls from a man who would simply appear one day if I didn't answer him within an allotted amount of time.

Most everything was already packed and ready to go from the night before. All we had left to do was load the SUV, pile in, and head home sweet home. And then hope against hope Nolan wasn't about to face justice, Black Hat style.

We rolled into Samford under the cover of darkness, which worked for what I had planned.

It was late enough I shouldn't have to worry about Mrs. Gleason until the morning. None of the lights were on in her house, and her rocker sat empty. Since she wasn't on patrol, our butts ought to be safe.

Asa parked off the main road, and the three of us ghosted up the driveway, as stealthy as possible.

Colby, in hairbow mode, quivered against my scalp. "Do you smell that?"

The guys inhaled but shook their heads. I didn't bother. If they couldn't pick it up, I didn't have a hope.

"What you got, Shorty?" Clay kept his eyes on the trees nearest the house. "And is it dangerous?"

"Sugar," she breathed. "Lots of it."

Leave it to a moth to ferret out the sweet stuff.

"That's what he was tossing in the yard?" I tried to wrap my head around that. "Granulated sugar?"

Salt, sure. That made a certain amount of sense. Sugar? That made none whatsoever...

...unless you were attempting to lure a moth with a sweet tooth outside the wards.

A hummingbird feeder with a nectar might have tempted her, but I wasn't going to offer him any tips.

Within sight of the house, Asa inclined his head. "I smell him."

"I don't sense any magic." Clay scratched his bare scalp, as his wigs were still boxed to avoid more smoke contamination. "None."

"He's been camped out for days," I reasoned. "That gave him plenty of time to set a circle."

Though he must either be a gifted practitioner, or his circle was old enough its signature had faded, if Clay couldn't sense it. As a creature animated by magic, he was more sensitive to it than the rest of us.

"The smell is human," Asa countered. "A human who hasn't showered in days."

"You take point." I scanned the area. "Your nose will be faster than my security feed." I put my hand on his arm. "Just don't shift until we know what we're up against, okay?" I worried my bottom lip with my teeth. "We need to keep this low-key until we determine who and what we're dealing with."

A shadow passed over his features, there and gone before I could peg its cause, but I had a good guess.

"Hey." I yanked on his arm. "You smell a human. That's why we need to be daemon-free. If this goes south, I'll be the first to welcome your other half to the party."

With a lightness to his movements, he slid out of my grasp to begin his hunt.

The three of us spread out, keeping to the deepest shadows, which meant we would be all but invisible to a human. If that was what we were dealing with. Veering away from the house, Asa prowled into the backyard, weaving through the trees.

A silent gesture caught my eye, and Asa pointed to the same spot where Nolan had been hunkered down since I left. As far as I could tell, he was totally oblivious to our arrival. He lay on his stomach, in the grass, with a tripod set up in front of him. One with a fancy telescoping lens. He swept it left to right, panning the yard and the house.

For a human, he was remarkably quiet and still, but I suppose that came from years of stalking wildlife.

The three of us stopped a yard away from him, silently conferring, and came to the same conclusion.

Nolan Laurens was plain vanilla human.

"Hey, Nolan." I kept my voice conversational. "Whatcha doing?"

A surprised yelp burst out of him, and he flopped onto his back, caging his head in his arms for protection.

"That's not going to help you." I looked him up and down. "Why are you on my property?"

Arms lowering, he stared up at me as if he were seeing a ghost instead of the owner of the land where he had been squatting without permission.

"Just taking some pictures." He eased up slowly, demonstrating more techniques he must have learned in the field about how not to spook wild animals. "The area is so lovely."

As someone who grew up down the road, he'd had plenty of time to document Samford. I wasn't buying this burst of nostalgia.

"The girls think you're in Africa." I cut through his BS. "Also? My property is wired for surveillance."

Expecting Clay to step in, I was surprised when Asa came to my side without the usual slouch he used to ease others' worries. The effect on Nolan was immediate. His knees shook, and I worried for his bladder.

"You're trespassing." Asa flashed a police badge. "You are aware that's illegal?"

"You're Rue's cop friends." Nolan blasted Asa with a smile that trembled around the edges. "I appreciate everything you did—"

"Why are you spying on Rue?" He made no effort to diminish himself. "After everything she's been through with her ex, I'm sure you understand why it concerns us to discover a strange man hiding out here while she was gone."

"Whoa." He raised his hands, palms out. "It's not like that."

"What is it like?" Clay folded his thick arms across his wide chest. "From here, it looks like enough to bring you in."

The color drained from Nolan's cheeks, and he took a healthy step back before his gaze dropped to the thousands of dollars in camera equipment he would never see again if he bolted. He relaxed his stance and kept his hands where we could see them. He fought the twitch in his legs, proving he was a man used to facing his fears and knew better than to run from them.

"The girls told you I'm a wildlife photographer." He addressed his defense to me. "Okay, well, they sent me a picture when you guys were moving Hollis Apothecary from your kitchen to the shop." He wet his lips. "Hear me out. There was a moth. This *huge* white moth. I couldn't tell if it was in the house, the glare was terrible. Either it was resting on the glass inside the living room, or it was right outside."

A sour taste filled my mouth, and I could have kicked myself for not seeing it sooner.

Power increased as it reached back through generations. Nolan was Arden's uncle, therefore he had more magic than her. Enough he could see through the wards to spot Colby in the window. Enough he had groped the ward without realizing what kept repelling him. Enough to cause me big problems.

Goddess bless, what a mess I had made.

On the heels of that revelation came another. The shock of awareness when I shook Nolan's hand wasn't a glitch in the bracelet. It was my instincts warning me I was in the presence of another witch. He wasn't powerful enough to warrant that kind of buzz. So maybe the bracelet helped, a one-two punch I misinterpreted at the time.

"I thought you were here for Arden," I said flatly, "for both the girls."

But their abduction must have only been the tipping point in his decision to verify the photo's authenticity.

"I am." He pulled a hand through his greasy hair. "I thought—"

"—you would put in an appearance, raise their hopes, then ditch them to pursue your real goal."

With my hectic schedule, he could have been creeping around the edges of my property for days before he pulled his prodigal-returns act with the girls. He must have hoped to finagle an invitation to the house under the guise of seeing where the girls had worked for so many years, using his charm to grease the wheels. Then the case lured me away, and he got an even better deal. Carte blanche on my property.

And, as a bonus, he could have asked the girls to call him with a heads-up when I started home for any number of flimsy reasons. Such as making an empty promise to honor our missed breakfast date in the future.

"I saw this moth in South America, a white witch moth, and it was huge. More than a foot across. They're gray and white, with a zigzag pattern on their wings." He sliced his hand through the air. "Never mind. Not important. The point is— There are no moths native to the US, let alone Alabama, that size. And it was snow white."

"Can I see the picture?" Asa held out his hand. "I would like proof that what you say is true."

"Sure. No problem." He pulled out his phone and scrolled through his gallery. "There. See?"

Asa accepted the phone, waved Clay over, and they pretended to compare notes.

"The moth is outside the house." Asa glanced over at Nolan. "It's an optical illusion. It was closer to the camera than you might think. The glare makes it hard to tell, but the moth was maybe four feet from the lens. With the house behind the girls, who are standing closer, the moth is in the middle distance."

"I thought that too," Nolan gushed, "but I had a friend analyze the photo who—"

Unable to hold it in a moment longer, I blew my top. "You did *what*?"

"—says it's definitely not in the foreground. It's in the background, with the house."

"You set up camp to stalk...a giant moth?" Clay's laughter rumbled through the night. "Seriously? That's what you want to go with?"

"Do you know," Nolan asked, "what a discovery of this caliber could do for my career?"

"Yeah, make you a laughingstock." Clay wiped tears from his eyes. "I thought you were a serious wildlife photographer, but you're a cryptozoologist wannabe. You're out here in the sticks, hunting Moth Man."

"During your stay, have you seen any evidence of this moth?" Asa arched an eyebrow. "Even once?"

"No." Nolan rubbed the back of his neck. "I haven't seen it." He turned to me. "Please, Rue, let me stay. I won't get in your way. You won't know I'm here. I'll camp here a few more days, to be sure, then you never have to see me again."

The insanity of this situation caused me to forget, but now I remembered. "Mrs. Gleason shot you."

"I know how she operates. I'm wearing a Kevlar vest."

"She shot you in the butt."

"Yeah." He twisted around and lifted his shirt. "I had a fix for that." His butt was totally flat. A pancake. I gave him a once-over when we met, and I would have remembered if he suffered from pancake buns. "I shoved an insert down the back of my pants. I still had to pick buckshot out of my lower thighs, but it would have been worse without it."

"Mrs. Gleason does have a thing for shooting people in the butt," I admitted. "She shot Clay too."

"She shot her husband three times." Nolan dropped his shirt and faced us again. "Granted, she only mistook him for a prowler the once. The other two, she caught him having an affair with members of the Yard Birds. Former members, I should say."

If I was going to keep living in Samford, I had to research Alabama's Stand Your Ground laws.

That, or pray cadaver dogs were never sent to investigate our shared property line.

"Even if I didn't mind," I began, "and I do, the girls would see it as a betrayal on my part if I sided with you and your cover story. I would have to tell them, and I'm not going to heap more stress on them by explaining how you lied and used them. That means you have to go."

A muscle ticked under his left eye. "It's only a few—"

"I've been stalked, hunted, and surveilled for too long." That much was the truth. "I don't want to jump each time the moonlight hits your camera lens or get woken up by my surveillance app when you get too close to the house. I want a normal life, and a guy hunting a moth in my backyard is not normal."

"Gather your things." Clay snapped his fingers at Nolan. "I'll escort you off the property."

"Good night, Mr. Laurens." Asa passed Nolan his phone. "I hope you appreciate how lucky you are that Rue doesn't press charges. Given recent events, people in this town are overprotective of her just now."

About to open his mouth and dig his hole deeper, Nolan froze when Asa flowed like smoke to his side.

"You don't get to claim insult or injury for what was done to Arden or Camber. They endured it. You didn't. You can't play that sympathy card. Not when you've just admitted you came back, not because of the girls' tragedy, but for your own selfish purpose."

Mouth twisting with a too-human snarl, Nolan took a step toward Asa. "I didn't say that."

"Does this sound familiar?" Clay pressed a button on his phone, and Nolan's voice spilled out into the night. The whole conversation. With lines plenty wide enough for the girls to read between. "This is a confession. We've got you on trespassing. Worse, we've got you attempting to use the girls to get your way after you admitted you didn't come back for them."

As damning as it was for Mrs. Gleason, I wasn't too worried. It was much worse for him.

"You recorded that on my phone," he realized, staring at it like he was holding a snake.

"I wanted you to have a copy. I texted it to Clay, Rue, and myself."

Asa smiled, and Nolan shrank from it. The step his anger allowed him turned into a retreat. "Do we have an understanding?"

"You're blackmailing me?" He choked on a shocked laugh. "You're cops."

If he knew who he was really dealing with, he would shake their hands for getting off with a warning.

Then again, if he knew who he was really dealing with, we might have to kill him to get rid of him.

"We're not blackmailing," Clay said. "We're suggesting. That you leave. And don't come back."

Turning to me, who he must have pegged as the weak link, he begged, "But the girls—"

Nolan had a whole family here in Samford, but he defaulted to the girls every time. He had weaponized them, used their victimhood for his own gain, or tried to, and I was done playing nice.

"The girls haven't seen you in seven years. You've basically missed one-third of their lives. You don't visit or invite them to visit. They're used to your relationship being transmitted over FaceTime." I nudged his knapsack with my toe. "In point of fact, they have no idea you're here. None. Because you lied to them."

"It's your fault Arden wakes up screaming in the middle of the night," he hurled at me, fists clenched at his sides. "It's your fault Camber is a shadow of her former self. You did that to two bright, smart, funny girls."

"You're right. I did. They got caught in the crosshairs of my life, and I regret that more than you can ever know."

Owning up to my mistakes confused him a bit, but he pressed on. "I'm Arden's uncle. I have the right—"

"Look, I'm tired, I smell like smoke, and I'm out of patience. You could have asked for permission before assuming my relationship with the girls granted you the right to be here."

A low rumble left Asa's chest as he sensed my annoyance. Or perhaps it was the daemon itching to get out and rip off Nolan's head then scream at it in his signature finishing move. Right about now, I was game for some cork popping and cathartics.

I'm a white witch. I'm a white witch. I'm a white witch.

Murder was wrong.

Granted, Nolan *was* trespassing...

No, no, no.

I loved the girls too much to take one more thing from them. Even if it was an uncle who put himself above his family, above the law, and above common sense.

"Clay," I said before I got mean, "be a dear and escort Mr. Laurens to the end of my driveway."

"Come on, buddy." Clay slung an arm around his shoulders. "We're friends, right?" He all but dragged Nolan down the road. "Let's you and me have a talk about boundaries and what happens when you cross them."

"What about my equipment?" He struggled to break free. "It's my life. My livelihood. You can't keep it."

"We'll have it shipped to your hotel, on our dime, assuming the address you email me is out of state or country. Consider it an insurance policy." He strong-armed Nolan farther down the drive. "Or, if you prefer, we'll drop it with Arden and her mom, and let you sort out the mess you've made. Let you make amends before you vanish on your family for another seven years."

The fight drained out of him then, but I didn't trust the hard set of his jaw when he fell in step with Clay.

Once they got a safe distance out, I leaned my shoulder against Asa's. "He won't let this go."

I knew the type. He was a hunter. He might shoot film instead of bullets, but he lived for the rush of discovery, taking the perfect shot, doing what few others could, and then raking in the acclaim for it.

"We have a week to set up deterrents in case he returns." Asa wrapped an arm around my waist. "We won't let him expose Colby. Or hurt the girls through you. Don't let him get under your skin."

"What happened to the girls *was* because of their connection to me. He wasn't wrong about that."

"He also used their pain to capitalize on an opportunity for himself. He didn't come here for them."

I noticed he didn't say it wasn't my fault, and I appreciated that. I liked that he didn't lie to make me feel better or make excuses for me that wouldn't change a thing.

Bottom line: I wanted a normal life.

To make that happen, I had brought normal people into my life to learn their ways.

Because of that, I had put normals in the path of paranormals, and that only ever ended one way.

Maybe if I had loved the life Colby and I built in Samford less, I would have moved on and spared this town from my problems. But I had put them on the map by coming out of retirement, and I owed these people protection from whatever may come.

Never in a million years did I think saving Colby would spin so far out of control. I didn't regret it. Not for a second. She was, literally, the light of my life. But it's like the saying goes...

Two can keep a secret if one of them is dead.

David Taylor might be dead, but he seeded Black Hat with unrest before he got vaporized, and that meant Colby was at a greater risk than ever.

"Let's fetch the SUV." I forced myself to straighten. "Mrs. Gleason will come looking if it's still there in the morning. Usually, I would trust her to remember what you drive, but she's always got a hair-trigger when I'm away."

Between the three of us, we were going through SUVs like tissues, but the entire fleet was identical.

Hand in hand, Asa and I strolled to our current ride, which required a wash ASAP to rid it of telltale gore. Clay stood in the center of the road, legs braced, watching Nolan hoofing it, daring him to try something.

"There are no fancy ride share apps in service this far out in the boonies." I considered his options. "He's got a long walk ahead of him, unless he cons whoever dropped him off into picking him up, and I bet you a dollar he paid someone at his hotel to drop him off with a smooth lie to avoiding driving his rental."

The neighbors would tell his family if they recognized his ride, or him, and he didn't want to risk that.

"Is it safe now?" Colby whispered from on top of my head. "Is he gone?"

Quickly, to prevent any escape attempts, I let myself into the SUV, and the guys joined us.

"Stay put," I rushed out as I slammed the door. "We need to keep a low profile the next few days."

A tickle across my scalp told me her wings had wilted at the sentence I had handed down.

"You've got Ace and me for a week." Clay leaned forward. "Are you telling me we can't have fun, even if we have to stay indoors?" He shook his head. "And here I thought you were the mighty Orc Bane."

"You really mean it?" Hurt underscored her fragile hope. "You're staying?"

"Nothing in this life is certain but death and that homemade is always better, but I'll do my best."

"Okay." A breeze stirred my hair as his intentions registered. "We're going to have so much fun."

Across from me, Asa smiled a little smile. I was grateful he didn't mind Clay being Colby's obvious favorite. I got the impression he appreciated any distraction that let us spend more time together.

Alone.

Warmth spread through my cheeks as I imagined having Asa under my roof for a whole week with nothing to occupy our time... except each other.

After Asa parked the SUV, I collected the grimoire from the floorboard and walked Colby into the house. While she powered up her gaming rig, I locked the grimoire in the safe, then stepped out to help unload.

Clay skirted us, carrying his wig boxes, cooing under their lids about the tender care they would receive.

As soon as he entered the house, Asa pinned me against the open rear hatch with his hips.

"Yes?" I tilted back my head. "Can I help you?"

"I would like to kiss you." He searched my face, his eyes going soft. "Do I have your permission?"

Unsticking my tongue from the roof of my mouth, I managed, "Yes."

He leaned down, his scent washing over me, filling my head. He brushed his nose against mine before he glided it over my cheek, along my jaw, nuzzling until he could inhale the vulnerable spot beneath my ear.

Fever warm lips brushed over that delicate skin when he spoke. "Thank you."

Withdrawing in a rush, he loaded his arms with luggage and left me standing there on wobbly knees.

Seconds later, Clay returned for his bags, read my sorry state, and clucked his tongue. "Told you so."

"I don't understand daemons." I glared at the front door. "He asked to kiss me, but then he..."

I flung my arm toward the house, making it plain Asa got me hot and bothered then split.

"Try smearing frosting on your lips." He winked. "Or maybe chocolate sauce."

"You are the worst," I huffed, still tingly all over from how Asa left me. "The absolute worst."

"I told you to leave Ace alone, and you chose to hear it as *I hope you and Ace bone.*"

"I can't help myself." Heat lit my cheeks like beacons. "He does *this*, so I have to do *that*."

"Have you considered turning the tables on him? You do *this*, so he must do *that*?"

The lightbulb moment he inspired blinded me for several seconds. "You might be on to something."

What better time to turn the tables than during his weeklong Thanksgiving stay?

Asa thought he had seven days to cash in his smooch voucher, but I bet I could punch his ticket in one.

Let the games, and the turkey basting, begin.

ABOUT THE AUTHOR

USA Today best-selling author Hailey Edwards writes about questionable applications of otherwise perfectly good magic, the transformative power of love, the family you choose for yourself, and blowing stuff up. Not necessarily all at once. That could get messy.

www.HaileyEdwards.net

ALSO BY HAILEY EDWARDS

How to Rattle an Undead Couple #9

The Potentate of Atlanta

Shadow of Doubt #1

Pack of Lies #2

Change of Heart #3

Proof of Life #4

Moment of Truth #5

Badge of Honor #6

Black Dog Series

Dog with a Bone #1

Dog Days of Summer #1.5

Heir of the Dog #2

Lie Down with Dogs #3

Old Dog, New Tricks #4

Black Dog Series Novellas

Stone-Cold Fox

Gemini Series

Dead in the Water #1

Head Above Water #2

Hell or High Water #3

Gemini Series Novellas

Fish Out of Water

Lorimar Pack Series

Promise the Moon #1

Wolf at the Door #2

Over the Moon #3

Araneae Nation

A Heart of Ice #.5

A Hint of Frost #1

A Feast of Souls #2

A Cast of Shadows #2.5

A Time of Dying #3

A Kiss of Venom #3.5

A Breath of Winter #4

A Veil of Secrets #5

Daughters of Askara

Everlong #1

Evermine #2

Eversworn #3

Wicked Kin

Soul Weaver #1

Printed in Great Britain
by Amazon